S0-BZD-525

HONOR
THY
FATHER

Center Point
Large Print

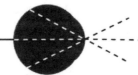

**This Large Print Book carries the
Seal of Approval of N.A.V.H.**

HONOR
THY
FATHER

ROBERT A.
RORIPAUGH

CENTER POINT LARGE PRINT
THORNDIKE, MAINE

This Center Point Large Print edition is published
in the year 2012 by arrangement with William Morrow,
an imprint of HarperCollins Publishers.

Copyright © 1963 by Robert A. Roripaugh.
Copyright © renewed 1991 by Robert A. Roripaugh.

The text of this Large Print edition is unabridged.
In other aspects, this book may vary
from the original edition.
Printed in the United States of America
on permanent paper.
Set in 16-point Times New Roman type.

ISBN: 978-1-61173-319-8

Library of Congress Cataloging-in-Publication Data

Roripaugh, Robert A.
Honor thy father / Robert A. Roripaugh. — Large print ed.
p. cm. — (Center Point large print edition)
ISBN 978-1-61173-319-8 (lib. binding : alk. paper)
1. Wyoming—Fiction. 2. Large type books. I. Title.
PS3568.O72H66 2012
813'.54—dc23
                                                         2011039978

Disclaimer

Although I have attempted to convey accurately the general geography and problems of one part of Wyoming in the late 1880s, the events in this novel are imaginary. The characters, as well, are fictional and are not intended to represent anyone living or dead, including the actual inhabitants of the Sweetwater country. The only exceptions are Ella Watson, known as Cattle Kate, and Jim Averill, who are mentioned in the novel and were hanged near the Sweetwater River during July 1889. As for the actual men who lived in Wyoming during the period covered in this novel—cowboys, homesteaders, politicians, ranch owners, and "rustlers"—they belong rightfully to history and the fading memories of their friends and families . . . And this book is dedicated to them and their descendants who, for better or worse, made Wyoming into a state.

"Honor thy father and thy mother"
stands written among the three laws
of most revered righteousness.
—Aeschylus, *Suppliants*

Honor thy father and thy mother:
that thy days may be long upon the land
which the Lord thy God giveth thee.
—Exodus, 20:12

Chapter 1

Maybe you know how it is. You can remember about a lot of separate things and people, but one particular time in your life stands out from all the other memories. And often that time keeps coming up in your thoughts like a big trout after a fallen insect where the Sweetwater River moves slowly around the far side of an oxbow. . . .

Sometimes I want to tell everyone in Wyoming just what happened to us one year—to Father and Senator Karr . . . my brother Ira . . . Leah Karr, who grew up with Ira and me . . . and to a few other people, too, like old Jules Lamar and his girl Mary. If I could tell everybody about that year I might quit thinking about it so much, though maybe no one wants to hear a story where good and bad are hard to untangle. If I had been to a college back East like my brother Ira, I might know how to explain it all so it would make better sense, but I was never much interested in books. Father used to say I took after him that way, and he was right, I reckon, because I started riding a horse when I was five years old. And by the time I was eight I was helping on roundups.

My father had lived in the Sweetwater Valley since 1873. He brought a herd of Texas cattle up the year before and left a crew of men to put in all the ranch buildings and corrals. While he was gone from our home in Texas, Mother died giving birth to me, so she never saw the Wyoming ranch. Relatives took care of Ira and me until we were old enough to ride to Rawlins on the train with Father.

I don't remember much about Texas except for the stories my father would tell about fighting Comanches or the early trail drives north with the cattle. He'd worked for Charlie Goodnight, and I can still close my eyes and hear Father tell about taking those longhorns past Fort Concho and Horsehead Crossing . . . how Oliver Loving hid for days from the Indians along the Pecos . . . how Mr. Goodnight, who wouldn't let his men drink or gamble, found a new way through the mountains to keep from paying a toll, driving past Las Vegas, Raton Pass, and the Sangre de Cristos, or sometimes along the Rockies, even getting up to Cheyenne in those early years.

I used to like playing out one story by myself— I would be Mr. Goodnight or my father bossing a big herd up the trail. If nobody was watching I'd ride out among those Texas steers and pretend to drive them somewhere, but they were always pretty wild and most of the driving went on in my head. Father caught me at it one time, and I was scared of being in awful trouble, but he just teased me about it for a long time. I can recall that part of it clearly . . . even now. I didn't scare any more of the steers, but I was still crazy to be with a trail herd. And I spent a lot of time around the bunkhouse, listening to the talk or tagging after our foreman, Finn Rankin, who came up the trail with Father and worked for us a long time before being fired. I remember thinking that I would bring cattle up the trail someday myself and have a ranch as big as Father's. . . .

Ira was different, I guess. He always stuck pretty much to himself, and Father used to say he never knew what my brother was spending so much time thinking about, and I didn't know either. Ira also worked a lot with horses. Even Father had to say he was a good hand with them, but he handled them differently than most people did. The custom was to let them run in the rough country until they were four- or five-year-olds, and then get a bunch together and break them out quickly. In a week or two a good bronc rider would have them bucked out and ready to be ridden on roundup. "Nothing like plenty of hard work to make something out of a horse," Father used to say, "or a boy either."

But Ira, in the summers when he came back from the boarding school in Pennsylvania, would get in a few three-year-old colts and start gentling them. He'd talk softly, tie up their hind feet and rub their backs with a gunny sack, and let them get used to a saddle, until when he rode them they would hardly buck at all. They made good horses by the time they were four or five, but Father wouldn't ride any of them, because he said they were lady-broke and didn't have enough spirit left in them to buck on cold mornings. Ira gave two of the best ones to me when he started college, and I always felt a little ashamed about riding them.

Then there was the way Ira liked to go off to hunt by himself or with Jules Lamar, an old wolfer homesteading on some good water for Father. We used to eat a lot of game meat, and it wasn't much trouble for someone to ride out a little ways from the ranch and kill a deer or an antelope. In an hour or so you could come back with the hindquarters tied onto your horse. Unless you were like Ira and always brought the whole carcass back—stringy forequarters and all.

Of course we ate plenty of beef, too, and it sometimes was slick or didn't carry our brand. That was the way it had been in Texas and on the trail drives, and nobody thought anything was the matter with it, though I heard Ira argue with Father about it in the spring of 1889. I guess I was seventeen and Ira was twenty then, and he'd just come home after the winter quarter of college to help with roundup. Most of the hands were out at the line camps riding bog. A couple of our cowboys were helping the cook skin out an unbranded beef by the meat house, and Father and I had just ridden into the corral as Ira was saddling up to take one of his rides by himself.

When he saw my father, Ira turned around slowly to face him. "It wouldn't hurt us to eat some of our own beef," he said.

"What are you getting at, son?" Father asked him. "I reckon there's a lot of people eating our beef now, and that's the way it's always been. You know nobody ever eats their own brand if a maverick's handy."

My father was a tall man, and he rode his slick-fork saddle straight up with a long stirrup. There weren't many men who argued with him. At least I hadn't heard many do it like Ira was doing it now. Father had a long face, weathered brown and grained like the walnut in an old gunstock, but what I can remember best about the way he looked then was the shadows in the deep hollows of his eyes, as if he'd not slept for a long time. Actually it was just the shape of his face—high cheekbones, jutting nose and chin, all laced with harsh lines made stronger by those hollows around his eyes.

I watched him sitting there on the Texas bay horse in his old boots, California pants, gray flannel shirt open at the neck with the vest of a dark suit over it, and narrow-brimmed hat of gray felt with no creases in the crown. I remembered hearing the men talking in the bunkhouse about the way he'd started growing the mustache after Mother died. It was heavy and seemed now to lay against his face like a dark scar. . . .

"No," Ira said finally, "and I know some people around here don't butcher their own brand ever. But that doesn't make it right, does it? If somebody borrowed one of our horses and didn't return it, would it matter whether he expected you to borrow one of his the same way? The horse would still have our brand, and you'd say it was stolen by a horse thief."

"You're talking about horses and I'm talking about cows," Father said. "Is that the way they've been teaching you to think at that school, son?"

Ira was looking right into his eyes then, and I felt as if I hadn't ever really seen my brother before. Or maybe, I thought, I had suddenly grown older while watching the two of them facing each other in the too bright, dusty sun that cast the shadows of corral poles into bars by Ira's soft boots. I wanted to tell them both to stop arguing, but I knew Father wouldn't have tolerated my butting in.

"It's not just the school," Ira said. "You see and hear things while riding out on the train from the East. Everything's being settled up all through Nebraska. It will happen here too."

"Maybe," Father said. "Maybe not. But what's that got to do with butchering a beef?"

Ira turned back to his horse and began pulling the cinch latigo tight in that slow, gentle way he had when doing anything around a horse. "If more people come into this country there'll be more cattle, more brands, and more ways to fight over the land and stock. Why can't we avoid trouble before it comes to us?"

"That same way you break those young colts," Father said softly. "Rub them, and talk to them, and tie cans onto the saddle, until they won't buck at all when you begin to ride them. That's a way to stop trouble before it starts, son. But it's a damn poor way."

I heard Ira say, "I think we should try anything which has a chance of stopping men from killing each other. There's already some bad feeling between men like you and Senator Karr and the newcomers trying to get started on Antelope Creek or near Green Mountain. And if we're more careful about butchering only our own brand, we won't have someone stealing our steers when even more outfits move into the country."

Father stood up in his stirrups and then swung down from the bay in a smooth, long-legged motion that I'd never been able to imitate. He had an effortless way of doing anything with cattle or horses—things he'd learned gathering wild longhorns in South Texas after the war and making the drives clear up into Montana.

15

Watching him bluff out a nervous, switch-tailed horse in the corral, or hind-foot a steer that had to be doctored in the sagebrush, I often worried that I'd never have a chance to learn even half of what he knew. And here Ira was, arguing with him about how to keep out of trouble.

"Ira," Father said, "I haven't read many books since your granddad moved the family from Virginia to Texas. But I haven't seen many men that could step back from trouble and still keep their pride. Or their belongings. The Tyrrell men haven't bred any killers yet, but they respect themselves enough to stand up for what they believe. Even if it's sometimes wrong."

I can still recall the way Ira's face looked when he heard my father say that—it was as if he'd been slapped. There was a softness always in his face, a refinement of the high Tyrrell nose and full mouth, a lightness of skin that wouldn't disappear until the end of the beef roundup, when he'd been in the sun for weeks. And now it seemed like he'd been struck, perhaps more by the edge of disappointment in Father's voice than by the words themselves.

I watched a little cone of dust funnel up in a whirlwind off in the sage. It formed up, dry-looking and moving quickly over the heat-distorted land like a man riding hard, and disappeared into the crumbly sandstone bluff on the far side of the river. The white, bonelike

16

cottonwood poles of the corral glared into my eyes, so that I lost sight of the whirlwind. The heat of the packed ground seemed to burn up through my boot soles, and still Ira hadn't spoken.

"It isn't just the Tyrrell men who respect themselves," my brother said at last, leading his horse toward the corral gate. "It isn't just the Tyrrell men who are going to want some of the land here. The homesteaders won't be much more right than we are. They'll clutter the land up, fence it off, rip it up, and graze too much stock on it. But there won't be enough right on either part to be worth the fighting. You pushed the Indians onto the reservations so you could run cattle in here, and we're going to be pushed in turn. Who can honestly claim grazing rights on a quarter million acres of public land?"

"I can," Father said abruptly. "The land's for those who know it, respect it, deserve it. Yes, by God, for those who love it!"

"I love it too," said Ira. And he walked by us, leading his horse through the sagging pole gate.

Chapter 2

I recall standing there with my back against a hot corral post while my father stared at Ira, who had begun to ride north past the log barn toward the horse pasture. The men helping Cookie must've heard the argument, but they didn't even glance up when he rode past. Before Father moved, Ira had ridden through the meadow edging Longs Creek and out where the land flattened away from the ranch buildings and sagebrush spotted the greening buffalo grass.

Then Father turned and began unsaddling with his face shadowed by his hat so I couldn't see his expression. He didn't speak until I started to unsaddle also. "Won't need you this afternoon," I heard him say.

"All right. I can take care of the horses," I told him.

"I'll make out, son," he said almost gently. "Thought you might want to ride over and see if there are any late calves around Willow Springs."

I knew he wasn't asking me and that he wasn't worried about calving, either. "No trouble to ride that way," I said. "Some of our old cows over there didn't winter too well." I started to say that none of the cows had done well since the big die-up two winters before, when we lost a third of the cattle and counted ourselves lucky. But I saw Father's face then and didn't say it. I just mounted Blacky and rode out from the corral after Ira.

The men had the beef skinned out when I passed the meat house. They paused, rubbing bloody hands on their overalls as I passed.

"Wondered what happened to that old bull died last winter by the river," I told them, watching the cowboys grin and Cookie pretend to scowl.

"Sure now, Mart," one of the hands said. "Told Cookie here it wasn't right. But guess he figured froze bull was okay since the magpies always fatten out on it."

"Should have throwed the bull away and butchered them magpies for Cookie," the other cowboy said earnestly.

"Thought we ate some squallers last night. Couldn't sleep none and woke this morning starved for ripe meat."

"If you spot any more ripe beef like this here, better stake a claim on it, Mart. Cookie told me he don't have to waste any pepper on bull's been range-cured with the juice in it."

I grinned as Cookie winked at me and growled the two men back to work. "Man's got to put up with a lot round here from you pie-biters," he said. "Wouldn't be bad if you knew dead bull when you wolfed it down. Quit jobbin' me and rig up the gambrel."

I felt better for a ways, but I couldn't help thinking back on Ira's argument with Father. I'd heard them disagree at times since Ira started school back East, but this one and the one last spring that caused Finn Rankin to get fired were different. My father never said anything about the arguments directly, but I knew how bad he must've felt. He'd counted on Ira taking hold of the ranch and running it the same way he had for ten years. And they'd been rough years, too.

The first trouble had been with Indians drifting off the reservations to hunt and, if they got a chance, killing cattle like they'd once killed the buffalo. Then everybody overstocked and overgrazed the land—even though there was still lots of open range—until the cattle market was ruined for several years. There had been mavericking and plain rustling because the big English-owned companies looked like easy pickings and their hands had been branding slick calves for themselves. I knew Father's men had been paid five dollars a head to brand mavericks for us—before the territorial legislature passed a law against mavericking in '84. And I knew the TX cowboys still rode out early each spring and marked slicks with our running iron . . . despite the Maverick Law.

I figured Father was right, and a man had to fight for things if he wanted to build and hold a ranch. I guess we thought the same way most of the time. Maybe that's why I was ashamed sometimes about Ira. It wasn't that he was a coward or anything like that, but he figured different from the people I'd been brought up to admire. Most of the hands felt uneasy around him, because he couldn't joke with them and didn't swear or talk a good story like cowboys were used to doing to make the hard work pass easier. But then he was my brother, and I knew he was smarter than me about lots of things. . . .

I found the tracks of Ira's horse crossing Longs Creek and turning east toward Willow Springs. The new grass was light green for a ways along both sides of the narrow stream. Then the sage began again and the sandy soil was still moist from the last wet snow, so it was easy to follow the hoofprints leading out of the swale.

In March the wind usually blew hard from the west—feeling like it was sharpened on the Wind River Mountains and the edge of Beaver Rim. The wind was what made the Sweetwater country good for cattle. Most winters it blew the snow off so that cows could live without any hay. And usually there would be a warm chinook when you needed it most. There was none in the worst months of '87, and the cattle drifted south toward Red Desert and starved until they ganted up, humpbacked and bony as sage roots, and piled into ravines or creek bottoms to die.

But the March wind was laying today. I heard a meadow lark flute from across a far draw, and I was glad to be riding somewhere, listening to old Blacky snort as he did whenever he wanted to jog-trot and smelling the range so clean and sharp like it always was at green-up time. The weather reminded me of the spring two years back when Ira and me had ridden along the river past Split Rock to see the Devil's Gate.

That day we'd climbed up hard rock beside the steep notch the Sweetwater had cut in the rounded granite hills. On one side of Devil's Gate you could see the valley spread out smoothly from the river and never stop until it hit the shadowed mountains past Bothwell, Independence Rock, and the CY outfit on Bessemer Bend of the Platte. Southwest was Green Mountain and north was the Rattlesnakes, red granite sticking up from the rangeland like a big lump on an old bull's back. But best of all was looking west, toward Father's ranch, and seeing the Sweetwater curl like blued steel through the valley in oxbows that held swollen fingers of meadow and clumped willows.

Off there a ways was the land where our longhorns had rustled to stay alive that first winter up from Texas. Just thinking about the ranch had made me feel taller and yet ache inside—like I had a lot of growing up to do before I could feel right about ranching down there along the river.

Ira had sensed that something was making me quiet, and he'd taken me down to look at the ruts where the emigrant wagons passed. He showed me some graves along the Oregon Trail and told about the Mormons who died near there one winter on the way to Salt Lake with wooden carts they pushed by hand. He talked about other things he'd read or heard from old Jules Lamar, who'd guided emigrants over to the Snake River country.

"I guess that's interesting all right," I told him. "But I can't see much point in getting excited over a thing that ended thirty or forty years ago."

"Nothing ended with the Mormons or the other emigrants," Ira said. "People will always be looking for a place or a way of life that suits them better. I suppose the emigrants intrigue me because they were trying hard to make something new from their lives. Of course they didn't succeed completely, but making the effort was the important thing. A person living here now has to make the same effort to move ahead of old ways of looking at things."

He sat there for a while staring out at the river and thinking something over to himself. Finally he said, "That's one reason why I can't go along with Father's view that a few men have a right to control the Sweetwater Valley for over seventy-five miles from the mouth of the river. When there weren't any other people in the country, it might've made some sense, though I can't see where white men had the right to take this land from the Indians to begin with. But now a lot of new people with rights as good as those of any early rancher are coming in. I think everyone should start using the land here in fairer ways and acting more civilized toward each other when problems come up over mavericks and homesteads."

My brother had gone on talking for quite a while, and I only remember part of what he said. I know he talked about the college, what his life there was like, and how he might go on to law school someday. I could see how important schooling was to him, though I wouldn't have enjoyed being shut up in some building listening to an old professor rattle away at me, learning some foreign language I'd never speak anyway, or reading a lot of books instead of getting out in the open where a person could think clearly. Ira even mentioned a poet he liked, whose name was Whitman, and recited parts of his poetry from memory. He was especially fond of a poem called *Passage to India*. Once a long time afterwards I looked it up in a library and found the part he had recited at Devil's Gate that day. It went

Sail forth—steer for the deep waters only . . .
For we are bound where mariner has not yet
    dared to go,
And we will risk the ship, ourselves and all. . . .

And he told me about other writers he admired—men named Rousseau, Bronson Alcott, Wordsworth, Henry George, Browning, and a few more that I've forgotten.

"Don't you care any about the ranch?" I had asked him when we rode back that afternoon. "I know you're learning a lot at that college, but cows and horses are important, too."

"I like the ranch, Mart. What made you think I didn't?"

"I don't know. I just had that feeling up at Devil's Gate."

Ira smiled. "You've heard Father talking about me. He and I don't see things the same way. That doesn't have anything to do with my feelings about the ranch, though."

"He's counting on you to run it someday," I blurted out. "That's why he sent you off to school. It pains him when you talk back to him, and he's always favored you since Mother died bearing me—"

"Don't talk that way," he interrupted sharply. "I don't want to hear you saying a thing like that. It's something you imagined yourself."

"Finn Rankin said it. He came on a trail drive with Father after it happened. Father told him his wife's dying was like a crooked poker game where a man lost everything he'd ever worked for. I don't blame him for feeling cheated. You're older than me anyway, so it's right you should take over the ranch."

"Forget that kind of empty talk, Mart," Ira had said. "Finn gets away with it because he has been working for Father ever since the TX was started.

He has hung onto Father's shirttail so long he thinks himself to be a big cattleman too. . . ."

As I rode up into the last valley before Willow Springs, I couldn't help thinking that Finn had been right. Father tried not to show it, but he favored Ira, strange ways or not. When Finn and my brother had quarreled last spring on roundup, Father fired him—top hand, foreman, and trail pardner or not, he'd given Finn his time. Maybe Ira was in the right when he wouldn't let Rankin, who'd been in charge of the roundup, put our TX brand on a couple of slick steers he knew were strays from over on the Powder River. But I figured it was like Rankin had often said in the bunkhouse—"Longest rope marks the maverick." I would bet a good stake that those two slicks were now on Finn Rankin's homestead south of Antelope Creek and carrying his brand.

Just before I topped-out on the ridge, I heard the shot. It echoed a little and there wasn't another. I figured it for Ira's .38-55 Ballard, so I wasn't surprised to see him riding down Willow Springs Canyon toward a freshly killed antelope buck, whose white belly and rump glistened among the dull rocks and sage in the shallow valley. By the time I rode up, my brother had started skinning the buck. He spoke little as I began to help him, and when the antelope was gutted and cooling out he didn't seem to want to talk.

Ira had brought a curved-stem pipe back from the East that spring. He filled it now, and when it was lit he smoked and then passed it to me. I had rolled some cigarettes in the bunkhouse and didn't think much of a pipe, but I puffed away with him.

"Do you want to take a few shots with the Ballard?" he asked me finally.

I nodded, wishing it was a Colt six-shooter instead of an old single-shot Ballard like nobody in our country used any more.

"Let your elbows slide down farther over your knees," Ira said, when I was sitting on the ground and aiming at a rock across the canyon. "A rifle's an instrument and needs a rest. Now take a good breath and let about half of it out before you tighten up on the trigger."

I shot three or four times with Ira coaching me. The last time I fired, that white rock disappeared. It was an accurate rifle all right—heavy enough to point solid and fixed up with a tang peep sight. Our closest real neighbor to the east, Senator Wallace Karr, had bought it for Ira several years back when he was serving in the territorial government at Cheyenne. It was supposed to be a present, but even though the Karrs were good friends of ours, Ira wouldn't take the rifle unless Mr. Karr let him pay for it.

The Senator, his wife, and daughter Leah usually came to our ranch when Mr. Karr and

Father threw their outfits together at roundup time. For a few years they had been almost the only ones in the roundup district. Then several large cattle companies moved in and started operations, though some of them were wiped out by the blizzard of '87. And now more ranchers were getting a start. Moses Ethridge and the Thompson brothers between Mr. Karr's place and Bothwell belonged to the Stock Association, so they rounded up with us. Bobby Dutton, an Englishman ranching northeast of Bothwell, did too. But lately some other men who weren't Association members had come in. A drifter called Jack Stenger had opened a saloon for the cowboys on the river between us and Mr. Karr. Seth Daniels and a bunch of ex-cowboys had started homesteading to the south on Antelope Creek. And since last spring Finn Rankin had joined them. People said it was getting worse crowded up on Powder River, though.

"Did Father send you over here for some special reason?" asked Ira when I was handing the rifle back to him.

"He sent me to check the cows around the spring."

"I see."

"It wasn't my idea to follow you," I told him. "Something's been bothering Father lately."

Ira knocked out his pipe and booted dirt over the embers. "Things can bother a person all right.

It might be losing a foreman who knows too much about the way you handle cattle. Or it could be worrying whether old Jules Lamar will really sell you his homestead on the best spring in the country after he proves up on it. I suppose there are plenty of things to worry about."

I didn't like to hear him talk about Finn Rankin as if he'd had no part in getting him fired. "We better get on to the spring," I said. "I don't care to be riding all the way back after dark."

"All right, Mart," my brother said pleasantly, as though I was his own age. He wrapped the meat loosely in some clean burlap sacking he'd brought and tied it across his saddle. Then he looped the hackamore rein over his little mare's neck and climbed up behind me on Blacky. The mare followed us with her ears pricked forward like a big bay dog. . . .

Chapter 3

Before long I saw the slabs of rust-colored rock behind Mr. Lamar's cabin. The spring, obscured by a clump of gnarled willow trees, made a patch of green near the base of the sandstone slabs. Jules had built a round corral with a pole wing parallel to the rock, so that stock could be run easily into the enclosure. The sod-roofed cabin was made of untrimmed logs chinked with clay, but despite its roughness, the cabin, like the corral and adjoining pole shed, looked well built and permanent.

Jules Lamar stood inside the cabin door, the barrel of his rifle glinting in the sun and then disappearing when the old man recognized us. I glanced back at Ira. "Hate to try a sneak on him. His eyes may be getting bad, but there's nothing wrong with his ears and nose."

"I doubt if he even thinks about being careful any more," my brother said. "It's as natural with him as putting on his hat when he goes outside."

I waved one hand at Mr. Lamar. I didn't see his girl Mary anywhere, and I hoped everything was all right.

"'Lo, boys!" the old wolfer called out. "Tie up now, tie up."

"We can't stay long, Jules," Ira said. "We were just riding by."

"The hell with riding by. Tie up, boys! What's the matter with the mare? Looks like she's packing a corpse."

"We brought you some goat meat, Mr. Lamar," I told him.

"Goat meat, is it?" He must've been seventy that spring, but I remember how his laugh rang out like the report of a buffalo gun. "Was raised on goat meat cooked in wolf fat, boys. Rest your saddles a spell."

Lamar was still a large man, but the skin and flesh seemed to have shrunk over his heavy-boned frame. He wore Arapahoe moccasins, thick wool pants, and a faded Hudson's Bay mackinaw. Between the coat collar and his winter cap of sealskin, the old man's weak eyes seemed to gaze through us and on down the canyon. His beard was lead-gray, like his eyes, and carefully trimmed.

"Mary'll be pleasured to see you," he was saying. "Stepped down to the spring for water."

I turned in that direction and saw her walking up the path worn between clumps of sagebrush. She stopped momentarily when she saw Ira and me, smiled, and then hurried toward us.

"Let me help you," I called, going to meet her.

"Hello, Martin," she said as I took the water buckets. "You and Ira can stay tonight?"

"I reckon not this time. I've got to look at some cows around here."

"The cows are all right. I looked already for new calves today. This is the first time I've seen Ira since he got back."

I shouldn't have minded the way she said that, but all of a sudden I felt bad and a little touchy. "He hasn't been home but a few days, Mary," I said abruptly.

She didn't notice anything in my voice, and I was glad. I'd spent nights that winter, in the room I had to myself when Ira was at school, lying awake and thinking crazy dreams about me and Mary Lamar. I was a little ashamed about them, too. Although the hands often talked wild things about women they'd met in Miles City and Rawlins, or made jokes about Ella Watson over at Bothwell, I figured this was plenty different. But I wasn't going to let anyone know about the hurt and pleasure mixing me up each time I saw Mary.

She didn't call out to Ira, or hurry to the cabin either. That wasn't her way, I knew, but I hadn't known enough girls to tell whether it meant anything or not. Of course Leah Karr was a lot different, because she'd been sent away to school like Ira. Watching Mary walk along beside me, sleek braids of black hair swinging against her shoulders in the long-sleeved blouse and wearing a blue cotton skirt above deerskin leggings her father had traded for at the Arapahoe Reservation, I thought she looked more a woman than Leah, who was two years older and wore fine dresses from St. Louis or Chicago.

Mary's mother had been an Arapahoe, and the Indian showed mostly in her oval face, thrusting cheekbones, and deep brown eyes that seemed to see everything without moving much. She was turning eighteen that spring, and from the side her features, the delicate nose and small, serious mouth, reminded me for a moment of a young boy's face. But there was nothing boyish about the way she talked or acted—maybe being half Indian and living alone with her father had made her grow up more quickly than Leah or the few girls I'd met when visiting in Rawlins. . . .

"Hello, Mary," I heard Ira say from the cabin door.

"I'm happy for seeing you," she answered quietly.

That was all they said on meeting after seven months apart. But to me it was the same as if they had said a lot more things that I didn't want to hear.

"Hell, boys," said Lamar, filling the coffeepot and stirring up the stove. "Here it's near roundup time and your dad hasn't been by for two-three months. He break his back this winter?"

"He's all right," I told him, "but he and Mr. Karr were gone to Cheyenne almost a month for the Association meeting."

The old man snorted to himself, and I saw his eyes burn fiercely as he stared into the flames he'd poked up under the coffee. "Association, is it? He didn't use to give a damn for associating with the lords and earls. First time I seen your dad, there wasn't a fence between here and Canaday, and he didn't need any hired detectives to protect his caddle from any man—red or otherwise. Just shows how times change for the worse in a country."

Ira listened politely, but I said, "He hasn't changed any. Maybe the country's different from the way it was, but he's not afraid of rustlers, or the Association either. And a man has to stand on one side of the fence or the other."

"Sounds simple enough, young hoss," Mr. Lamar said. "Might be that neither side's worth more than a pack of last summer's skunk hides. Reminds me of when I had to pick whether to trap wolves, hide hunt, or go hungry. Nothing shined about any of them, but you're not going to starve out another man by killing wolves. Can't say as much for taking buffalo tongues and hides, or making a passel of laws that splits the local residents into hoss thieves and caddle detectives."

It sounded to me like the same kind of talk Ira had been making, and I began to see why they'd always been friends. With Ira the ideas came mostly from books, while Lamar figured like an Indian or wild animal that always had the run of the land. I kept quiet, and by the time we finished the pot of coffee it looked almost four o'clock by the sun. When we got up to go, Mary said she would ride down to the end of the canyon with us. My brother helped her saddle up a horse in the round corral, and I watched Jules cut some steaks from a hindquarter of the antelope we'd brought.

He kept talking while he worked—half to himself and half to me—and it took a few minutes to catch the drift of what he was saying. "Don't judge I'm going against your dad, son," he told me finally. "I promised him I'd prove up this place and put her into the TX someday if he needed more water. This wolfer thinks more of him than he does of any another man on the Sweetwater, but I ain't the sort to agree with a thing if it sands my craw."

Mr. Lamar fixed his eyes on me then, and it seemed to me they were the same narrow, cold gray 'as those of the animals he'd shot snarling in his traps for more years than I'd lived. "Tell your dad to keep Clayt Paulson away from here. Hear me, son? He'll know what I mean. Tell him I know coyote sign when I cut it sneaking around here. Specially if it's made by the kind working for Karr."

I knew Clayton Paulson was one of the Association detectives—paid mostly by Mr. Karr, I'd heard—and that it wasn't my business to ask any questions. So I nodded and thanked the old man for the coffee.

"You boys both come back soon," he said before we rode off. "Gets a shade quiet for Mary and me until roundup starts. Much obliged for the goat meat, too."

"I'll ride by in a few days, Jules," Ira said. "I brought some things for you and Mary from the East."

"Don't forget what I said for your dad." Mr. Lamar was looking straight at me again.

"I won't forget," I said, beginning to anger a little. And I knew I wouldn't forget—the words or the look on his face when he said them in the cabin.

The three of us rode abreast, while Mary talked to both Ira and me. She stopped her horse on the canyon rim above where my brother shot the antelope. The sun going down behind the Rattlesnakes yellowed the sage and grass for as far as I could see, making the land look fresh and new, like you'd never before seen it or the flint-horned Texas cattle grazing there. Color flared over Mary's skin and turned her skirt to a sharp, vivid purple that hurt my eyes.

"I'm going on to the ranch," I told her and Ira, trying to make it sound careless.

"Wait a minute, Mart," Ira said. "There's no hurry."

Mary tried to make me stay there longer too, but I didn't want to listen to her talking with Ira. "I've got things to do," I said. "See you at the ranch."

"Good-by, Martin!" I heard Mary call as I loped Blacky along the ridge, and I pretended not to hear her. . . .

By the time I was in sight of the ranch the light had almost been washed from the sky. The range looked dead and treacherous now—like it was in winter when it could kill a strong steer or a man easily enough. Our corrals, the horse and saddle sheds, narrow bunkhouse, the log headquarters—they all seemed to fade and shrink once the sun went down. I guess I wasn't feeling too happy, either.

I unsaddled and turned Blacky into the horse pasture. There was no light in the house, so I went to the bunkhouse kitchen, where Cookie was making up a list of supplies he needed for roundup.

"Grab some coffee," the tough little cook told me, bending back under the lamplight. "Damn this paper scribbling."

Nobody remembered what Cookie's real name was—maybe he wanted it that way—but he'd worked in a Confederate officers' mess during the war and cooked for Shanghai Pierce afterward in Southeast Texas. He kept to himself, and when he spoke in the bunkhouse it was mostly to make a sarcastic comment on the crudeness of some hand who needed taking down. But he seldom flared at Ira and me, and I knew it wasn't because Father was his boss. I always guessed he felt responsible for us, since we had no woman around to help raise us.

Cookie looked at me more closely when I didn't pour any coffee. "It ain't coyote poison. Just made it up fresh."

I shook my head. "I drank some a while back with Old Man Lamar. Is Father gone somewhere?"

The cook licked the tip of his stubby pencil. "Gone to Bothwell. Didn't say why."

"Will he be back tomorrow?"

"Didn't say. I didn't ask him neither, Mart."

I kept thinking of Mary and Ira back at the canyon. Remembering them together there almost made me hate them both. And now my father was off somewhere, too. During the last year he'd been making more trips than before to Bothwell or sometimes to Rawlins. "Association business," he'd told me once. Tomorrow he would probably stop at Mr. Karr's ranch to finish plans for the spring roundup. Sometimes when he came back from a trip like that, he'd brood for several days and hardly talk with anyone. Then all of a sudden he would appear in the bunkhouse, hooraw with the cowboys, and play cards all night long, until the cigar smoke filled the whole place like gray dust. . . .

When I started to leave the kitchen Cookie said, "He did tell me Miss Karr and the Senator was coming in a couple of days. I got to send a man to Rawlins for some fancy grub. That's why I'm stockin' up for roundup, too. Damn nuisance when a crew bellyaches if they got to eat flour, beans, and bacon. Wasn't that way ten years ago when cowboys was men."

Then he squinted up his eyes in irritation. "Little argument this afternoon in the corral . . . Your brother gets his tail twisted sometimes, don't he?"

I nodded.

"He's a thinking boy, Ira is. Most men around

here don't give a damn about anything but how many cows they got or fencing themselves off a little dab of ground. I seen 'em kill each other over cows and fences some places in Texas. I told you how your uncle got himself lynched in that kind of foolishness. Might be Ira's got sense enough to fall clear if a bronc goes over backwards with him."

"Meaning what?" I asked him.

"Meaning you ain't," Cookie muttered. "Kids and most men is damn fools."

Chapter 4

On the first night that Mr. Karr and his daughter Leah were at the ranch, we all gathered in the front room after dinner. Light from two kerosene lamps on the fireplace clung to the whiskey in the glasses Father and Senator Karr held. My father's hands were rein- and rope-roughened, the Senator's strong but white from wearing gloves. I remember thinking how close their drinks looked to the color of Leah Karr's hair as she sat in a rocking chair near the Senator, her head bent and cheeks glowing with firelight. Ira came back into the room and leaned over to hand her a cup of tea. From across the room I saw her lips move and Ira, his dark suit looking unfamiliar and out of place to me, talked easily with her.

"I say it all changed when the Swan brothers failed in '87," Mr. Karr was telling Father. "It was not the bad winter alone that ruined so many of us. Afterwards we were hurt by the English-owned cattle companies when they liquidated their holdings and dumped stock on the markets. My steers that had brought nine dollars a hundredweight at Chicago in '82 went for a dollar two years ago. I thought I had been wiped out, but somehow I kept going."

A square-built man of fifty-seven, Mr. Karr often reminded me of the Shorthorn bulls becoming so popular on the ranges then. He suggested the same blunt compactness and careful breeding. There was a story about him which made the rounds of the bunkhouses in the territory—how Karr, a Kentuckian, had quarreled with chunky Major Frank Wolcott over the Civil War, picked the ex-Northern officer off the floor of the Cheyenne Club, and held him sputtering while he finished making his defense of the South's position. Whenever I heard the Senator talk with Father about the cattle business or homesteaders, I wondered if the story was really true. I realize now it possibly could have happened, for Mr. Karr had a conviction about right and wrong which was not bluster but an aggressive confidence in himself and the other older cattlemen.

"The foreign companies were sure to breed

trouble," said Father, reaching out to light the Senator's cigar and then firing his own. "There was bound to be mismanagement. You recollect how they tried to tally cattle on the Swan holdings by dabbing paint on each cow. And they thought they had above 120,000 head to mark at the time!"

"I remember well, Martin. Their manager was serious about it, too."

"Naturally the rain washed the paint off the critters, and the Swan stockholders in Edinburgh never got their close count."

"They had 120,000 head on paper only," Karr chuckled. "When Swan and Sturgis failed, it was the end of an era."

I heard Ira speak to Mr. Karr, ignoring Father's stern glance of warning. "I think another era is about to end also," he said.

"How's that, Ira?" Karr asked genially.

"The open-range philosophy of the strongest person controlling the land is going to give way," my brother said. "Father and I disagree about it, but I won't be sorry to see the end of illegal fencing and suitcase homesteaders proving up on land for us."

Mr. Karr was momentarily startled. An odd smile was forming beneath his cropped, gray-flecked mustache. I noticed Father's mouth harden, as though he was angry or ashamed. The two men were both about to speak out, but the laughing voice that seemed like music in the slab-walled room belonged to Leah Karr.

"Ira always was frank, Father," she said. "You and Mr. Tyrrell are so used to having your own way with all your horses and rough cowboys that neither of you can discuss something objectively any more."

"Now, Leah," Karr sighed gruffly.

She looked at my father in mock protest. "Really, Mr. Tyrrell, if it weren't for the chance to hear a fresh opinion from someone, I would have gone with Mama to Denver for the summer."

"I reckon if you stay here long you'll hear plenty of fresh opinions," Father said less severely.

"I might just stay longer then," she said, with a little smile that seemed half to herself. "Of course, your opinionated son will have to talk more to me than he has so far this spring."

Ira acknowledged this pleasantly enough, but he quickly turned back to Mr. Karr. "I intended no offense," he said. "I'm not suggesting that Finn Rankin and the homesteaders on Antelope Creek are right either. But we shouldn't act like outlaws to get our way."

"We have tried to act like honorable men." Karr frowned. "It has not been enough to protect our herds. I would be one of the last to say the laws should be broken by honest ranchers. But there isn't much law out here. I will not sit back and watch my property and stock preyed upon by range tramps or vagrants who will never make a living tilling grassland."

"I think we are destroying ourselves, sir," Ira said. "We should stop trying to hold more range than we really need and begin developing hayland and improving smaller herds. If we did that—"

"I don't think this is the time to discuss your reforms with Wallace," Father broke in. "Hear me, son?"

"All right, Father." Ira did not flinch under his eyes. "Excuse me," he said to Mr. Karr and Leah. He walked from the room but didn't seem angry.

I waited while the conversation between the two men started up awkwardly. Leah came away from the fire and sat beside me. "Martin, take me for a walk later," she whispered. "Will you, Mart?"

I smelled the perfume she'd never used before and saw the clean line of her throat in the high-necked silk dress. She was not so painfully slender as Mary Lamar, and watching the light reflected in her sage-gray eyes, I wondered if she felt the same way about Ira as I did about the half-breed girl. I guessed that she did.

"We can go now if you like," I said, feeling happier.

"Yes, please. . . ."

Leah told her father we were going for a walk

and followed me out the front door. I smelled the corral and saw squares of lamplight filling windows in the long bunkhouse. It sounded like the hands were deep into a stud-poker game. A horse whickered near the saddle shed, and off by the bluff above the river I heard an owl in the cottonwoods.

"Wait here and I'll go find Ira," I said.

Leah pretended not to understand. "Don't you like walking with me? Your brother's probably reading some of his precious books in his room. I think he's mad at me."

I knew she was teasing me some way, so I decided to play along with her game. "I reckon so, Leah. He uses up the kerosene some nights and I don't get much sleep."

"Poor Mart," she said gaily. "Your brother's making everyone unhappy, isn't he?"

"It's not really his fault," I told her. Sometimes hearing things like what she'd just said made me want to stand up for Ira. Not against Leah, for she was on his side, but against Father and Mr. Karr. Against Finn Rankin and some of the cowboys in the bunkhouse who made talk behind his back. I guess maybe I didn't want to be ashamed of him. . . .

I said, "It seems like everybody thinks my brother's not enough like Father. I don't figure that's his fault. He's got his own way of looking at things is all."

Leah smiled and made me sit down beside her on the seat of our buckboard. I watched the grass stretching out to the west and shining like cartridge brass in the moonlight. Off behind me a long ways was the cabin where the Lamar girl lived. I closed my eyes for an instant and wished it was Mary sitting with me, and then I wouldn't have to say anything or want to do anything but watch her looking off at the land like she could hear it breathing. But now I just heard the dying-out wash of the river and Leah Karr talking.

"I thought I understood your brother as well as anyone. I thought that until he came home this time. I guess I was wrong, Mart."

"Maybe it's what school does to a person," I told her uncertainly. "I wouldn't know much about that, though."

She shook her head, and her hair flashed like the mane of the sorrel gelding she used to ride all the time. But all those years she and Ira and I had grown up together, riding and being Indians or trail drivers at her ranch or ours, seemed like they happened with someone else.

"I didn't really want to go to school back East," Leah went on. "But I know now it would be just the same if I'd stayed here those five years. You know what I mean, don't you, Mart? He wouldn't . . . he wouldn't like me any better for having stayed here."

I saw what she meant then, but I didn't know

anything to say. She could tell I didn't want to speak and turned away.

"I guess I have my answer," Leah said finally. "I suppose I had it before—the first night Father and I were here. Sometimes a girl has to act foolishly, though."

"Look," I told her, "this isn't doing any good. You should be talking with Ira instead of us sitting here augering about schools and all. It's just crazy talk, and if Ira knew you were here he'd be out already."

I jumped off the seat before she could say anything and ran back to the house. Ira was there in our room, but he wasn't reading—just lying on his bunk and looking up at the rough-boarded ceiling.

"Come in, Mart," he called to me. "Is the party going strong?"

"Father and Mr. Karr are still talking," I said.

"I thought so. Where's Leah?"

"She's been outside talking with me."

He nodded and reached for his pipe.

"She's growed up some," I said.

"Yes, she has." The match flared yellow in the dim moonlight let in by the window and open door.

"She's been hoping to talk with you," I said. "She's sitting out in the buckboard now."

Ira looked at me without showing up anything, but I felt a little guilty about sticking my nose into his business that way. "That's fine, Mart," he said. "Come on and we'll all walk down to the river. Do you remember how we used to ride our horses in swimming?"

"I'm not going just now," I told him.

He was moving toward the door. "Of course you are. You've nothing else to do, have you?"

"No, but I'm not going now."

I couldn't see his face clearly, but I knew he was watching me. "You're not angry about anything, are you, Mart?" he asked.

"No. Not now, anyway," I said.

"I'm glad." His slight frame filled the doorway, and then I heard his footsteps moving around outside the lean-to which had been added to the house for our room. His steps were light and certain on the ground, like Mary Lamar walking in her moccasins and very different from the forceful thrusts of Father's boots, which left a deep imprint of heels in the earth like a shod horse.

I lay on the coarse blankets in my underwear, and in the quiet I could hear the voices of Father and Mr. Karr and the snap of pitchy pine in the fireplace. Everything around me seemed to be lulled by the damp spring night. And yet my breath felt heavy and out of beat with the house sounds and the night, too. I didn't know what it was galling me—Leah, the talk of Father and the Senator, or the memory of Ira and the girl

47

skylined on the canyon rim above Lamar's homestead. I didn't like myself any better for hoping Ira and Leah would marry sometime.

After a while I began figuring I should leave the Sweetwater. I reckoned I was old enough and smart enough to make a hand somewhere else. Everybody said the trail from Texas was petering out, but cattle were still being brought in from Oregon. A man could go to Baker City with a foreman for one of the Wyoming outfits and make the drive back. That Snake River country would rawhide a man into forgetting about lots of things. And there must be other places to go where there were cattle and good grass, even if Jules Lamar said different.

Maybe I could . . . Oh, to hell with figuring like a punk kid, I thought angrily. I knew I probably wouldn't run away from this valley. Or from the Lamar girl and Ira either.

I shut my eyes and after a while everything seemed better. . . . I thought I was walking along the river with Mary, and when we stopped by the cottonwoods, the owl flapped off and turned back low above the willows and came straight at us. I could see its yellowish eyes burning like moons and the tufts of feather growing into horns. I felt the beat of gray wings and saw, crooked in the feathery-legged talons, a buffalo skull like those bleaching out everywhere along the Sweetwater. All at once I saw it wasn't really an owl but a red-necked, ugly-headed turkey buzzard that smelled a week-dead steer carcass . . . its eyes piercing hot and accusing . . . and then it was gone. And I lay alone in the sweet grass along the river and listened to the cattle bawling off in the direction of Willow Springs Canyon. . . .

I woke up knowing there was someone outside the lean-to. It took me a few moments to be certain I wasn't dreaming still, and then I heard cloth scrape gently against the logs. I waited, my breathing sounding louder the more I tried to control it. When I recognized the lowered voices of Leah and Ira, I was all right again.

"Thank you for walking with me, Mr. Tyrrell," Leah said. "I enjoyed it, even though I forced you into saying things you . . ."

"I'm sorry, Leah."

"You needn't be. I know you never said we were anything more than two friends who grew up together out here. Those letters you sent when we both were off at school last fall should have been clear enough for anyone. I was the one who was thinking about marriage." Her voice seemed to me to have a tone of forced gaiety that made me glad I couldn't see her face. "I suppose I took Father's jokes about having you for his foreman too seriously. I thought you would like a chance to run a large ranch. I thought we could . . ."

"I couldn't be your father's foreman," Ira said.

"He and I would never agree on how to operate a ranch, and I'm not interested in becoming a successful cattleman on the Two-Bar-K. I have to go my own way now and decide what I want to make of my life. And I don't believe you could be happy living in Wyoming the way I'd have to live if I didn't work for your father."

"Once I thought I could, Ira. Wasn't I foolish?" Leah laughed then, but it sounded a lot different than I'd remembered from summers before.

"I wouldn't call you foolish," said Ira. "I still value our friendship, Leah. And I won't be forgetting you."

"No," she said, so low I figured she was walking away. "I don't suppose you will. Good night, Ira."

I heard my brother walk to the door and step inside quietly to keep from waking me. I thought he was going to lie down on his bunk, but the next thing I knew he was back outside, and I smelled his pipe. He must've sat out there smoking for a long time, because I went to sleep before he came to bed.

When I woke up the next morning I saw that Ira's bed had been slept in. But he had ridden out early by himself, and the packages on his shelf that he'd brought back from the East for Jules Lamar and Mary were gone.

Chapter 5

I spent the next day away from the ranch putting out salt for our cattle that were grazing toward Beaver Rim. It suited me to ride by myself, leading the pack horse with the block salt in canvas panniers swaying across his back. The new calves looked slick and clean in the sun. Most of our cattle over here were brockle-faced Shorthorns from Oregon, and some of them would crowd right up around me at the salt licks. When I had my own ranch, I decided, I would have all Texas cattle—none of these "pilgrim" cows raised in a honyocker's barnyard.

"I'll have a hell of a spread, too," I said angrily, and old Blacky flicked his ears back.

"You, Blacky!" I made him walk up and headed back toward the river. The sun was getting noon hot, and I was sweating in my wool shirt. If it hadn't been for the cooling wind over the moist range, I might have called it summer weather. And if I hadn't been thinking about where Ira was, I would've enjoyed looking the country over.

A band of sheep were moving along the other side of the Sweetwater when I got there. Behind them a herder drove a team hitched to his wagon, and a couple of stringy dogs followed the sheep like coyotes. The herder waved, and I rode opposite the wagon until I came to a crossing. The river was high and dun-colored with runoff from the mountains. I saw the herder stopping and rustling together a fire while his sheep watered. He beckoned me across with his arm, so I unpacked and hobbled the other horse. The crossing was firm-bottomed but deep. It gave me something to think about besides myself—the river pushing Blacky downstream farther than was good and me, holding my boots in one arm, feeling the suck and chill of numbing water. But I felt better for the danger and hell of it.

The herder was a one-eyed Mexican no taller than the backs of his slouchy team. His fire was going strong when I rode up to the wagon. He was watching me from his good eye while he fiddled with a fry pan and an iron pot hooked over the fire. Both dogs squatted out of rock range, staring at me suspiciously.

"She is roily bitch." The little Mexican's voice was shrill, and he rubbed one hand nervously against his dirty-bearded cheek.

I was still sitting my horse. "It's high all right," I said, eying a ewe pelt stretched out over the side of the wagon frame. The smell of sheep drifted back from the woollies spread out along the river like a dirty bed-tarp.

The herder began to nod, his blue-skimmed eye shining out sullenly below the crumpled black hat. "Dry yourself, *amigo*. It is time for eating something. One hates to eat without company if another man is near."

When he straightened up over the fire, I saw a six-shooter butt with the bluing worn off protruding from his waistband. It looked like he'd been driving horseshoe nails with that old Smith and Wesson. I got off and tied the black horse to a wagon wheel. The Mexican was frying antelope chops and warming a pot of beans. After I dried out my pants and pulled my boots back on, he climbed into the wagon and brought out two tin plates with thick slices of bread on them.

"You know this country well?" he asked when I began to eat.

"I reckon so," I told him. "Our ranch is down-river a ways."

He guessed what I was thinking and grinned agreeably. "I take my sheep through. I go away from the river south of the Split Rock. My boss, he tells me the country is good there only for the sheep. No?"

"Maybe. But I know a man who is running cattle there now."

He kept grinning, but his tongue moved over his lips as if he was thirsty. "Is it true? I was not told this."

"The man's name is Mr. Wallace Karr. His brand is Two-Bar-K."

"*Señor* Karr? I hear of him. He owns land there, this Karr?"

"He's bought up several homesteads," I said. "I reckon he owns enough land there to figure on saving the grass for himself."

The Mexican blinked his good eye slowly and mopped his plate with the coarse bread. "He have the sheep too?" he asked finally.

"No, just cattle. Most of the sheep outfits are farther south."

He did not look at me. "It is land of the government, I am told."

"Some is."

The dogs hadn't come any closer since we started talking. I was just as glad they didn't, for they looked more snaky than the herder himself—and much less sociable. I found myself wondering what my brother would've said to the Mexican about running sheep on government land. Probably Ira would be all for it and encourage the old bastard to have at it, but I wasn't about to give out any damn-fool opinions about those woollies.

"My boss, he thinks it unfair for one man to keep others from the land of the government." The herder shrugged carelessly. "Me? I only drive the sheep where I am told. It is foolish to quarrel when you own nothing. If one has meat and a little wine in the winter, what more is there? Surely I cannot become more poorer."

"I guess not," I answered, thinking he was right on that last point, anyway.

I had finished eating, and it was a ride of several hours back to the ranch. As I was about to stand up, I saw something flash on the smooth ridge to the north, where I had ridden to reach the river. At that distance it was hard to be sure what it was—a mirror maybe, or field glasses—but I was almost certain a man was up there.

I looked back at the fire. "Thanks for the feed. I've got more riding to do this afternoon."

"I will warm up the coffee." He started for the wagon again. "Why ride so soon? Besides, I have talked to no one since leaving Lander."

I could believe it all right, but I shook my head. "Much obliged. Next time I'll sample your coffee."

"*Bueno, bueno.*" When he spoke again, the Mexican's voice became pleading. "You will tell the man Karr where I go with the sheep?"

"No," I said. "He'll find out anyway, though."

"I must pass through land he owns to reach the land of the government. Maybe at night. There might be trouble."

"Why did you tell me where you were going?" I asked him.

He gnawed the corner off a dry plug of tobacco and exposed brown teeth in a smile. "Why not, *amigo*? You are Martin, a Tyrrell boy, no? I have an acquaintance with your brother. Tell him Pete

Rodriguez asked about his health. We are old friends."

"I didn't know that, Mr. Rodriguez." I walked over to untie the horse. "I'll tell him I met you passing through."

"*Si*, do that." He spat into the fire. "He will remember me well. Say to him that Pete Rodriguez the sheepherder passed by here today on his way to the land of the government."

I pulled the cinch tight and rode away toward the river. I didn't think he really knew Ira, yet I couldn't figure how he knew my name. I finally decided he had been talking with somebody who had described me to him. When I looked back from the riverbank the Mexican was sitting by the fire with his back humped over and looking much like his two dogs that were still watching me. I didn't figure I owed him anything, but I didn't think I would tell anybody where he was going.

Father never tolerated a blab-mouth, even if the talk was something he wanted to know about. He always said a man's business might be straight or crooked, but he had a right to live his own life without a lot of loose talk and foolish rules. I knew Senator Karr didn't like the way Father couldn't go along with the Two-Bar-K's rule against gambling on roundups. Father said he'd put up with that foolishness working for Charlie Goodnight, and he was damned if he'd make a man sneak off from camp to play cards. It still angered me to think of what old Jules Lamar had said about Father and Clayt Paulson. Mr. Karr might have a cattle detective snooping around, but I didn't think Father needed one. . . .

I took off my boots again and recrossed the river without any trouble. Then I repacked the rest of the salt on my other horse and started up toward the ridge where I'd seen the flash before. It was farther away than it looked, and when I finally got off Blacky to look around on top, I didn't really expect to see anyone. I had to look around a long time before I found any sign, but there were hoofprints coming just far enough over the ridge so a rider could see the sheepherder's wagon without getting off his horse or showing up more than the top of his head. The horse was unshod. It could have been a stray getting up on high ground to look around, but I figured a riderless horse would have topped out completely on the ridge.

I mounted up and followed the horse tracks. In the flat below they led off toward our ranch, but after I'd gone a far ways down a dry creek bed and around the edge of some jumbled granite hills I knew I'd have to give it up. The rider, whoever he was, knew his way through the roughest country on our range, and he was sticking to what cover there was like an old buck deer. And it wasn't the best plan those days to follow a man too carefully just to see if he carried a pair of field glasses.

By the time I'd backtracked enough to put out the last blocks of salt, it was close to four o'clock. Blacky was getting tired and cranky, though I hadn't moved him out of a walk all day. He twisted around while I was laying out salt and bit a patch of hair from the neck of the squealing pack horse. I had to whomp Blacky's belly a couple of times with the instep of my boot before he calmed down. It didn't help things any.

Riding for the ranch, I watched the sun go down far enough to brighten all the colors of rock, land, and sparse grass. I'd heard some people call this the lonesomest country they'd ever seen. I wouldn't argue with them about the way it looked in winter. But other times there was plenty to see and think about. A man could look around and see all that sky opened up and washed with blue, except to the west where it was getting yellow-orange and violet now, like it was smeared with wildflowers. In the rough sandstone or granite country were yellow-gray badgers and rabbits with rust-tinted fur that was hard to tell from the rock. You'd see red-tailed hawks hunting sagebrush gullies for meadow larks or mottled sage chickens moving down in huge flocks each morning and evening to water on Longs Creek or the Sweetwater.

And sometimes like now—when the color was

firing the range and you saw antelope trailing sunlit dust as they ran, black-horned and drifting away over the grassland like white-splotched tan ghosts—I could almost see what Ira meant about nobody having an exclusive claim to this much land. But I didn't figure it should be sheeped-off or plowed under, and then abandoned to go weedy and sterile like some old homesteads I'd seen near Green Mountain. And I knew that I, like Father, would fight for our range if it became necessary. A man had to hold some things for himself and, right or wrong, stand up against those who threatened to grab them.

It bothered me, though, that maybe I didn't really understand too well what was happening to cattlemen like my father and Mr. Karr. Ira, with his reading and talking to old-timers like Jules Lamar, seemed to be trying to form something worth holding to from a change nobody could stop. Most everybody on the TX thought he was the dreamer and Father and me the practical ones. But maybe my brother was being practical in trying to avoid fighting over mavericks and range rights.

While unsaddling later in the corral, I wondered if that Mexican sheepherder named Pete Rodriguez or the honyockers on Green Mountain were also trying to keep trouble from flaring up. . . . I doubted it.

Chapter 6

When I turned Blacky loose he rolled and trotted off into the horse pasture, and the pack horse followed him, whickering loudly. The hands, back from the line camps for roundup, were eating in the bunkhouse kitchen. Father and Senator Karr, his dress clothes of the evening before replaced by an old tweed suit and high riding boots, were standing by the chuck wagon, which was blocked up for repair of the rear wheels. I knew my father was proud of that wagon. It had come up from Texas several times with his trail herds, and was the only grub wagon in our roundup district that had been over the Goodnight Trail.

Mr. Karr nodded to me. "Good evening, Mart."

"Cattle looking good, son?" asked Father. It was his standard greeting when I'd been riding.

"Slicking off nice," I said. "Calves are doing proud too."

"It seems too bad that our cattle do as well with other men's brands as with our markings," the Senator said.

"Don't know that we'd be better off in another part of the country," Father commented to no one in particular. "Trouble follows cows, I'd say."

The Senator spun one wheel of the chuck wagon with his hand. The spokes blurred with motion and the hub sang in the greased shaft. Mr. Karr stared at the wheel until it slowed and the spokes were separate again. "I'm going to put an end to rustling on the Sweetwater," he said stiffly. "I despise a thief worse than a murderer. I despise a man who thinks one calf or one spot of ground more or less doesn't matter to the person who owns it or develops it."

I'd never known Mr. Karr to look so cruel and determined. Sometimes now when I see a picture of the Senator's oldest grandson I can imagine the exact expression again—and the rest of what Karr said that evening. "Carpetbaggers, fence cutters, rustlers—I hate a thief's guts. What I have now I gained without stealing. I will make these renegade cowboys and their nester friends honest or drive them from the country. And the Stock Association will stand behind me."

My father laid his hand gently on the wheel and stopped it. He was not looking at the Senator but past him to the river. His deeply sunken eyes were momentarily black as powder under his heavy eyebrows. I couldn't tell what he was thinking, but I noticed the Senator didn't press him for agreement.

"Friend of yours riding this way, Wallace," he said finally. "Sits a horse like Paulson."

Mr. Karr and I turned also then. The man approaching the ranch rode, as Father once said, like he was watching his shadow. Even at some distance he looked tall. He was taller than Father maybe and dark-skinned, like he might have Indian blood, though nobody seemed to know just where he came from. Some people said he'd been a Pinkerton man before coming to Wyoming, while others would argue that he had fought against the Apaches as a cavalry officer during the Geronimo outbreak of 1885. In the bunkhouse one night I'd heard a couple of cowboys swear he had killed his first man in the Texas brush country, close to where my father used to live.

"Gentlemen," said Clayt Paulson, when his horse stopped near the wagon. His frock coat and hat were dark—he might have been mistaken in town for a moody preacher or a doctor—and black pants were tucked neatly into tall, shotgun-topped boots. He wore no mustache, which was unusual then, and the bunkhouse wits said he was so proud of his looks he couldn't stand to hide any part of them. His lips and mouth were firm but, I thought, a little too small under a long, straight nose that was thin as the front sight of a six-shooter. His horse was a fine buckskin branded Two-Bar-K.

Mr. Karr's mood seemed to change once Paulson rode up, and he smiled broadly. "I thought I had seen that buckskin somewhere before. Were you looking for me, Clayt?"

"Something important came up." The voice

was low and soft, with a faint rasping undertone that clashed with his cultured speech. While he spoke, Paulson looked around guardedly at everything except the three of us standing by the wagon. It seemed to be a habit with him in the same way that a horse always inspects a strange corral—only Clayt Paulson was already familiar with every building and cow hand on our ranch.

"Well, let's hear about it," said the Senator. "Is it too serious to discuss right away?"

The stock detective's eyes lowered at Karr's joke and settled on Father as though Paulson had only then noticed his being there. "No," he murmured. "I think you both will be interested."

"Mart will turn your horse into the corral, Clayt," Father said. "I reckon I'll take care of some things in the house while you two talk for a spell."

Mr. Karr was insistent. "Wait until we have all three talked this over, Martin. There's no need for you to leave. Clayt said you should hear it too."

Father looked at them both steadily for a moment before nodding. I took the buckskin as soon as Paulson dismounted, led him to the corral, and took off the saddle and bridle. It was a good rig, made in Denver with matching rifle scabbard and saddlebags. The rifle was a long-barreled Winchester .44-40, model 1873. A pair of field glasses were thrust into one saddlebag that hadn't been strapped shut. I wasn't much surprised.

When I walked back to the chuck wagon Father was squatting on his heels and drawing in the dirt with a stick. Senator Karr and Clayt Paulson stood with their backs against the wagon. Paulson was the only one who noticed me, but he didn't stop his talk.

"I had thought the setup looked suspicious," he was saying. "Volanski had been selling beef in Rawlins for a year, and the hides he showed were getting worn out from being carried back and forth to town. But I had not caught him at anything before."

"There are others like him in the Green Mountain country or on Antelope Creek," Mr. Karr put in. "Look at Averill and Ella Watson with their operations at Bothwell. They are all damned hard to catch and impossible to convict in the local courts. This Russian squatter Volanski is shrewder than many of them."

Paulson's large eyes were mottled yellow like agate. When he began talking again his eyes became alive with flecks of light, as if the detective was angry or drunk on bad whiskey. "He was not so shrewd this time. I was hidden and watching him the other day. He and his boy gathered in their milk cows and those six head of poor steers they run. A Two-Bar-K stray was with the other cattle, but they cut it out that evening into their baling-wire and matchstick corral by the milking shed. I knew then what the play would be."

"Did you stop them?" Mr. Karr spoke jovially, but I knew he wasn't joking now.

Paulson shook his head. "No. I thought it best to see how they would operate."

"Good man," agreed Mr. Karr. "Not much chance for a jury around here to do anything but acquit him, anyway. One damned rascal protects another when a case comes to trial. What did Volanski do with our steer?"

"He, his wife, and the boy worked at night in the shed. I got close enough to hear them talking while they butchered the steer. The next morning Volanski left for Rawlins in his wagon. Later the boy took the hide up the mountain wrapped in gunny sacks and buried it. They had cut the brand out—burned it in their stove, I think."

"Were you sure the steer was a Two-Bar-K?" Father asked quietly.

Paulson smiled. "The left ear was grubbed off. I saw the brand clearly when they put the steer into the corral. Did you think I wasn't positive about it?"

"A man can make a wrong guess sometimes. Of course this doesn't look like it leaves much room for doubt . . ."

"We have been suspicious of this one for a long while, Martin," said Karr. "The Association is getting together a list of other rustlers along the river also."

"And then what's the call, Wallace?"

"The Association is still working on a plan to eliminate troublemakers," Mr. Karr answered. "If we had ten more men like Clayt, there wouldn't be a rustler left in the territory."

Father didn't smile. "I reckon not. Sorry to have interrupted your story, Clayt."

"There wasn't much more to it. I followed Volanski into Rawlins and found out where he sold the steer carcass. Quite a horny crowd lives in that community. I am sure Volanski goes there every week, and according to the talk in the saloons he brings a beef at least once a month."

"We will deal with Mr. Volanski as soon as the roundup is over," said Karr.

Paulson didn't seem satisfied. "May I ask how?"

"I will have to think a little, Clayt."

"I have a way that is certain."

Mr. Karr laughed, while my father looked up carefully at Paulson. I thought he was exerting an effort to keep from speaking angrily to both the other men. But then he seemed to gain control of himself. "I guess that's all settled," he said, standing up and rubbing out his scratches in the ground with one boot toe. "Anyway, I reckon it's about mealtime. We better not keep our new cook waiting tonight, either. Mart, show Paulson where to wash up, and I'll ask Miss Leah to set an extra place."

I knew Cookie and Slat Honeywell had never been very friendly with Clayt Paulson, and that many of the hands hated him. Maybe the men's feeling was why Father had invited the stock detective to eat at the house instead of in the bunkhouse. I guess he figured it was best not to take a chance of stirring up the hands just before spring work began. Cowboys were a touchy bunch some ways—they were wild often, but most of them were hard workers in a dirty business. Whether they'd ever vented another man's brand or not, they resented an Association snooper like Paulson.

"Thanks for taking care of my horse," Clayt said when we were walking around to the pump.

"It wasn't anything," I told him.

"I saw you eating with a sheepherder down on the river this noon," he said. "I didn't wait to ride in with you because I noticed you had salt to put out."

That wasn't what I'd expected to hear, and his saying it straight off put some slack in my rope. "That's right," I answered finally. "I figured it was you up on that ridge with those glasses."

He hadn't expected my reply either, but he covered up smooth enough. "You don't like me very well, do you, son?"

"I don't know you very well."

He pumped water into the brass washpan and took off his hat and coat. "I don't blame you any for feeling the way you do. There is considerable talk around the country about what a coyote I am. But no one can catch a coyote unless he can think and act like one when necessary."

He looked much younger in his shirt sleeves and bareheaded. The holster and cartridge belt around his waist had been saddle-soaped recently. His .44 was well cared for, unlike a cowboy's battered Colt or Smith and Wesson handgun.

"Maybe it's needed," I said, watching the far end of the horse pasture where Ira was riding in on the little bay mare. He's been there all day, I thought. He's talked with her and maybe taken her for a ride, and given her some present like I never thought of doing. . . .

"We could try being more friendly." Paulson dried his face deliberately. He'd already noticed Ira too. "I might not be as black as some people would like to believe."

"Maybe not," I said.

Clayt Paulson didn't press the matter, but carried his coat and hat into the house while I washed. He might or might not be all black, but I had to admit he was smart. You had to give him the credit there all right. I'd have to wait and see about changing my mind as far as he was concerned.

The others were seated when I entered the long area in our headquarters that was both living and dining room. Leah had put one of Mother's embroidered tablecloths over the slab table and gotten out the Tyrrell family chinaware, that wasn't used unless a woman was present. I sat down at the end of the table just as Leah came in from the kitchen with the last hot dishes of food. She had on a plain blue dress and a big white apron that made her look different, not any prettier but more like a working ranch woman. And her face was tempered with some resolve to be gay that seemed out of place to me after what I'd heard the night before outside the lean-to.

Ira entered just as Leah was leaning over Paulson to pour coffee into his cup. She paused, looking directly at him in the doorway and then smiling at Clayt's compliment on the meal. I won't ever forget her expression, which was, I realized later, a challenge meant for Ira and Paulson both. Watching my brother, I knew he was troubled by something in Leah's shining face. And yet he didn't avoid her eyes.

"We were almost going to stop waiting for you," she said, her cheeks flushing as she turned away from him to finish pouring the coffee.

"I'm sorry to be late," Ira said to her. "I didn't know we were having company and one of your dinners."

"Clayt here will sleep in the extra bunk with

you boys," Father said, passing the platter of beefsteak to Leah, who was sitting down beside me.

Clayt Paulson stood up slowly as Ira walked to the empty place at the end of the table. He held out his hand to my brother. "Back from school again, I see."

"That's right. I understand you're still riding around after rustlers." Ira shook hands with him, but he made no attempt to hide his coldness toward the taller man.

The meal was good, but I had a feeling that none of us were thinking about food. Leah managed to keep the conversation alive by asking Clayt for his opinion on the last big party at the Cheyenne Club while the Stock Association was meeting and whether the Natrona County seat should be in Casper or Bessemer.

While the uneven light from the kerosene lamp distorted his face at the table's head, Father nodded politely at the proper times in the slow conversation and stared down into the Tyrrell chinaware. I wondered what he saw there to make him so silent. Perhaps it was some memory of my mother, the woman I'd never known . . . or something I couldn't even guess. But I thought the lines and shadows, the heavy mustache masking his mouth, the eyes that looked even larger by lamplight, gave the impression that he might be haunted by guilt or remorse in this house built among the Indian camp sites, the emigrant trails, the hollow buffalo bones and cattle skulls littered along the Sweetwater like a taunt to the ambition of any one man. . . .

Ira ate quickly and excused himself before Leah served the pie and second round of coffee. After the meal I went out to the corral and tried to work on a hackamore bosal I was braiding from rawhide. I had an awful wanting to ride over to see Mary on some excuse or another, but I knew it wouldn't have been any good, feeling the sulky way I did. I couldn't help hating Ira a little and then myself too for being so small about him and Mary. It wouldn't have been so bad if I hadn't some things to keep remembering about her . . . like what happened the fall before, after Ira'd gone back to college in Pennsylvania. . . .

I'd been riding a half-broke horse Father had given to me. We'd already trailed cattle to Rock Creek for shipment East, and I hadn't any special work to be doing. So I rode that horse along the river every afternoon. This time I'd rode farther than usual and met Mary riding back with a sack of grub from the little store Jack Stenger ran along with a saloon that the cowboys called a "hog ranch."

Of course my horse had to shy and almost buck me off when he saw that lumpy sack tied behind

Mary's saddle. I got him stopped finally, though he was still trembling and tossing his head.

"Is your horse always so unfriendly, Martin?" she laughed.

"Guess he's not used to girls dressed up like men," I told her.

But she kept smiling. "How can I ride without pants, Martin? And wouldn't a skirt scare your new horse more?"

"He's not scared," I said. She made me feel foolish sometimes, and now I couldn't think of much to say. That made things worse.

"Why haven't you come to Willow Springs lately?" she asked. "My father says you must have a girl friend at Bothwell." She laughed again. "Is that true?"

"Sure," I said. "I thought everybody knew about it. There's a couple of sisters in Rawlins that Ira and I met last Fourth of July, too. Then there's a Shoshone girl at Fort Washakie and a preacher's daughter in Lander . . ."

"I thought so," Mary said, and I judged she might be a little more serious. She got off her horse and tightened up the cinch of Lamar's old, black-worn saddle. "My father will be glad to hear you're so busy."

I started to get off too, and when I had only one boot in the stirrups my horse jumped, got frightened seeing me halfway off his back, and began to buck. I lasted out two stiff jumps and got piled down into the sage. The lead rope on the hackamore pulled free of my belt, and Mary was able to catch my horse before he could quit bucking and start to run. She rode back leading the snorting animal, but she wasn't laughing at me.

"Are you hurt, Martin?" she called. "You fell so hard."

I rolled onto my feet and brushed some of the dust off my pants. "Served me right, I reckon. Thanks for catching the bronc."

When I had the lead rope in my hand she dismounted again and pulled her saddle off. "I think you hurt yourself," she said. "I'm sorry I made your horse afraid."

"It's just his ornery nature," I told her. "It wasn't your fault." I did feel shaky, but I didn't want to show it. I unsaddled and then hobbled both our horses. We sat there along the river in the warm sun.

"Don't you get lonesome living out here?" I asked her after a while.

Mary gazed down at the green water bending around through marsh grass and willows. The sand under shallow water was shining cleanly on the near edge, and across the river two red-winged blackbirds fluttered up with flashes of scarlet like blood against black feathers and disappeared again into tall reeds and cattails. They sang over there, out of sight and sounding wet and heavy like a part of the moving water—wonk-la-*ree* . . . wonk-la-*ree*. . . .

"I'm used to living here, Martin," she said. "I don't need many people around to be happy, and if I feel lonesome I can ride out to watch the cattle and try to find some bird or animal I haven't seen very often. Your brother has always come over to talk to Father and me, and even you aren't so busy that you don't stop by every once in a while. But that cabin is the place where I was raised. How could I be more happy living far from there?"

"I don't know," I said. "I guess growing up in a place makes a person like it, even if it's some god-awful place like London or another one of those smoky cities with the people all crowded up like bees in a hive."

Mary nodded and rested her chin in her cupped hands. "Once I left my father and mother alone out here and stayed for almost a year on the Arapahoe Reservation. Father thought I might enjoy living with my mother's people. Everyone was kind to me and I learned to work with leather and beads, but I felt like I was shut up in a big jail made and owned by the government. Then my mother died and I had to come back to take care of Father at Willow Springs. Since then I haven't left him or the Sweetwater. I think people are foolish to believe a strange place can make them more happy. A person is contented when he lives at peace with himself and the things around him. . . ."

That was something to think about all right. "You weren't very old when your mother died, were you?" I asked.

"Only nine or ten. She had caught the lung sickness long before . . . what my father calls consumption."

Then I told her about my mother dying, though she must've heard all about that from Ira. It was good to talk to someone like Mary, who would listen as though what you said was important to her also. She had good sense and made everything sound simple and right. And being half Indian had given her a dark sort of beauty that made my throat tighten a little when I looked at her for long.

"I feel a lot better now," I told her, flipping a rock out at the water. "I'm going to come back here sometime and take a swim in that big bend of the river."

The corners of her eyes crinkled up. "Why don't you do it now? I'll watch the horses for you."

She meant it, I knew, and the way she said it was like a dare. I figured a swim might clear my head, so I left her and went down to some willows and took off my clothes. Then I swam down into the big hole. The water wasn't too cold and I dived around some, showing off.

"Come on!" I teased her after I'd been in a while. "It's not very deep, so it won't matter if you can't swim." Then I drifted up against the near bank, never thinking she'd really do it. But it wasn't long until I saw her swimming down, her hair loose and shiny around her laughing face as she dog-paddled like a beaver.

"I can swim, Mart!" she called. "Better than you, I think. . . ."

She'd surprised me all right, but I went out halfway to meet her, and we ran a race back to the bank, laughing and splashing water around like we were just kids again.

We reached the riverbank, breathing hard, and clung to an old willow tree. I remember how water drops beaded on her shoulders and thick hair in the sunlight. I felt tired and warm watching her there in the water beside me, brown arms reaching up to the dying willow and her eyes partly closed against the sinking sun. I wanted bad to touch her, hold her against me, and never let anybody hurt her.

Mary had seen me watching her and half turned, putting one hand on my shoulder. "I beat you, Martin," she said gently. And we held each other there, her wet mouth by my ear, while the sun spread orange like a range fire across the sky above the riverbank. . . .

After a while I put the hackamore away. My fingers were clumsy, and I remembered Cookie saying a man had to be at peace with himself to work rawhide into something worth having. Maybe I didn't like wondering why I'd never had sense enough to tell Mary the way I felt about her. Anyway, I went back to my room and lay down. I wasn't very tired from riding, but I figured I might get sick of lying there thinking and be asleep by the time Ira or Clayt Paulson came in to bed.

Chapter 7

When I woke up early in the morning, Paulson was gone. From the noises outside I knew the hands had eaten already and were gathering their bedrolls and personal gear for roundup. Ira and I dressed without much talk, and when we got to the table Leah Karr was fixing flapjacks, bacon, and eggs she'd brought with her from the Two-Bar-K.

Father looked tired, and I thought he must have slept little. He and the Senator were driving to Rawlins that morning for mail and supplies. Ira was quiet and thoughtful. I saw Leah watching his back from the kitchen, as if she was looking for something important in the set of his shoulders.

"Ira," said Father when we were seated.

It sounded harsh the way he said it, and I glanced down at my brother. He'd put on Levi's and a fresh work shirt, but the clothes didn't seem right for him. They were too new. He had shaved that morning, and his face appeared thinner and paler than ever.

"Ira, I want you to ride back to the Karr ranch with Miss Leah today," Father said. "She's decided not to stay until the roundup's over this year."

"All right." Ira nodded slowly without looking up.

"I want you to ride out with the grub and bed wagons this afternoon," Father told me. "You'll be in charge of our outfit on the way. Wallace's foreman will run things until I come out tomorrow."

I knew he was deliberately putting me in charge instead of Ira, and in a way I couldn't help feeling a little happy about it. It was Ira's own fault for not acting like a real cowman, I told myself.

"My foreman Roan Meyers and six men are to meet you at the Red Rocks beyond Willow Springs," Mr. Karr said. "We are going to work my range last this year."

I said, "I'll see to it we start in time to meet them before dark."

Father laid his knife and fork across the edge of his plate. "I reckon we should make a decision about Finn Rankin and his friends," he told the Senator. "They're likely to cause trouble when we don't let them round up with us."

"I'm afraid they will, Martin. I do not like those untrustworthy cowboys like Rankin and Seth Daniels any more than you do. I have always said that. But if we don't let them come on roundup with us, they will make an early gather by themselves next spring."

"The Association doesn't recognize most of their brands," my father pointed out bluntly. "It's illegal to even let them gather cattle with us."

I saw the Senator raise his eyebrows at that. "You might call it that, I suppose. But I think we also have to be practical about the matter. We have only a few Association members in this roundup district, and we would be shorthanded if any trouble started."

"They'll try to cause some kind of trouble before long," answered Father. "You recollect how Daniels tried to stop us from putting the Association brand on those mavericks that strayed near his place on Antelope Creek last year. I figure they'll keep on crowding us one way or another—especially if we let them on roundup."

Mr. Karr smiled agreeably, but I could tell he hadn't changed his mind. "Of course I realize it's a delicate situation. But I still feel we must be practical. If we let those renegade cowboys round up with us, we can keep an eye on them. And when the right time comes, I believe the Association will be able to handle them. Besides, would you care to be the one that prevents them from joining our roundup, Martin?"

Father looked around at all of us. "I don't believe I'd be afraid to stop them," he said. "I don't reckon it would hurt to show them where we stood. As I recall, you and me both voted for the Association's roundup regulations, Wallace."

That was all my father or Mr. Karr said about it. But I wondered if something had come between the two men that might destroy their friendship. I hoped not, because I'd always admired Mr. Karr, who had given me my first man's saddle, a slick-fork much like Father's.

Father and the Senator drove off in the buckboard just after daylight. I watched them go, both sitting stiffly on the seat in the cool air like the uneasy figures you see in old newspaper pictures. Past the corral my father reined his team into the wagon ruts that curved through morning-dark sage toward the river, and the Senator raised his arm once in a farewell to Leah, who stood alone on the headquarters porch.

When I started toward the bunkhouse, I heard her call me. The sun, tipped over the Rattlesnakes like a bloody moon, hurt my eyes as I walked toward her.

"Why did he do that, Mart?" she asked in a strange voice.

"Father, you mean?"

"Yes . . . what he said to Ira."

"I don't know, Leah. It doesn't mean anything. Ira knows that."

She shook her head. "He has never given Ira a chance. How does he know your brother doesn't fit the ranch, when he won't give him an opportunity to use any of his own ideas?"

"He likes Ira," I said. "That's why he tried too hard to change his ideas about the ranch."

"That's difficult to believe," Leah said coolly. "He's only driving Ira farther away from all of us."

I didn't answer her. Cookie was out scrubbing down the chuck wagon with a broom and lye water. Slat Honeywell and Whitey Pence were saddling up to bring in the horse herd they'd been shoeing all week. "Guess I better get to work," I said. "It was a good breakfast you fixed, Leah."

"Just a minute, please." She hadn't moved on the porch since we started talking, and the way she looked made me a little uneasy. "Things aren't the same now between your brother and me. I wanted you to know."

"I guess I'd figured that. I'm sorry, though."

"Are you, Mart?"

I felt uncomfortable standing there, with the sun burning my eyes because I had to look up to see her. For a moment I wished I could say something to hurt her—I hadn't been the one who broke up her and Ira. "That stock detective works for your dad, doesn't he?" I asked.

Her eyes widened a little. "I don't really know about that. He has been a friend of Father for a year or two. My father's very fond of him."

"He said he wanted to be my friend too," I told her.

"Why not, Mart?" She smiled faintly. "You don't have many friends out here, do you?"

"I don't need many."

"Clayt always has been polite to me. He wants to quit detective work someday and start a ranch of his own in New Mexico."

"Why not?" I gave it back to her as a mean joke, but I was sorry when I'd said it. She turned away from me, not standing straight any more like she had when cooking breakfast at the stove.

"Don't turn against Ira, or Clayt either," Leah said, stepping back to the doorway. "They need friends as much as you or I do."

I thought of saying that Ira had a friend all right—a couple of them, in fact—at Lamar's homestead. But I couldn't do it.

Leah said, "This country is changing some way. I can feel it in Cheyenne and driving from Rawlins to our ranch. People on the trains coming west look so hungry when they talk about the land they're going to settle out here. They think men like Mr. Tyrrell or my father, who risked their lives building ranches here, should be punished or driven out now that the country has been developed and made safe."

"Talk's cheap," I said.

"They mean it, Mart. Without the protection given us by Clayt Paulson and the Association, we would all have nothing now."

"I reckon that's true. Only—"

"So don't condemn a man like Clayt too quickly," she went on. "He's a good man doing an unpleasant job. Won't you try to give him a chance?"

"Maybe I will, Leah."

"And please don't let Ira down. . . ."

She had a point about Paulson and his job, I thought afterward, riding out with Slat and Whitey Pence after the horses. But I wasn't sure it was a very good point. Ira and Old Man Lamar didn't cotton to the detective at all, though they had strange notions about the big cattle companies claiming more land than they had any right to. It looked to me like Father should mistrust the detective for a different reason. From what Cookie had told me once, he shouldn't like the way Paulson talked about having a method of dealing with rustlers that was "certain." Clayt's meaning was clear enough, and some people would tell you he'd already taken care of several men in Texas and Wyoming that way.

Father would have a good reason for not liking talk about that kind of killing. As near as I could tell from Cookie's story, the Tyrrells, like a lot of other cattlemen, had got their start by working the Texas brush country for mavericks that weren't always on their land. Father's oldest brother had been surprised one night, with a holding pen full of longhorn cows and slick calves, by men from a neighboring family who were said to have branded their share of Tyrrell cattle. He'd rasped the hoofs of the calves tender, so they wouldn't be able to move back to their own range, and already branded some of them. Cookie said my uncle had been roped around the neck, dragged through the chaparral until dead, and strung from the gate of that pen as a threat to the other two Tyrrell brothers. It must not have worked very well, because my father and the younger uncle were well liked in the country, and one of their friends joined them in carrying out the Texas custom of paying back the death of a relation.

That part was just hearsay, but Cookie thought two or three men had been killed before the other family moved on farther west—looking for better range, they said. My father had been married several years by then, and made cattle drives with Goodnight and by himself. It must not have been long afterward that he started the ranch on the Sweetwater and I was born. . . . And now we were having trouble that wasn't much different from the kind Father had known in Texas.

I guessed that how you looked at the rustler problem depended on a lot more than you'd think just to hear Mr. Karr talk about it. A hired watchdog like Clayt Paulson, backed by the Association, could see it simple enough maybe—a man was guilty or innocent, depending on reports given him from Cheyenne, and if a man was said to be guilty, Paulson would dog the "rustler" until he saw something suspicious going on. But I didn't see how my father could see it that simple after his brother had been lynched and men killed in the feuding that followed. Anyway, I wished he would keep Clayt Paulson off the TX. . . .

If I was going to stay on the ranch, I'd have to decide where to stand on a lot of things like that. The easiest way would be to pull out for some new country until I knew my own mind for sure. But I'd been through that kind of thinking before without getting anywhere.

"Old Mart there's got the sleepin' sick," Whitey hollered at Slat Honeywell as we got the horses bunched and headed in. "Ought to squaw-hitch him in the saddle, so he don't drop off and get trompled."

Slat's teeth flashed in skin tanned like work-glove leather. He'd ridden for my father longer than anyone else at the TX. He always wore yellow galluses and a dingy white shirt. Although he never talked much, he was the best hand with cattle on the river. Slat's white mustache was thick on each end like a steer's tail, and when he looked at you his eyes were creased in wrinkles like he was still looking into afternoon sun on the cattle trail north.

As far as size went, Whitey made about two of the older hand. He was big-boned and red-faced, with surprising strength under the flabby flesh padding his frame. A year or two ago he'd drifted in with a herd of cattle from Oregon. He still rode a center-fire saddle and carried a long braided rope like the Mex hands used in California. Most of his talk was either bragging about his skill with horses or playing a joke on someone which usually ended up with a touch of meanness. I didn't really have anything against him, though.

"Listen now, Mart," grinned Whitey. "I know how you feel. Here's a young fellow just got his growth stuck off where nothing happens for excitement all winter 'cept the snowballs hittin' your dad's caddle in the ass. Now I say let's you and me go over to Bothwell or Stenger's first chance after roundup and sample the booze and heifer meat."

"Maybe sometime, Whitey," I told him polite enough. "The way you boys look after going to Stenger's isn't much of an advertisement."

He snorted in a friendly way. "Some's hung up for a spell, but not old Whitey. . . . Why, hell's prod, Mart, what's the use of ridin' your butt raw all year, 'less you socialize a little?"

There wasn't any easy way to answer that, and I kept quiet. Anyhow, Slat was riding around to get in front of the horses and lead them into the corral wings, so I didn't push them for a while.

"See that blaze-faced black?" Whitey reined in abruptly beside me, and his horse threw his head up, banging the Mexican bit against his teeth in a way I didn't care for. "Your dad bought him along with some mares this spring from Mose Ethridge."

The horse was big, with a swinging hammer-shaped head lined by a crooked white splotch like a broken nose. He ran in a heavy-footed lope, biting the horses jostling against him with a snaky twist of his long neck. I didn't like the looks of him.

Whitey pursed his mouth sagely. "Slat and me named him Moonlight. Got to watch yourself when you climb aboard that bronc or damned if he don't give you a screwin' that won't stop."

I caught a brooding in Whitey's voice that sounded like he was working up to something. "I guess you've already knocked some of the meanness out of him," I said, looking dumb.

"Oh sure, sure. He's just right now for the gov'ner's wife to mount, Mart. We threw him to get the shoes on, but that only gentled him more." He winked elaborately at me. "Was you needin' a stout circle horse in your string for roundup?"

I saw what was coming then. "Forget it, Whitey," I told him. "I'm not going to ride that hammerhead."

"Why, I wasn't suggestin' that. Naturally, being a good rider like your dad, you could stick him . . . but I wasn't thinkin'—"

He broke off, cussing as the horse herd veered away from the trail, spooked by sage chickens flushing up noisily around Slat's gray gelding.

"Head 'em, head 'em!" the old hand yelled, and we had a hard time bunching and lining them out again. They were hairing off and spring fat. And when it looked like we had them started, Moonlight rolled his eyes and turned back, bucking and cutting wind as he ran.

When we finally got the horses into the corral, they bunched up in one corner and milled nervously. Moonlight edged himself far away and watched us with bear-small eyes over the neck of another horse. Whitey and Slat were rolling cigarettes and looking over the saddle stock. I saw Ira walking toward the corral like he wanted to talk to me.

Whitey saw him coming and busied himself with the tobacco and brown cigarette papers. "Good morning, Ira," he called pleasantly. "Nice weather for roundup, ain't it?"

Ira nodded. "Whitey . . . Slat." He turned to say something to me, but Whitey spoke first.

"Got some new horseflesh, Ira. I was wondering what your opinion would be about that white-faced black in the corner."

I watched Ira glance at Whitey and then at the Moonlight horse. "I don't think much of him," Ira said quietly.

"Well now, I'd say he ain't a *puny* bugger. You got to allow he's got meat on him." Whitey smiled apologetically. "Nothing like those colts you been raising, though." He looked to Slat for backing, but Honeywell only squatted down against the corral poles, staring at the shifting horse herd.

I could tell Ira hadn't missed the emphasis Pence put on the word "puny." But he seemed to be waiting, as though curious to hear what else the cowboy was going to say.

"A little exercise's all old Moonlight there needs. A good rider would quiet him down like a suckin' colt."

"I'm sure you'll quiet him down," Ira told him, looking over pointedly at Whitey's saddled horse that moved nervously on the end of a tie rope looped around the top corral pole. The horses in his string usually became switch-tailed, galled, or cold-jawed.

Pence ignored this. "Since you been to school and everything, I figured you might educate old

Moonlight a little. Course, he's a mite stout and mean spoiled . . ."

"A spoiled horse needs training instead of being jerked and spurred, Whitey."

I wished Ira hadn't said it that way. For Whitey—and most of the other hands too—it wasn't a question of what Moonlight needed. They saw a horse as another tool a man needed. Although they might make a pet of a horse they owned, most cowboys wouldn't see anything wrong in roughing up a spoiled company horse while bucking him out for the hell of it. That sounded sensible to me too. I thought gaining the respect of the hands was much more important to my brother than a bad horse getting completely soured. But Ira didn't seem to care what the cowboys thought of him.

"Sure, sure." Whitey winked. "I was just thinkin' you might like the practice, since you ain't been spurrin' anything 'cept a school desk all winter."

Ira was calm enough. He just shook his head and asked me to come over to the house when I was finished at the corral. Then he started to walk away.

I watched him a moment, wishing I didn't feel ashamed. "Rope out that black for me, Slat," I finally said.

Honeywell stared at me until I asked him again. After that he dropped his cigarette in the dust and got his rope.

"Don't be foolish, Mart," Ira called to me.

"I didn't ask for any advice," I said.

Whitey stood there grinning and scratching his red neck. When Slat had roped the horse he brought over my saddle and hackamore. He and Honeywell had to tie up a hind foot to get the saddle on. Then they put a blindfold over Moonlight's eyes and took off the foot rope. I didn't look at Ira again, but I knew he hadn't left. It was a long step and swing up into the saddle. I tried to think of nothing but the stretched-out, lowered neck of the quivering horse. He was straining beneath me with the effort of sensing my movements as I settled in the saddle. It seemed a long wait while Slat pulled the blindfold, and when he stepped back Moonlight didn't move. . . .

I didn't spur him, but with a squeal he suddenly began to buck in the same spot he'd been standing. The saddle leather jarred into my crotch, and that ugly head—teeth and tongue showing—swung out to the sides in rhythm with the stiff-legged bucking. When he began to spin around I thought I had him licked, which sure suited me then, because he'd almost had me a couple of times and my nose was starting to bleed. A stout horse, I knew, could scramble a man's guts if he bucked hard enough and long enough. But I wasn't going to give the thing up now and let Pence get the satisfaction of pulling something on me as well as on Ira. I knew I wasn't the rider my brother was, but I was mad enough at Whitey, and Ira too, that I didn't care.

Maybe I would've ridden that horse down if he hadn't started bucking toward the side of the corral, making Whitey and Slat jump up the poles to get out of the way. The next thing I knew Moonlight banged my leg against the corral. That loosened me. All he needed then was a couple of good stiff jumps to jar me off. I fell against the bottom of a post, and the horse stepped on me, kicking that sore leg again.

I was still lying there when Slat came over. "You hurt anywheres, Mart?" He didn't touch me, but he was frowning and awfully serious.

"I'm all right." I got up on my knees, feeling my right thigh hammer. "Lost my breath's all."

Whitey came over too, but Ira was still standing halfway between the corral and the house. "Well now, that was some ride." Whitey grinned. "Thought you had him rode down for a spell."

"Joke's over," Slat told him flatly. "Go pull the boy's saddle off that horse before he rolls on it."

"Hell, Mart there's all right!" But Whitey went over to get a rope.

I stood up, bracing myself against the corral, and moved a little without putting any weight on the one leg. Then I pushed my hat back into shape. I hobbled across the corral and let myself out the gate. Ira stood there waiting for me. He looked as angry as I felt.

"Did you prove something, Mart?" he asked me.

"Maybe I did," I said abruptly, walking on past him.

"I thought you had grown up," Ira said. "There was no need to play the fool for Whitey."

"Let me alone," I said. "Just let me alone from here on."

He suddenly looked hurt and didn't say anything else. I limped around to our room, where I could look at my leg without anyone seeing me so close to bawling. By the time I rode out with the horses and wagons for roundup, it didn't hurt . . . not quite so much, anyway. . . .

When supper was finished that night at the Red Rocks, the hands settled down around the fire for a session of hoorawing each other and swapping stories. A few men spread out a bed-tarp away from the circle of firelight and began a game of monte. Most of these cowboys were from the Two-Bar-K, making the most of Mr. Karr's not being there yet.

The Senator's foreman, a big man from Montana named Roan Meyers, laughed out from time to time at the joking. He was a cowboy's foreman who knew how to work his men without seeming to drive them, but I'd heard him sucking up to Karr enough times to figure him for a company man underneath the drawling laugh and red fringe of hair sticking out from his pushed-back hat.

I left the fire and went over to where I'd put my bedroll and saddle, off a ways from the wagons and fire. A few of the horses being herded by the nighthawk had been belled, and I always liked to listen to that sound coming lonely across the swells of rangeland like some kind of strange bird singing. Blacky was a shadow out beyond my bed where I'd staked him. He stood there with his head up, watching me so that mostly what I saw was his eyes like chips of waxed horn.

I wondered why I hadn't turned him out with the horse herd. Thinking about that, I rubbed the back of my leg. The ache ran through my whole leg, but I wasn't going to ask anybody in camp for advice on how to ease it. I could hear Whitey Pence talking a low story for the Two-Bar-K hands and Meyers' snorts of laughter punctuating it. Enough words carried to tell me it was about Ira not wanting to ride that spoiled bronc.

"Looked us right in the eye and said there wasn't no point getting his pants dusty on old Moonlight. . . . I 'lowed the hoss needed educatin' and maybe he'd be the one to book-learn him. But Ira wouldn't even take a squint at him. Said a spiled hoss needed training instead of jerkin' and spurrin'. 'Well yes,' I told him, 'but maybe you might care for the practice since you ain't rode nothing all winter but a damned school desk.' Anyhow, we just meant to hooraw him a little."

"Hell of a way to treat the boss's son, Whitey." It was Roan Meyers talking. "Haven't you got respect for Mr. Tyrrell? Even a good bull can throw a muley calf some spring."

Slat Honeywell grunted. "That Mart's got sand. He was up that gelding's back before Moonlight got his ears laid back proper. Rode him down, I'd say, and curried the burrs out of the old bastard's hide. Just bad luck he got throwed."

"See the muley calf's face when he seen Mart get trompled?" Whitey chuckled softly. "Looked plumb angered about it all. Hell's prod, a man ain't been piled up a few times hasn't got his growth yet. Mr. Tyrrell can still top a mean one hisself if he has a mind to. But this muley calf—"

There was a crash of tin plates in the roundup pan. "Can't you birds talk something else!" Cookie yelled at them from the chuck wagon. "I'm damned if you don't sicken my guts with it. Bunch of gossipy hens cacklin' around here. Somebody grab a flour sack and help dry these plates."

"Aw hell, Cookie!"

"You'll do fine, Whitey."

"Damn me if I wasn't just tellin' what happened."

"Bring that coffeepot around while you're up, Whitey!" someone laughed.

"Man at the pot!"

The talk shifted then, but I wasn't really listening any more. And I didn't like what I'd heard, either. I suppose I'd been proud of trying to ride that Moonlight horse, but I wondered now if I hadn't done it to make Ira look bad. You've sure done it, I told myself, whether you meant to or not. I had to admit that maybe I'd been trying to get back at him for seeing so much of Mary. What did I expect, anyway, since I hadn't done anything but moon around over her?

After thinking that over awhile, I decided what I was going to do. First I got a fresh shirt from my war bag and cleaned up as best I could. Then I saddled Blacky, led him farther away from camp, and rode west for Willow Springs. . . .

The moon, lopsided now and distant-looking in the early evening, gave enough light so I could tell where I was going. All the noise around the wagon faded out quickly, but for a long ways I still heard the belled horses grazing over to my right. My leg felt fevered, and the country I rode through was unfamiliar in the night, like I'd seen it before in a dream. I kept thinking about what I'd say to the girl, but I didn't really know yet. Space and time swallowed me up, while Blacky's hoofs marked the distance like heartbeats. It seemed a longer ride than I'd remembered.

Following a cow trail down into the canyon, I smelled the wood smoke and then finally saw it pluming up from the cabin's flue. My saddle jolted from side to side as the horse felt his way on the trail through sandstone outcrops weathered off into slabs and crumpled ledges. The spring was below me to the left, with the willows dark against the rock. The moon was just high enough to turn the willow leaves slick and shiny on the near edge of the spring.

I pulled up in the shadows, thinking of how Mary was in the cabin there, and how her face would look when she came out to ask me inside. Something kept me from going right on down, though—the looks of things was a little wrong, but it was a minute before I saw the movement in the willows. Then I thought—I guess he'd been on my mind—that the dark shape was Clayt Paulson watching the cabin.

But the form divided and became two shadows. Ira and Mary Lamar, I thought bitterly.

They were walking back from the spring, and I heard their voices without recognizing any of the words. They seemed to be laughing together. At the side of the cabin, where there wasn't a window, they stopped. Her face caught the light momentarily as the two shadows merged for what seemed a long time before drawing apart. When they walked around to the cabin door and pulled it open, I saw them clearly in the kerosene light flung in an oblong through the doorway. The door shut, and that was all there was to it. . . .

I felt myself shiver, and I remembered stupidly that I hadn't brought a jacket. For several minutes I sat there, staring down at the smoke from the cabin that trailed up and dissolved into the clean night sky. I'd forgotten all about my sore leg when Blacky shifted his feet impatiently and my weight bore down on it. I almost cried out. But it was at Ira and the girl . . . at myself for not seeing before that I was just a green kid who hadn't grown up yet.

Riding back toward the roundup camp, I knew I was jealous of my brother. And I felt empty inside from being a fool over a half-breed girl. I wondered if admitting to myself how I felt about her and Ira was a sign I had begun growing up a little.

All of a sudden I was in a hurry to get started with the spring work.

Chapter 8

That year our spring roundup began on the Powder River, and we worked west almost to Beaver Rim and south to Green Mountain. Only a few years back there had been twice as many outfits rounding up each spring—that was before the winter of 1887, though. Now there was us and the Senator, the Thompson brothers, Moses Ethridge, Bobby Dutton, and sometimes one or two others. The roundup districts were being set smaller by the Association, but each year you'd run across a few more little homesteads thrown up along the river or back in some canyon that had water and was on the edge of land claimed by larger cattlemen.

It made you wonder if Leah Karr and Ira weren't right, and the country was changing faster than anyone realized. . . .

The cowboys working for the outfits in our roundup district always seemed glad when we moved out in the spring with the wagons and horse herds thrown together. They were free of the long winter holed up in some god-forsaken, dirty cabin. Free of doing nothing in some dead little town or riding the grub line from ranch to ranch, eating and moving on somewhere else in the worst weather. Before roundup they usually had shined up their bits and spurs and polished any silverwork on their bridles, chaps, and saddles. It was quite a sight to see all those hands start out on the first morning's circle, showing off a little and riding fat horses that had haired off so they shone like satin in the sun.

But the work soon settled down to long monotonous hours gathering cattle in the rough granite mountains and badlands north of the Sweetwater. When the cattle were driven down to the wagons each day, the worst part had just begun. The cows and calves had to be cut out and held together for branding—what I always thought was one of the dirtiest jobs on the cattle ranges.

Even though Ira was a good roper, Mr. Karr as roundup foreman had him rastling down calves with the younger or less experienced hands. His job meant throwing down the calves dragged to the branding fire by several ropers on good horses and holding them until other cowboys branded them to match their mothers, earmarked them as further identification, and castrated the bull calves with careful slashes of sharp knives. The work was dusty, hot, and tiring. Even now I can close my eyes and imagine the way it was— calves bawling under the knife, the stink of glowing irons searing hair and hide, ropers shouting out the brands for the fighting calves they dragged up through the dust, the bloody pieces of flesh cut out in earmarking piled to keep count of the calf crop, a whitish scattering of testicles thrown down in the burning afternoon. And my brother Ira, sweating and calm among the cursing, manure-splattered rustlers who looked and smelled like wild cattle at the end of each day's branding. . . .

As we worked up the Sweetwater, I began to wonder if my father resented the way Mr. Karr had given Ira the dirty end of the stick. If he did,

Father never showed it, so that I finally realized he might have asked the Senator to put him rastling calves like a green hand who couldn't sit a cutting horse and heel a calf with a lasso.

"Ira's getting a bad deal," I mentioned to Father once. "The whole branding crew is pouring it on him just like he was some dumb kid."

"I hadn't noticed that," Father replied evenly. "I reckon a little hard work won't hurt him, though."

"It's not the work I was thinking about."

"What was it then, son?"

"Roan Meyers has charge of the branding crew," I told him, "and he's never liked Ira. He's got the others riding Ira too. I guess you know what it's like when they can have some mean fun with the son of one of the owners."

Father glanced hard at me. "I know what it's like. And I told Wallace to put your brother with the branding crew. I reckon he'll learn a lot this summer."

I just shook my head. "He's stood up to it already," I said. "Why don't you let him trade jobs with me for a while? I don't care much about being nighthawk. Anyway, he's a better rider than I am."

"He'll stay with the branding crew," Father said bluntly. "I'd like to see him learn that things aren't always the way they seem in those books he's been reading."

So that was the end of it. And maybe I really wasn't too sorry about seeing Ira getting a raw deal. At the time I thought Father was more concerned about whether Finn Rankin, Seth Daniels, and the Antelope Creek bunch would try to force their way into our roundup. I noticed he never talked about this with Mr. Karr any more, but I heard him discussing it with Moses Ethridge and a couple of the other owners and managers who stayed with the roundup for several days.

Finn Rankin never showed up, though, at least not that spring. Enough happened anyway before roundup was over. . . .

One evening when we had worked back near Willow Springs, Mary Lamar came riding toward camp while I was taking the horse herd out to graze for the night. When she got close enough to tell it was me, she rode over so I had to talk to her.

"I have to speak to Ira," she said. "Would you ask him to come out here for a minute, Martin?"

She was being friendly enough, but I hadn't forgotten about her and my brother being together so much. "Sure I can," I told her. "I guess it don't make a damn whether these horses scatter all to hell or not."

Her eyes looked big and full of hurt after I'd said it, and I told myself I'd paid her back a little for that night at Lamar's cabin. "I'm sorry I bothered you," she finally said, her voice gentle.

"It isn't a bother. I'll go get him for you, if you'll make a bargain with me."

She looked up slowly, her eyes deep brown and soft now. "What is it, Martin? Aren't we still friends?"

I felt cold inside and a little crazy in the head. "Sure, we're friends," I said. "It's just that I don't want to bother you and Ira, so I won't be hanging around Willow Springs any more."

Her face looked troubled and a little puzzled. I thought she was trying awfully hard to cover up the way things were for her and my brother.

"I don't understand," she said. "I think you and Ira are my—"

"He is," I cut in angrily, "but I'm not. I don't want to feel like some damn fool kid around you two. So if you'll stay out of my way, I'll stay out of yours. That's an easy enough bargain, isn't it?"

I couldn't look at her face after that—for fear she might be crying or, much worse, glad I'd said it. I turned Blacky and spurred him so he jumped and even pitched a couple of times in surprise. When I'd told my brother about Mary being there, I rode back and drove the horses off without looking at her then either. That was worse than anything else, and all night long, with the horses grazing ahead of me in the moonlight, I felt lonely and ashamed. In the morning as I helped Cookie hitch up the chuck wagon, I told myself it was all finished and the hell with Mary and Ira. For some reason that didn't make me feel any better. . . .

And so the work continued for a couple more days, as the weather grew hotter and the Rattlesnake Mountains shimmered through heat waves in the afternoons until you thought that cracked granite could be a swollen, sun-lazy rattler lying in loose coils down the valley. Ira never talked to me about his feelings toward Mr. Karr, Roan Meyers, or—the one who must have hurt him the most—my father. But his silence and withdrawal from the life of our roundup camp gave me a mean feeling of being evened up some for losing Mary. After all, I began to tell myself, he probably deserved the taking down for trying to tell a cowman like Father how to run the TX.

Then one noon, when I was watching the cowboys fill their tin plates at the chuck wagon, Roan Meyers rode in and told the Senator and my father that he'd been in a gunfight with a man trying to brand a Two-Bar-K calf in a sagebrush draw over toward Willow Springs.

The Senator was indignant and loud. "They are rustling under our very noses now. I suppose the man got away, Roan."

Meyers looked pleased with himself. "He didn't get away. I saw to that, Mr. Karr."

104

"Good man!" the Senator cried. "Did you know this ex-thief?"

"Hell yes," nodded Meyers. "I surprised him with the calf all tied down, and he took a shot at me. Right off I saw what was going on and got my Winchester ready. He shot again and missed, but I didn't."

"Who was it, Roan?"

Karr's foreman glanced over at Father. "Old Man Lamar," he said. "I left everything just like I found it, so you can take a look at how he was operating. Had a cinch ring and a little fire built to heat it with."

"Old Jules Lamar?" Senator Karr said, looking astonished. "Of course we better ask the sheriff to come out from Rawlins and have a look ourselves. You say he shot at you first, Roan?"

"Scared the hell out of me, too."

My father had been listening without changing expression. "I reckon we better take a ride over there," he said. And then I saw a shadow of anger touch his lined face under the hatbrim.

I watched him, Mr. Karr, Roan Meyers, Moses Ethridge, and foremen from the other outfits on roundup saddle horses and ride out of camp. After that, without a word to anyone, my brother Ira saddled up too and followed them.

I couldn't really believe any of it had happened. But a couple of hours later they all rode back with the old wolfer's body across the saddle of the bony horse I'd seen so often in the corral at Willow Springs Canyon. . . .

We buried Jules Lamar wrapped up in a bed-tarp. The sheriff and coroner had been brought out from Rawlins to make everything legal, but they talked mostly to the Senator and agreed it looked like good riddance of another rustler. I saw Ira interrupt a time or two and heard his voice, sounding cold and edgy like it was someone else talking, as he argued against Mr. Karr. All the while the sheriff kept nodding and smiling at the Senator, as though they were having to be patient together until the foolishness was over with. The coroner, a skinny dun-faced man wearing old checkered trousers, had already made up his mind about what had happened and was trying to supervise the two cowboys who dug clumsily at a shallow grave off in the sage.

Father and I were standing together away from the others when Ira left the sheriff and came over. His face was pale but streaked with sweat and grit. He kept his eyes on Father as he walked up, as though he was looking for some sign from him. When my father turned away and gazed off to where the grave was being dug, Ira seemed to be disappointed some way.

"I suppose you want Jules to be slandered this way," he said angrily.

Father kept looking at the two hands bent over the broken patch of sandy ground like tired farmers. "I didn't see the thing happen and it was none of my play, anyway. That doesn't mean I wanted it to happen, though apparently that's what you're thinking."

"I wouldn't say you wanted him shot down. But Senator Karr is making Lamar out to be some kind of rustler who had been blacklisted by the Association. According to him, Meyers had seen Jules branding Two-Bar-K calves before. I wouldn't think you would let Karr slander a man who worked hard for you and . . ."

"And what, son?" asked Father, turning back to Ira.

"And agreed to squat on a piece of government land for you when you wanted to control more water."

"That had nothing to do with Lamar's getting shot the other noon."

Hearing my father say that gave me a strange feeling, almost like the two things really had been connected some way. I watched him more closely now, thinking his face might show me whether he or Ira was closer to the truth. It was the first time I'd ever had a doubt about Father not being in the right, and I wanted him to say or do something that would prove to me, as well as to Ira, how wrong it was to question his word about anything.

Ira wouldn't back off. "Nothing to do with it? You shouldn't lie to me."

My brother had spoken so bitterly that I didn't

realize at first what he'd implied. And then I couldn't believe anyone would say this to Father or, if anyone did call him a liar, that he would accept it calmly. But now he seemed to be looking right through Ira at something shadowy and far away, which he alone could make out among the distant shapes of his drifting cattle.

"You shouldn't let Karr slander a man who honored you," Ira went on without hesitation. "No piece of land or water hole is worth that. Nothing Senator Karr and the Association can do for you is worth that, either. Or would you disagree?"

When Father finally did answer, he spoke as if they were talking about something completely different from Lamar's death. His voice was even, almost gentle. "I reckon you've a right to talk to me the way no other man would, son. We've been short with each other quite a few times, but I figure we both said what we thought and felt better for it. Now let me tell you something and be done. I worked out here these sixteen years to give you and Mart a start I didn't have. A man has to work for something, and after your mother died there wasn't much I wanted any more. But I figured you and Mart would need this ranch—and it was the only thing I knew to give you. I sent you to school, Ira, so you wouldn't have to learn everything the hard way and could balance out the things I taught Mart by showing him."

He raised his voice slightly, and I thought there might be some pleading to what he said then. "I want to sign the place over to you two at the end of the year. Both of you can manage it together, or we'll decide on some arrangement that suits you. I'll stay on or leave—whichever way you boys think best."

I knew he was saying that last for Ira's benefit, and I wondered if the whole thing was his way of trying to settle his differences with my brother. I couldn't help being a little hurt that he would go that far, and I remembered again what Finn Rankin had said about Father favoring Ira, who looked so much like our mother. . . .

"I'm asking for your answer," Father said, looking over at me. "How about it, Mart? Would you be willing to take over the ranch and run it together with Ira?"

I hesitated for a moment as I thought about what he was offering. I knew what the TX meant to him and what it would come to mean to Ira and me. But I wasn't sure that I could work with my brother, either—at least not until I felt different about him and Mary Lamar. Besides, I knew we had some opposite ideas about running a ranch, and that I might not get along with him much better than Father did. When I finished thinking of all the problems, though, I had to admit I couldn't refuse Father what he asked. I was his son—and admired him much more than he maybe realized—and I said, "I'm willing if Ira is."

Then I saw something come alive in my father's eyes, and I figured he thought there was a chance now that Ira would also agree. I even thought that myself, until Ira began talking again.

"Your ground doesn't mean that much to me," he said. "Even if you signed over the ranch to Mart and me, we would have to live with a lot of things like what just happened to Jules. Or the way you've let the Association send Clayt Paulson all over your range looking for so-called rustlers, when everyone knows you built your own herd by branding mavericks. But I shouldn't speak for Mart. I'll just say that you better give the whole business to Mart if he wants it, because I'm sick to my stomach of the way you and Karr hold onto your land."

"I reckon there's another side to it," said Father.

"I'm sure of that, but it's not much better. Finn Rankin's crowd are just as greedy, and they'll find some way to fight over the land and the cattle too. They've learned some good tricks working for members of the Association."

"You think my offer over," I heard Father say. "It's not a matter to decide after a man's been killed. We can talk it out more definitely another time."

"No," Ira told him straight. "It wouldn't be different to me then. I'm finished with the TX. Give it to anybody you want to, because we don't owe each other anything."

"Wait a bit, Ira," I said. "I'd always planned on us working together here, and you used to figure on it too. Don't you remember the way we decided to work up some hay meadows along the river so we could carry more cows through the winter? There's other things you told me about doing to the ranch when you finished school and the three of us could work together here."

Ira knew what I meant all right, but he shook his head. "It wouldn't work out now, Mart. You two will make out better than the three of us would, anyway."

Father bit down on his lower lip and pulled his hat farther down over his eyes. I heard the murmur of Senator Karr's voice mixed with the assenting comments of the sheriff as they talked in the shade of the grub wagon. I still recall how close the bawling of calves sounded that day . . . the clear ring of the two spades when the silent cowboys struck solid rock in the hard ground where Lamar was to be buried . . . the heat and emptiness of the land . . .

"You're decided then," Father said curtly, so that I knew it wasn't meant as a question.

"Yes, I am."

"All right, Ira," he said. "You should draw pay at the ranch for the work you've done since you came home this spring."

"I haven't done enough work to matter, but I'll pick up some of my gear."

Father lost control of himself then. "The devil you say! You'll pick up your time too, like any other man. I'm still running this ranch, and you'll do as I say until you're off it. Which will be damned shortly." He drew himself erect in the sunlight, so that every wrinkle and crow's-foot in his face was clearly etched on dark skin. "Like you said, we don't owe each other anything. Hear me, boy? Once Jules is buried and you've got your time, I'll have only one son."

He turned to me, his hand shaking slightly as he gestured toward the cattle. "Who told the men to let the herd drift before we've finished working it? Ride out and tell Slat to throw them back and hold them together. There's still half the afternoon left for branding, and by God we'll use it!"

And Father walked away from us and moved in long strides toward Lamar's grave. He took the shovel from one of the men and began to dig with hard, regular strokes—as though he could slice the ground into a form that pleased him better. I wondered if he might be punishing himself for something, but I didn't know.

Soon afterward Ira rode off to the east, and by the time everything was ready for the burying he was back with Mary Lamar riding beside him. A few of the men who had known Jules well rode over and spoke awkwardly to her. Mr. Karr had already sent Roan Meyers back to the Two-Bar-K. Now he walked up to where Mary sat her horse, and I figured he was trying hard to tell her how terrible he felt about the shooting. It made me uneasy to watch him talking to her that way, but at the time I supposed he was trying to do the right thing.

Ira and the girl stayed back while the old man's body was carried over in the gray tarp and lowered to rest. The coroner made the readings in a high-toned, singsong voice, and I figured Jules would have felt uncomfortable hearing him. But he finished quickly. The grave was filled in silence, and then the coroner wanted to put up some kind of cross to mark the grave. Father glanced back at Mary, and when she shook her head he cut the coroner off abruptly.

The cowboys stood around bareheaded, squinting up at the sun and gazing off away from the small mound of fresh dirt. And then one by one they left to catch fresh horses in the rope corral strung up beyond the wagons.

Ira and Mary Lamar were gone by the time we started working the cattle again. They seemed to just disappear, though I thought once when I looked up from holding a cut of cows that I saw them riding toward Willow Springs. I was too busy to look very carefully, and my father kept the work moving at that rate until roundup was finished. I'd never seen him drive the men or himself that hard. We finished one week earlier than usual, but two of the younger hands quit because of run-ins they'd had with Father, who took over the job of roundup foreman after Mr. Karr had to return to the Two-Bar-K on some business matter. . . .

Two days after we'd pushed our cattle deep into our own range and gone back to the home ranch on the river, my brother rode up to the corral leading a pack horse. We greeted each other, but it wasn't until he was sorting out his belongings in our room that he said much.

"Where do you think you might go?" I asked him, when the strain was gone between us. "You can say it's none of my business if you want— I'm just curious about it."

He smiled at me. "I'm not going anywhere, Mart. We'll still be able to see each other sometimes."

"Well, you're not staying around here, are you?" I asked in surprise. "I know you better than that, and besides you're packing like somebody who won't be back for a while."

"No, I won't be back. I'm going to break horses and raise a few good colts at the Lamar place."

I nodded, trying to act calm. "That makes sense, I guess. The only thing about it is that Father planned on adding that land to the TX. Maybe he's changed his mind now, though."

"I don't think he's changed his mind," Ira said, "but he hasn't mentioned anything to Mary about wanting to buy it."

"I reckon he wouldn't bother her just now," I told him.

"Jules' death didn't bother Senator Karr at all. After he left roundup, Karr talked to her for a whole evening and tried to get her to sell the homestead to him."

I didn't like the sound of that. "He knows the arrangement Father had with Jules. Trying to buy that homestead isn't like Mr. Karr, is it?"

Ira picked one of his books off the shelf. It was a copy from the works of a man named Emerson, and he held it thoughtfully for a minute before packing it with other books in an old powder box. "I suppose it isn't, Mart. But sometimes I've found I didn't know a man nearly as well as I'd thought I did. I don't believe I would expect the Senator to be as perfect as we thought he was when we were boys."

That was a polite way of putting it, but I took the advice for what it might be worth. "I see your point," I said. "Why don't you let me help pack something instead of just sitting here working my mouth?"

"Thanks, but there's no hurry," Ira said. "By the way, is Father here this evening? I didn't notice him when I rode up."

"He's gone to Bothwell again. Why don't you stay tonight and get your pay in the morning before you ride off?"

"I wasn't thinking about any pay," he told me. "It's just as well he isn't here, because we've both said all there is to say. And I want to be back with Mary before it gets too late."

"Sure, sure. I guess she gets lonesome without Mr. Lamar. It won't seem right to ride over there and not find him at the cabin." There was something about our conversation now that wasn't easy like it had been at first. I'd figured Mary would probably go back to her relatives on the Reservation near Lander. Apparently she hadn't, and Ira was talking about raising horses on the homestead and being back with her before it got late. A card was missing from the hand I'd been dealt. And now I wasn't sure I wanted to see that missing card.

"I think you've got a good idea about trying a horse outfit there," I said. "With all the settlement going on in Lander Valley and little cattle outfits starting up every day, you ought to do all right. I've been thinking lately how that old dun mare of mine is too old for riding any more. You could take her off my hands and let her throw a few colts for you."

He looked pleased at the offer. "Thanks, Mart. I might take you up on that once I get things started. I think we'll get along out there."

I let that "we" sink in a little. Maybe one of Mary's relations or someone else was going to live with her. Maybe it meant something else, I thought, as I tried to get a grip on my thinking. "I'm glad to help," I told my brother. "You and me don't always agree, but that doesn't matter too much. Taking that mare would be doing me a favor, since I can't look after her very well any more. . . ." Stop running off at the mouth like a damn fool, I told myself, wondering if Ira had already noticed something was the matter from the way I talked.

If he did figure I was getting upset, my brother didn't show it. Maybe he didn't want to take any chance of hurting my feelings, and after all he didn't really know much more than Mary did about what I felt for her. He looked down at his small hands that were just starting to tan. Then he stood up and began to move around the room. "I better tell you about Mary and me, Mart. After Jules was buried I asked her to ride into Lander and marry me. . . ."

Somehow a thing said isn't quite so painful as a lot of crazy guesses about what might happen. I hadn't any claim to Mary, and I wouldn't blame her for hating me after I'd said what I did when she came to see Ira on roundup. But it still wasn't easy to think of her marrying with Ira. If I'd been older I could've told myself a lot of bad things about her to make myself feel better. As it was, I just sat there and felt pretty low.

"Mary decided not to rush things too fast," Ira went on, "and I think she is right. I once promised Jules I would look after her if it ever was necessary. I intend to do that, Mart, and I hope she'll want to marry me after she's had a chance to get over what happened to her father. I wanted her to leave Willow Springs for a while, but she insisted on staying."

"That sounds like her," I said, trying to keep the conversation from getting more awkward.

He nodded, thinking hard on something. "I've tried never to lie to you, Mart, and I don't want to start now. You know the kind of talk that would go around if she and I lived out there without marrying. Mary and I talked it over and decided to let people think we were married. That would also give her some protection from anyone who might have ideas about taking Willow Springs away from her."

"You mean Mr. Karr and Father?"

"Yes. . . . That water might be tempting to someone else, although I was thinking mostly of how that homestead lies between the Two-Bar-K and the TX."

"All right," I said. "If that's what you and Mary want, I won't tell a soul anything different. I thought both of you might be thinking about marrying, and I imagine she'll be your wife before the summer's gone. Tell her I'm . . . Hell, you know the right thing to say for me."

Ira guessed I was taking it all right and got busy with his packing. I sat there watching him and making empty talk about the roundup and asking him questions about his horse ranch. When he got his gear packed I helped him carry it to the corral and load it on the pack horse.

"We'll expect to see you whenever you're out that way," Ira said. "Mary made me promise to get you to come see us soon."

"Sure," I said. "I'll be around so much she'll throw me out for certain." I watched him ride off, and then I took my Stevens rifle and went hunting along the river. The rifle was a .32 rim-fire with tip-up action that cost over ten dollars new, but a rifle didn't seem of much importance any more.

There was still light when I started, but down by the river I saw the crimson brighten in the sunset and then darken out. Once I caught a glimpse of a coyote's thin, yellowish form slipping up into the rocks on the far bluff, but I didn't have any chance for a shot. When it got dark I sat down and waited for the moon to yellow up huge and bright-looking over the river. I was thinking about Ira and the Lamar girl, though I'd told myself it wouldn't help any. That was settled for good and all. . . . The late autumn afternoon with Mary down along the river in the silvery willows and cattails couldn't matter now. Not with old Jules Lamar gone and Ira staying with his daughter on that two-bit homestead. . . .

Finally I got hold of myself and walked back up toward the ranch. I was getting sick of my own thoughts. The sage had a thick sheen of moonlight on it, and our buildings looked much bigger than before, like they might still be standing when I was long since dead—"gone under," as Jules had called it. This was a feeling I hadn't understood before, and it somehow made me feel closer to Father. Maybe I felt that way because of losing Mary and seeing Ira kill some hope that my father had been holding to for a long time. I only wished Father hadn't let Mr. Karr say the things he did against the old man. . . .

Chapter 9

Father didn't come back from Bothwell that night. In the morning I rode the country over toward Beaver Rim, just to be keeping busy. I made it a point to stay away until supper, but when my father was still gone I ate with the men in the bunkhouse kitchen. He did get back right at dusk, though, and I was at the corral when he unsaddled. Tall as he was, he seemed to lift his saddle up effortlessly with one hand, slip the blanket under his arm, and slide off the bridle in one smooth, silent movement so quick that a strange horse would stand for a minute afterward without a quiver, thinking he hadn't finished the job.

"Reckon you expected me yesterday," Father said, without looking around to check his guess about the footsteps he'd heard as I came up behind him.

"That's right," I said, "but everything has been quiet enough here, I guess."

He stepped by me on his way to the saddle shed. I thought I smelled whiskey on his breath as he passed, but he gave no other hint that he might have been drinking heavily. So I decided I'd been mistaken.

"You sure there's nothing I should know about?" asked Father. "You're looking poorly tonight."

I didn't think he could really tell how I felt. You never knew with him, though. "There's nothing much happened," I said. "Ira rode over last night and picked up his things, but you knew that was coming."

He glanced sharply at me, his eyes fierce for a moment as he tried to judge the way I'd said it. I meant the words to cut both ways, and I think he realized that. But if he did, he didn't comment on it. "Did you pay him the wages he had coming? I won't have a man who works for me leave here broke."

I started to say Ira probably didn't look at what he'd done that spring as working for Father. Instead I told him, "No, I didn't pay him. You've never fixed it up for me to write any checks on your bank."

"I will," he said shortly. "Where's Ira gone?"

"The old Lamar place," I said.

He came slowly from the saddle shed. "And where then?"

I told him about the horse ranch and afterward, when it had to come out anyway, about Mary Lamar staying there with Ira. I didn't let on they weren't married, though.

"He thinks to shame me," Father said, like he was speaking to himself. "I reckon he's going to live out there half starving and try to show how I've been unfair to him."

"I figure he just wants to be let alone," I said. "He wants a chance to use his own ideas—without the Association or anybody else to answer to."

Father frowned. "There's no place you can live without answering to someone. That's a thing you've got to realize before you can act the part of a man. People haven't changed much from what they were in Bible times. The same things itch at them and make them do wrong to one another. A man can't figure people to be perfect, because he's going to get a disappointment and be taken down a peg. I'd say to measure a human by the way he gets along with things the way they already are. Not by how much he can change them clean around."

I found myself going along with that all right, but I was sure Ira wouldn't accept it. Neither would Jim Averill, who ran his store and post office next to Ella Watson's place at Bothwell, and a few others who were considered "troublemakers" because they'd homesteaded on good rangeland along the Sweetwater and up on Powder River. I'd heard the Association was out to get them all, so I hoped Ira wouldn't be getting involved with their kind now. But there wasn't much I—or Father either—could do if Ira threw in with the crowd of discontented nesters and laid-off cowboys that hung around Bothwell or Jack Stenger's saloon and talked fight against the cattlemen.

Father's bay sniffed out a dusty spot in the corral and then knelt down to roll. He bellied up three times before going clear over and rising on his front legs. When he shook himself the dust powdered down from his hide, and he snorted at us, impatient to be let out into the horse pasture.

Father had been watching the bay too. Finally he sighed tiredly and shook his head once. "I hadn't thought Ira would stay in the valley . . . but I suppose he's thinking to shame me."

"I don't fault the girl," I finally said. "Mr.

123

Lamar had asked Ira to take care of her—she never tried to turn him against you or the TX."

"I wasn't faulting her, son." He moved toward his horse by the corral gate. "In the morning I want you to take Ira his time."

"All right." I nodded. "You probably want something to eat now. I can turn your horse out."

"I reckon not," he said. "You go on with whatever you were doing. I'll eat directly."

I saw him standing with his arm around the bay's neck and left him alone there. He didn't come in the house for a long while, and when he did I was lying in my bunk. As I waited to go to sleep, I thought I heard the clink of a bottle against a glass in his office. Pretty soon I couldn't see any stars through the open door—just a heavy gray-blue of sky clouding over and then jagged veins of heat lightning far away. Later I was sure Father was still moving around in the house, but finally the rain came down slantways against the lean-to. I lay in the cool, fresh-smelling night, and when I went to sleep I dreamed about Mary again. . . .

In the morning I ate with the men and got my horse saddled before Father was up. I didn't see him before I left, but he sent Cookie out to the corral with Ira's pay—all in silver.

"Did he want me to tell Ira anything?" I asked the cook.

He was already stumping off toward the

kitchen. "That's a hell of a damn fool question," he growled. "Got my head bit off just for being alive this morning. Yeh, tell your bud I said to take his pay and buy a good .45. Then he can shoot hisself when one of those knot-headed broncs falls on him a hundred miles from hell."

That kind of talk wasn't a very promising start for my ride to the new horse ranch, but I hadn't really counted on enjoying myself. I put Blacky into a hard lope as soon as he got warmed up. The trail was softened by the rain, and his hoofs flicked up bits of sandy mud. Damp sage gave off a sharp, musty smell that I usually enjoyed—only I didn't feel too good about anything today. The sky was an even light blue, like it had been washed of clouds by the night's rain, and the Rattlesnakes looked roan-colored off in the east, like the hide of a newborn Shorthorn calf. Already the day was still and warming off enough to begin baking moisture from the rolling, tan land. I realized that the grass would be burning dry by nightfall, but now I didn't care much whether or not we had grass at the end of summer.

My mood wasn't any brighter when I rode down into Willow Springs. I was still remembering too clearly that night I saw Ira walking Mary back to the cabin in the moonlight. They had probably been talking about marrying then, I told myself, but I still felt my chest getting tight as I saw Mary walk from the door into the early sunlight, her hair shining dark, and stand there looking across at the corral where Ira was working with some horses.

When she saw me, Mary turned around slowly until she was sure who it was. Then she waved her hand once and began to walk lightly down the trail. I rode on toward her, thinking of what I'd said to her on roundup and dreading the talk that might come now . . . yet knowing I wanted to see her, too.

She hesitated when I got close, and then she ran to where I sat my horse. "Martin," she said, holding to one of my stirrups with her brown hands. "It's good to see you." She smiled up shyly, and I couldn't hold to my resentment of her liking my brother instead of me. I just felt a whole lot worse about losing her. "I made Ira promise to bring you over soon," she went on. "But I was afraid it would be a long time before you came. . . ."

"You didn't need to worry about it," I said, trying to sound careless. "I wanted to see those horses you and Ira are getting started on."

Her thin face looked the way I'd often remembered—like a hidden warmth was suddenly livening her eyes with quick pleasure and moving color into her face. "I'm happy for seeing you here, Martin," she said, looking down quickly at the stirrup. "After what you said that evening at roundup camp . . . I thought you hated me and nothing could be straight between us again. But we can stay friends, can't we?"

I never had been much good at pretending, but I figured I might as well try to act big about it. "Sure," I said. "Everything's all right now."

Mary nodded and released the stirrup. "I won't worry then. You must come for coffee before looking at Ira's horses. And I don't think you've eaten yet, either."

I reached down with one hand and helped her swing up behind me on Blacky. "Just coffee," I told her. "Next time I'll come eat all the grub you've got in the house."

"I'll make you promise," she laughed. "I know you'll cheat me unless I make sure that way."

We sat in the cabin for a while and drank the coffee that tasted just like the strong brew her father used to boil up. Somehow the cabin looked different than before, though. Mary had cleaned it so thoroughly that even the log walls seemed to shine. I saw all Ira's books arranged very carefully on neat wooden shelves above a small desk made from rawhide laced tightly to a pole frame. Scarlet Hudson's Bay blankets were stretched over the two wooden bunks in opposite corners of the room, and the whole cabin had a clean smell of pine shavings.

"Ira made the desk and shelves himself," she

said. "But he hasn't had time to do any reading yet. . . ."

I drained my coffee cup and changed the subject. "That ride was worth it just to drink coffee like this. How about another cup before I go see Ira?"

When Mary came back with the pot, she'd become serious again. I didn't want to ask her if something was troubling her, but after we sat quietly awhile she brought it up herself.

"Do you think I'm a stupid girl, Martin?" she asked, looking down at her hands clasped together in her lap.

"No, I don't," I told her. "Who said that about you?"

She shook her head. "Nobody said it, but many people think a half-breed girl who hasn't gone to school is sure to be stupid. It might be true."

"If that's so, I'm stupid too," I said. "I wouldn't worry about what some people thought." I saw what was troubling her, though. There was quite a difference between what she knew about and what Ira knew from going to school back East— between herself and Leah Karr, also.

"Forget about it," I went on. "If my brother thought you weren't suited to each other, you can bet he wouldn't be here with you. He's not the kind to let off half cocked like I am."

"Maybe he could feel sorry for someone," Mary said softly. "Couldn't that be true?"

"It could be," I answered, "but I doubt it. He's so damned honest it sickens me sometimes to think about him being turned loose in the dirty old world."

Mary mulled that over, the little lines in her forehead making her look appealing and very young. "Ira is honest like that . . . but I think most people don't know why he acts the way he does. He doesn't like to quarrel with Mr. Tyrrell and Senator Karr, but he has to do and say what he thinks is right. You and your father feel ashamed of him sometimes because he seems different and likes things you don't understand. I think both of you are wrong not to feel proud that he knows of books and the thoughts of other men."

"Maybe so," I said. "They say our mother was the same kind of person, though I didn't know her. Anyway, Mr. Lamar thought a lot of Ira, and I guess he knew my brother better than anyone else."

"Ira always liked to come out here," Mary said quietly. "I think your father is a fine man, but he never gave Ira the chance to make his own choices. But out here your brother was always treated like a grown man . . . and he was in many ways. Maybe that's why Ira still likes Willow Springs, where he is free to live his own life. I don't think he will always want to stay here, though. He wouldn't be satisfied if he had to spend his whole life as a horse rancher."

"That's probably true," I told her. "But you . . ."

When I didn't go on she said, "My father thought of Ira as his own son. That's why he asked Ira to take care of me if anything happened to him."

Hearing that last part made me feel alone and more than a little jealous again. I listened to a meadow lark whistle from back of the cabin, and then, like a bad thought against the bright morning, the rattling squall of magpies down by the willows. Mary was listening too, but not just to the birds, I thought. From watching her, I guessed that she sensed something I didn't in the dry air and rust-colored rocks of the canyon.

"Since my father was killed I've had some bad thoughts here," she finally said. "I can't really explain them, Martin, and I don't believe I'm afraid. Often the wind cries at night in the willows and the horses get uneasy, but maybe it has always been that way here. . . ."

"I doubt if any of it means much," I said quickly. "I wouldn't put much stock in how the wind sounds at night." That wasn't quite the truth in our country, I knew, but when she brightened up I was glad I'd said it.

"I better get over to the corral," I told her. "Ira'll probably think it's a preacher up here sitting around all morning." I heard her laugh as I stood up, and I figured things were closer to being all right for her than they'd been before we had our talk together.

"I'm your friend, Martin," she said at the door. "That's not a light thing to me. The things between us before weren't light either—though you may not believe me now."

"I never thought different," I lied. "Thanks for fixing coffee for me."

"You'll be back to see us soon, won't you?" She stood with her shoulders against the slab door and very straight, with the light angling over her face and bare legs to make her skin a warm light brown, like the color of native hay just before it ripens fully. "You must promise or I won't believe you."

"Sure, I promise, Mary," I said. When I'd gone a few steps down the path to the corral, I turned and saw her still standing there and watching me. "Only I'll take it back if you call yourself stupid again."

"I won't say that any more, Martin," she called.

Then I remembered the money for Ira, which I'd wrapped in my scarf and tied tightly in the slicker behind my saddle. "I brought something for Ira," I told her. "It's wrapped in my slicker. Would you save it in the cabin for him?"

As I neared the corral I looked back and saw her standing beside Blacky while she retied the slicker to the saddle strings. She seemed very small, and for some reason I thought of her lying in the dark cabin beside Ira as she listened to the wind crying through the willows by the spring. . . .

Ira had a big palomino cut out from the half dozen other horses and was working him separately in the round corral. When I got close I saw he'd gotten a halter on the gelding and was shifting him around to work a foot rope on one hind leg. One end of the soft-braided rope was tied in a bowline around the horse's neck. The slack was played out on the ground in a half circle by the palomino's hind foot. My brother moved him around a little until the hoof was over the rope, and then he smoothly tightened the rope, pulling the hind foot off the ground. The horse fought, swirling up dust in the corral, but Ira kept talking to him and soon had made the needed wraps to secure the foot rope in a sort of sling from hind foot to the animal's neck.

"Hello, Mart," he called to me when he'd finished securing the Scotch hobble. "Wait just a minute and we'll talk."

"No hurry," I said, squatting down beside the corral. There were several things I noticed while I watched him. That yellow horse, like most of the others in the holding corral, was two years or so older and a lot heavier than the horses he was used to working with at the ranch. It took quite a bit more time and strength to break a four- or five-year-old and make a good cow horse than it did to gentle a colt. And since Ira was shorter than me and a lot less stout, it was a hard way to make a living. That showed in my brother's face, but from the way he talked to the palomino and went about his work, it didn't look like he could be any happier no matter what he was doing. Some of the change might've been caused by his new life with Mary, of course. Still, despite his dusty, bone-tired face, he had a contentment in his voice as he talked to the horse that I hadn't heard when he was working for Father.

He let the palomino stand there on three feet while he went to one side of the corral and picked up a gunny sack. At first he held the sack out for the horse to smell, and then, holding to the halter rope, he began to rub the animal's neck and shoulders with it. The palomino rolled his sky-blue eyes and snorted, his hide quivering with each touch of the burlap. Before long he got used to it, though, and then Ira began to slap him lightly all over with the sack. The horse crow-hopped around the first few times, fighting the hobble as well as the flapping gunny sack, but he gave that up too. Ira didn't carry the lesson too far. When the yellow horse was good and tired, he took off the foot rope and tied him up to the top pole of the corral, so he couldn't get his foot over the rope if he took to fighting the halter.

Then Ira sat down beside me with his back resting against the corral poles. "I thought it might be you up there talking to Mary," he said.

"It was me all right. I brought your pay over from the ranch—left it up at the cabin with Mary."

He took off his brown hat and wiped sweat from his forehead with a shirt sleeve. When he pulled off his leather gloves I saw an ugly rope burn marking the palm of one hand in a raw, reddish welt. His shirt had been ripped halfway down the right sleeve, but Mary had mended it so neatly that it wasn't noticeable. I wondered if he might need that pay from the TX more than he let on.

"I should have known Father would get the better of that argument," Ira said. "You can thank him for me, Mart. Probably that will just make him angry again, but as you can see this sort of work is going to be slow getting started."

He wasn't complaining, I thought—just letting me know how things stood. And I realized Father must have known how it would be for Ira here, because Cookie had handed me what amounted to considerably more than three months' pay, even for a top hand. Again I felt that some deep thread of feeling existed between my father and Ira. It was strong enough to make them respect each other in spite of their opposite personalities. It was almost strong enough to make Father humble himself to keep Ira from leaving the TX. Anyhow, that doesn't make a damn to me, I told myself. But it did.

"What about you?" I heard Ira ask then. "I remember how you used to talk about seeing some new country before you settled down. Is that still what you want to do?"

I hadn't thought too much about my own plans lately. "I don't know for sure." I grinned. "I always figured I wanted to run a big ranch somewhere. Now I'm not so certain. I ought to know about something more than just punching cows in Wyoming. You've been to college and all that, but I haven't been farther than Cheyenne."

Ira didn't try to answer that right away. "I see what you mean," he said after a while. "Of course I can't see anything the matter with your staying on the TX. I went to college in the East because that was what I wanted most of all to do then. If you want to run a big ranch, I would think that was a good thing to do too."

"You might not like my way of running a ranch any better than you liked Father's way," I said.

"That would be all right," he said. "I don't think you would follow all of Father's ideas, but whatever you did would be up to you. I argued with him because I felt partly responsible for running the ranch. I still disagree with him about a good many things . . . but I'm through trying to make him change."

The way he was talking sounded a little unfair. "I reckon that makes sense to you," I said, "but he's still our father—right or wrong."

Ira looked at me with an odd smile. "He said he wasn't my father any longer, Mart. I would say he meant just what he said."

Father meant it all right. I was sure of that, yet his saying it was another sign of how important Ira was to him. I felt all mixed up from getting myself caught somehow between my father and Ira. I wasn't sure what to believe any more, for one of them had the advantage in education and the other in experience. They seemed to be tearing me apart with their disagreements. I didn't want to think about Mary's place in all this, either—though it was another part of the whole hurt.

"I want you to make up your own mind about the ranch and how to live your life," Ira was saying. "All this rustler talk will pass someday, but you'll still need to know what you believe in. Once you've decided, it shouldn't make any difference what anyone else—me or Father either—wants you to do. You'll go your own way. When that time comes you'll know it yourself, I think."

He stopped talking and looked up at the sun. I knew he didn't mean it for a hint to leave, but I'd already stayed longer than I planned. As I left to go back to where I'd left Blacky by the cabin, I saw Ira moving into the holding pen with his rope in one hand. It wasn't much past ten o'clock. I guessed it would take him the rest of

136

the day to finish sacking out those other six horses. I thought of that rope burn on his hand and how it would feel with sweat working into it while he held a stout horse at the end of his catch rope.

Running a big spread of my own didn't seem like much when I thought of Ira trying to support himself and Mary by breaking horses on that old homestead.

Chapter 10

That afternoon I found a note Father had left for me on the eating table at the ranch. Placed openly where anyone might have found it, the note read: "Mart, I've been called away on urgent cow business to Cheyenne. Don't expect my return for a few days, M. Tyrrell."

It occurred to me that the business must have been awfully urgent if he couldn't have told me about it before I left for Willow Springs. Of course someone could've ridden in with a message calling Father to Cheyenne, although Cookie said he hadn't seen anyone—just Father leaving on horseback by himself.

"Usually takes a buggy or the buckboard," Cookie told me, "but it's none of my damn business. I only cook here. Thank God for that, too."

I quit thinking about it then, for I didn't see

much use in worrying about my father as well as Ira and Mary. I was beginning to feel like an old woman from getting all bogged down in family business until nothing else seemed to matter. I figured this was a good time to quit feeling that way, before it got to be a habit. But still I didn't get much done that morning.

"Got a proposition for you," Whitey Pence said when I was eating the noon meal in the bunkhouse kitchen.

I let him go on without committing myself. I hadn't forgotten that Moonlight horse rawhiding I'd taken, though I guess I'd been as much to blame for it as Whitey was.

"This being Saturday I thought you and me could ride over to Stenger's tonight." Whitey kept his voice lowered so that the other hands wouldn't notice our conversation. "Be good for you, Mart. See some new faces and get away from the same old stud-poker game they play here every night. You're game to ride along, ain't you?"

A few days before I wouldn't have thought twice before turning him down. Now the thought of sitting around the empty ranch house, or listening to idle talk from the few hands who would be in the bunkhouse because they were too broke to go anywhere livelier, was pretty hard to take. I'd never been to Stenger's on a Saturday night, but this was as good a time as any to go. I figured I'd better keep both eyes open, though, if I was going with someone like Whitey.

"I might ride over with you," I told him. "But I won't guarantee anything about how long I'll stay."

"I knowed you'd go one of these times," Whitey said, grinning. "You never seen such a fine place as Stenger's on a Saturday night. It's still got the hair on and then some."

Something was making Whitey enjoy the prospect of taking me with him. Maybe it was his knowing how Father hated to have any of his hands go there. The man who ran the gin mill had never been friendly to the large ranchers. Some people said that Jack Stenger, like Ella Watson, put a herd of cattle together at the expense of Moses Ethridge, Senator Karr, and other Association members. If he had, he knew better than to tell anyone about it. Anyway, he had quite a reputation for siding with the rustler element and stirring up discontent among the cow hands working for the cattlemen along the river. Whitey could have been one of Stenger's friends, but I still didn't see why he was so anxious to take me there.

We left the ranch at six, and it took about two hours to ride down to Stenger's—a patch of meadow out in a flat, a corral with a pole shed, and a couple of poorly made log buildings. His place didn't look like much with all the yellow snakeweed crowding out the grass where the meadow had been overgrazed . . . and the sod roof of one cabin beginning to fall through at the eaves. Just beyond the pasture you could see another little cabin, and then the wrinkled granite hills began to push up through the rangeland on both sides of the river. As we got close the sunset gave Stenger's "hog ranch" a pleasant touch of reddish color, but when that was gone the whole layout looked drab and cheap, like it didn't really belong there cluttering up the view.

"Don't look very lively," Whitey muttered. "Couple of horses at the tie rack and not much noise inside. Old Jack must be holding a wake in there."

Whitey didn't tie his horse with the others, so I followed him around to the corral and we unsaddled there. He hitched up his pants and gun belt, tilted back his hat to a more rakish angle, and started for the front cabin.

"Shake this rathole back to life," he hollered at the door. "I didn't ride over here to dicker around with a bunch of rannies on their last legs. Who the hell's died, Jack?"

I heard a curt voice start explaining something about Jim Averill and the woman over at Bothwell, but the man broke off as I entered the building behind Whitey. I recognized the man who'd been talking as Jack Stenger, a medium-sized fellow with sharp features like those of a butcherbird—a stout hooked nose, heavy oval head topped with graying hair, and angular blackish eyes. He obviously wasn't very pleased to see me there, but he recovered enough to slide behind his plank bar with a nervous smile that he probably meant to seem friendly.

"Name it, gents," he said, pushing up the sleeves of a rumpled white shirt. "Not that there's any choice about your drinking here— wine, whiskey straight or fortified by river water."

"Straight shot," ordered Whitey. "It's the mixin' that makes a man sick."

"Mix mine," I said, not caring to agree with him.

When I had a chance to look around more carefully, I saw two men who sat in the corner at a card table made from packing boxes. One was tall and thin, with a growth of beard shadowing his face. The other was a small cowboy dressed up very carefully. His pant legs were folded inside shotgun-topped boots that came up to his knees. Both men spoke to Whitey and nodded at me, but I hadn't seen either one before. Like Jack Stenger, they seemed edgy about something.

As I lifted up my drink I saw a woman enter the door and walk quietly to a bench along the wall, where she sat and smoked a cigarette. The two men playing cards didn't pay any attention to her, so I figured she'd been around the place for a while. She was a Mexican woman who looked about thirty. I noticed that her dark cotton skirt was shorter than those worn by the women I'd known, and above it she had on a white blouse with low neck and short, puffy sleeves. Her face—which somehow seemed familiar—was almost handsome, though her skin had been roughened by smallpox.

Whitey hadn't seen her enter, but as he pushed his glass out for Stenger to refill he caught sight of her. "Damn if it ain't Jenny!" he called roughly. "Come here and take a drink with us, Jen. Didn't think you was here tonight."

The woman stood up and walked toward the bar. She was neither fat nor thin, and I thought the way she walked was a lot like the graceful way Mary moved. Only this woman wasn't shy at all—she watched both Whitey and me with calm dark eyes all the while she was coming toward us.

"What'll you have?" Whitey reached out to encircle her waist with one arm, but she slipped by him and stood on the other side of me.

"A little wine, I think." She smiled at Whitey.

He wasn't happy at the way she avoided him, but I could see he'd decided to grin and bear it. For now at any rate.

"You heard the lady," he told Stenger. "Pour her some red *vino* and give Mart here another shot with your damned river water."

I hadn't finished the drink I had, and I didn't let Stenger pour another yet. This wasn't the first time I'd tasted whiskey—we grew up pretty fast in Wyoming Territory—but with Whitey Pence for a pardner I wasn't going to rush things in a run-down "hog ranch" like this one.

"What is your friend's name?" the Mexican woman asked Whitey, after she'd sipped at her wine.

"Ain't been introduced before, have you?" he answered. "This here's the boss's boy, Mart Tyrrell." Whitey swept off his hat in a mock bow that didn't go over too well with me. "Meet Jenny Rodriguez of Rawlins, Casper, Bothwell, and other places of like stripe."

She didn't blink at the meanness of what he said. Maybe it was because she was surprised at finding out who I was. "You are the son of *Señor* Tyrrell who ranches here on the river?" she asked.

"That's right," I said. "Do you know him very well?"

I hadn't meant it to sound like it probably did, but she smiled quickly at me and shook her head, the slick hair waving prettily on her bare shoulders. "I do not think so. Of course everyone knows the name of your father, for he is a famous man. Are you an owner of many cows also?"

"I'm afraid not. You might say I'm just learning the cow game." I was beginning to like talking with her, for she seemed to be really interested in what I said. I didn't have any illusions about the sort of woman who hung around a road ranch on Saturday night, but I had nothing against her yet, either.

"Yes?" she said. "I think it will be different someday for you. Who can say?"

"It'll all be different out here soon enough," Stenger put in. "After what happened yesterday we'll have the army protecting a man who ain't a bullionaire . . ."

"What did happen yesterday, Mr. Stenger?" I asked, figuring it had something to do with what he'd been trying to tell Whitey when we first entered.

"Ask your old man," he said coldly, turning away from the bar to inspect his whiskey stock. "I got sense enough not to blab a bad thing around when it's bound to raise a stink that'll smell clear to Washington."

The men in the corner glanced at him when he said that, but it was plain they weren't going to elaborate on the trouble any. They threw down their cards and began to work on a half-full whiskey bottle between them on the table. The short cowboy looked at me for a moment and then spit deliberately out on the floor in my direction.

I wasn't growing very fond of them—or Jack Stenger either. But now I was here I wasn't going to let them bother me. I ordered another drink and kept talking to Jenny Rodriguez. After a while three cowboys I knew from the Two-Bar-K came in—straight from a line camp near the Red Desert, they said. They were dusty and dry after a long ride. A few drinks loosened them up a whole lot, and they began to sing "The Cowboy's Dream."

Apparently they didn't know about any trouble at Bothwell. At least their presence made me feel better, though I'd already made up my mind not to hang around Stenger's much longer.

Near midnight, when the five cow hands and Whitey were drunk enough to be reckless, the poker game got serious. I left all of them hunched over their cards and went out to the horses. I'd already told Whitey I was riding back to the ranch whenever the notion struck me. And I think he was relieved to hear it. Apparently he'd brought me there in hopes I would get drunk and give him and Stenger's crowd a laugh. But tonight he and the saloonkeeper had been wanting awfully bad to finish their little talk, and it was clear that I was cramping the conversation.

Outside the building the night was cool and very dark. The horses at the tie rack had settled down until morning, so they hardly spooked when I walked past. Behind me in the bar talk flared up, and then Whitey said something that made them all lower their voices. I heard Jack

Stenger call out to the Mexican woman—it sounded like he wanted her to leave too. Whatever the news was, it was going to get hashed over now.

I leaned against the corral, feeling the whiskey working in my head, and listened to Blacky snort softly at me, until the cool air steadied my thinking and I remembered the way I'd treated Mary when she came to talk with Ira at roundup camp. That made me wish pretty bad for more whiskey. When I was almost ready to saddle up I heard a movement in the shadow of the saloon. It made me jump a little, and I saw a figure move out in my direction . . . but it was only Jenny Rodriguez. For some reason my heart was pounding hard, so that it seemed to be beating right up in my ears.

"Martín Tyrrell?" she said. "Do you ride off now?"

I nodded. "It's late . . . and I wasn't exactly welcome in there, anyway."

The woman stood watching me with one hand on her hip and the other holding a corral pole. The curving lines of her body were outlined and shaped by the shadows. "Perhaps not in there," she said, "but that should mean little to you."

"I figured to let them have the place to themselves," I told her. "If it's a bad thing that's happened, I'll hear about it soon enough."

"Who knows? They are afraid of you because

of your father. But I think these cowboys are afraid of themselves also. Only some among them are thieves, yet they all must sleep in one bed."

"Aren't you afraid to talk to me about that?" I asked. "I'm probably out here spying for my father, like Stenger thinks."

She shrugged her shoulders gracefully. "What of it? Besides, I know your father. He often came to the eating place where I worked in Rawlins, and he stops here at times when riding through. I think he is a fair man, although Stenger fears him."

The woman stopped talking suddenly and came closer. "Martín," she whispered, reaching out to lay a light hand on my arm. "Will you come where we can talk?"

Something was troubling her, I realized then. Her voice sounded scared when she lowered it, and her eyes couldn't hide her fear any more either.

"All right," I said, wondering if I was being a fool. "Where shall we go?"

"The small cabin near the river is where I stay now. Those men in the bar will not bother us, I think."

"I'll leave Blacky saddled here and come down," I said.

"Yes, that is good, Martín." She slipped away from the corral then, and I only saw the faint glow of her white blouse as she walked toward her cabin.

I didn't think her being scared was an act, but I would've wanted to talk with her anyway. Maybe I'd eased an awful lonely feeling that night while listening to her in Stenger's saloon. And though it was clear enough what kind of life she led, Jenny made me feel like a grown-up man instead of a dumb kid. I thought there was something about her face and name I should recognize. And then I remembered the sheepherder I'd met on the Sweetwater last spring—Pete Rodriguez. There was a good chance for them to be related, and he'd said he knew my brother Ira. . . .

The cabin was still dark when I walked to the door, but she called quietly for me to come in. I couldn't tell much about what was inside—a bed, stove, table, and a couple of old chairs, I thought, and not much else. The one room smelled of flour and the woman's perfume.

"Sit here," Jenny said from the side of the iron bed. "Or would you rather use the chair?"

"No, here's fine," I said, sitting down by her. The flesh of her upper arm touched my shirt sleeve, and I felt her shiver once from the cool midnight air. There was a wool blanket at the foot of her bed, and I wrapped it around her shoulders. She stopped shaking, and I felt her relax beside me.

"*Gracias*, Martín," she murmured. "I am all right now."

We sat that way for a while, and then she asked, "How old are you? If you don't wish to say, that is all right."

"Seventeen," I told her.

She nodded. "You look much like your father. He is a handsome man also."

I decided to try a guess. "You look a little like your father too."

That surprised her. "You know of him?"

"Pete Rodriguez, isn't it? He runs sheep over toward the Red Desert."

"Yes." She paused, and then I saw her begin to roll herself a cigarette—like a man, only more graceful. She made a second one and handed it to me. The smoke was strong, and I figured she was using some kind of Mex tobacco. I liked it, though.

"Did your brother tell you about him?" Jenny went on. "No. I met him moving a band of sheep one time."

"He will never make trouble for the Tyrrells. There is an understanding about the sheep and where he will graze them."

"How's that?" I asked.

"You don't know? Surely your brother has told you this herder Rodriguez works for him. It is not known by others, of course, but even the sheep were bought by Ira Tyrrell."

I had trouble believing that, yet I couldn't see why the woman would lie about it to me. And

Pete Rodriguez had acted strange when I ate with him that noon. "Ira doesn't tell me much about his personal business," I said. "Likely it's true enough if you say so."

She drew nervously on the brown cigarette. "It is true, but I do not tell anyone except you. Have no fear of that."

All of a sudden Jenny flipped away her smoke and clung to me with both arms. "Oh, Martín, I am afraid!"

I tried to get her to tell me what was bothering her. But she began to cry and shake her head, pulling me down beside her on the bed. Finally she begged me to fasten the door to the cabin.

"They will kill me next," she whispered in the dark. "Stay with me a little, Martín."

"What are you talking about?" I asked her several times. "Who are you afraid of, anyway?"

But Jenny wouldn't tell me anything more. When she did quiet down, I was holding her, listening to the crickets singing outside somewhere.

"Forgive me," she said. "I am acting foolishly. . . ."

The long touch of her body was warming as a drink of whiskey. After a while I didn't want to move or have to think of anything except lying beside her in the dark cabin that smelled of flour and Mexican perfume.

What began to happen was like nothing I'd expected. She had slender legs and smooth skin where I touched her under the flaring cotton skirt. There was nothing shameful about the way she made a man feel. I didn't know much, but Jenny made it all right the way she held to me, moving herself easily. I did the best I could to play my part well, with the whiskey hammering in my head and a crazy jealousy of my brother . . . a hurt for losing Mary . . . mixing everything up as the woman beneath me whispered in Spanish and taught me what I'd only dreamed about before.

"*Ai*, Martín," she sighed, when it was over too quickly.

I can still recall how, before I left early that morning, she said, "Please don't forget Jenny Rodriguez. . . ." And I haven't, either. . . .

We lay together for some time without talking. Her face was broad and pitted-looking in the dim light, her liquid, shining eyes almost expressionless. She wasn't ugly to me, though. Then I began thinking of Mary living with Ira— only she seemed much less real now—and my brother owning sheep that people thought belonged to a Mexican herder. I wondered what it was Jenny was afraid of and whether it might be tied in with Stenger's hurry to talk alone with Whitey and the other cowboys.

"Listen, Jenny," I said at last. "I don't know what's bothering you, but I'd like to help set it straight. You trusted me enough to tell me about the sheep my brother bought. Just who or what is scaring you?"

I watched her raise her knees and pull the skirt down slowly to cover her legs. "I am not certain myself," she said. "I overheard talk earlier in the bar. I wanted to tell you, but I was unsure of your friendship."

"And you're still not sure?"

She smiled and touched my cheek with her fingertips for a moment. "Perhaps it is unimportant. I am not a woman of good name, and I wanted you to lie with me as you did. But it was not a trick, Martín."

"I never thought it was," I said.

"That is good, then. I would not want something to make you doubt what I'm going to tell you now."

I waited, trying to imagine what she would say and thinking once I heard footsteps outside. When I got up and walked around the cabin I saw no one. I came back feeling a little nervous myself and fastened the door again.

"You remember the two men with Stenger when you first came tonight?" Jenny said when I was sitting beside her.

"The unfriendly ones playing cards?" I asked.

"Yes. Those two were at Bothwell today when it happened." Her hands were unsteady, so that I had to roll the cigarette for her.

"What did happen?"

She waited until I lit the smoke and handed it to her. "A bad thing, Martín," she whispered, as if going over it again in her own mind. "The men were working for *Señor* Averill and the woman named Watson. Several persons came making trouble at the store, and when these two men got there to help they were attacked. Almost a dozen men had come for Averill and the woman with ropes and a wagon."

She sucked hard on the cigarette, then let the smoke drift aimlessly from her nose and mouth. "Do you understand my fear now? Although this man Stenger claims land and is hated by many ranchers, I have no homestead or cattle like Ella Watson. Yet some would call me a bad woman too. If this thing happened to her, why not to me?"

I knew she might be close to the truth there, but I didn't say so. And I kept thinking of those men with the ropes and wagon. In my mind one of them had already taken the tall form of my father. Couldn't that urgent business in Cheyenne easily have included an attempt to scare out those two homesteaders who'd been defying several big cattlemen by squatting in their front yard, writing scathing letters about them to the Casper newspaper, and supposedly encouraging cowboys to rustle calves for Ella's herd?

"*Ai*, Martín," Jenny went on softly, "a bad thing. These *hombres* in the saloon and another man were not able to stop what followed. Several miles from the store in a *cañon*, *Señor* Averill and the Watson woman were choked to death with the ropes. I think you call it the hanging."

"They hung them?" I'd never thought of it happening to a woman.

"Yes, the hanging for her too."

I closed my eyes, seeing the two bodies as they must have looked twisting around slowly on the taut ropes after it was done. I didn't want to ask the question, but it had to come out in the open sometimes and the asking wouldn't be any easier later on.

"Did either of the men see who was in on it, Jenny? Did you hear them say anything about that?"

She nodded before noticing the tightness in my voice. "Mostly ranchers of the Association, they said. . . . Your father was not there—I heard them mention that. The sick boy who lived at the store was taken away by the murderers, and I think the two men here are worried about their own lives now."

I said, "I don't blame them for that. Was Senator Karr at Bothwell?"

"I think he was mentioned . . . as was the man called Paulson. But I am not certain what was spoken about them. You were afraid that your father was one of the ranchers. Am I right?"

"Yes," I said.

Jenny began to laugh in a low voice, so strained and mocking that I wondered if she had gone a bit crazy. "You thought he might help choke the Watson woman? Can you really know so little about your father, Martín? He could never do such a thing to her."

Then she abruptly stopped laughing, and I asked, "Why are you so sure?"

Jenny Rodriguez slumped down on the bed, her voice cold and dead-sounding. "He visited her often at Bothwell when no one else was there to see. Why should I know about your father? I will tell you so that you will understand everything. It was a lie I told you earlier about not knowing him well. I was his woman for a long time in Rawlins, until he thought his friends were becoming suspicious of us. Afterward he found companionship with the Watson woman at Bothwell. I think lately he has not visited her, but who can tell? Is it a pleasant story, Martín? I have never thought so."

And early that morning, as I rode back to the ranch, I didn't think so either. . . .

Chapter 11

By August, with feelings still tinder-dry over the lynching of Jim Averill and Ella Watson in Spring Canyon, there was open talk against Ira along the river. Nobody would speak to Father about him, but I heard enough in the bunkhouse to realize that the Association cattlemen, after seeing how the hangings solved their problems at Bothwell, were set on forcing my brother, and everyone else who opposed them, to leave the Sweetwater. So I wasn't surprised that Mr. Karr's foreman, Roan Meyers, had been spreading stories about thieves moving horses through and out of the country by way of Willow Springs Canyon. I expected this kind of thing from Meyers, for he'd been bragging that he was the one who pushed Ella off swinging and kicking to her death. What I didn't expect, though, was the way Finn Rankin and his bunch went against Ira too.

"What's Finn got against Ira?" I asked Cookie one afternoon after work. "I know they had an argument on roundup, but Ira isn't riding for Father any more."

"Don't see it, do you, Mart," Cookie said. "Why don't you quit worrying about a thing you can't help anyways? Only a fool would give a damn what Rankin or any of them is sayin'."

"I asked you because I wanted to know," I told him.

"I see that clear enough. Everybody wants to know everything around here. The caddle are going to hell while people hang whores and spy on one another. Looks like you're going to be the same way as the rest of them, Mart." He broke into a crooked grin then and cut a chunk of plug tobacco. "You're ridin' straight for hell and I'm supposed to circle around ahead to haze your bronc through the gates. Fine thing to expect from an old bird like me, ain't it?"

I began to see that Cookie was trying to get under my skin, so I sat back awhile and watched him spit tobacco juice onto the hot, sandy ground behind the kitchen. The late afternoon air was dead against my face and clothing. Nothing anywhere seemed to be moving, and there were no clouds to relieve the monotony of glassy sky and glare of the sun. I felt sweat drying under the leather band of my hat. It would be even hotter now at Ira's ranch in the canyon, especially if you were working all day with green horses.

"I'll tell you what's the matter with Finn," Cookie said when he felt like talking again. "He's already rode over to argue with your brother. Wanted him to throw in with the little outfits that are trying to organize for an early roundup of their own next spring."

"He should have known that was a waste of time," I said.

"Should've, but he went anyways. Ira didn't want no part of it, so Finn figures he's squattin' on some good water for your dad or Karr. He's got the boys on Antelope Creek convinced your brother's really out there to snoop around for the big companies."

"Finn can't believe that himself."

Cookie nodded without much interest. "Probably he don't. I haven't noticed anybody being bothered about the truth of things around here. Rankin figures that if you ain't for him you're against him. Ira's going to be real popular out there with his two-bit horse outfit. Wish I had a piece of ground somewheres out in the middle of the Red Desert myself. Time I'd been there a week, people that never even met me before would hate my old guts. That's what owning a shirttail of sagebrush'll do for a man."

I looked around at the buildings of Father's ranch. "I wish Ira had stayed here. He didn't have any need to go off by himself that way and leave us shorthanded."

"No need, boy? You just ain't growed enough to see it. He's got a right to make do for himself without thinkin' the same way as you or your dad."

"I know that," I told him, "but he's only making more trouble for everybody. It's not fair to Father . . . or Ira either. What if somebody gets angry enough to kill him out there?"

Cookie's expression narrowed a little, and then he spit past me carelessly. "Which one you worried about—your brother or the half-breed girl?"

I didn't answer that, and the cook began to grin. "Hell, Mart, you're gettin' awful serious all of a sudden. I've seen this same kind of game dealt in Texas. Ways change in the caddle business and people got to change with them. It ain't worth fightin' over, but some men are never smart enough to see that when money's in their reach. Why blame your brother for being disgusted with both sides of it?" He stopped, staring out toward the river like he saw something unpleasant there. "Or maybe you're blaming him for something else. . . ."

I left the kitchen then, but what Cookie said went with me. I told myself the girl had nothing to do any more with my feelings about Ira. Hadn't I gotten over that? I told myself I had, anyway. And the next morning I took supplies out to Slat Honeywell at one of our line camps. I stayed there helping him out for a week, and when I came back in I'd had time to finish that rawhide hackamore bosal I had worked on for so long. Cookie grunted noncommittally when he saw it for the first time.

"I've seen worse," he said then, more kindly.

"I thought Ira might need a new one since he's working horses all the time now," I said.

"I was bettin' you wouldn't finish it. Kids don't have time to learn things with their hands no more, but maybe you ain't such a kid like I thought."

"Maybe not," I told him. . . .

The next day Clayt Paulson rode in to see

Father. They talked together for quite a while in the office, and after the noon meal Paulson rode off again on the Senator's buckskin. I didn't ask about their talk, but Father called me in that afternoon. He had changed into the range clothes he used for working.

"I want you to ride over Green Mountain way with me," he said seriously. "Clayt and Senator Karr will go along with us."

I nodded and waited to see if he was going to tell me anything more. He was deliberately choosing a thin Mexican cigar from the box on his rough desk. "You remember the homesteader named Volanski, don't you, Martin? Last spring Paulson was sure he was selling stolen beef in Rawlins."

I nodded again, remembering the conversation by the chuck wagon and my own talk with the Association detective. Some things had changed a lot in the six months since he ate with us and Leah Karr cooked the dinner in our kitchen.

"Now Clayt thinks he's caught this Volanski with one of our steers in his pen. He thinks we might find him butchering it this evening."

"I see," I said. "I'll get the horses saddled right away."

"Reckon there's no hurry, but we should be getting started soon. We'll meet Wallace and Clayt at the Two-Bar-K."

I stood up in the office. "Do you think the man

is really guilty the way Clayt Paulson believes?" I asked. "I'm not suggesting he hasn't butchered stolen beef, but sometimes a man has to feed his family."

"I won't argue with that, son." Father bit down firmly on the cigar as he watched me with deep-set gray eyes. I thought he was going to say something about Ira, but he didn't. "We'll just have to see what the situation is. Wallace has had much heavier losses from rustlers than we have. I'm in no hurry to condemn this Volanski, but it's not for me alone to decide."

Although he seemed to be finished with the subject, he didn't tell me to go. I saw the tired lines in his face that came when he wasn't sleeping well. His eyes shifted unconsciously to the daguerreotype of my mother on his desk. I looked at the picture too, and it almost seemed to be Ira's face that was framed there.

Finally his chair creaked and Father became aware of me again. "There's something I want you to know, Martin," he said then. "You listening close? This ranch is going to be all yours someday. Do you understand that? I've arranged it all with our lawyer in Rawlins. You're the only son I have now, and this land is going to belong to you. . . ."

His voice became harsh and then died out. I couldn't say anything, so I sat there waiting for him to let me leave.

"You won't go against your father, will you?" he asked suddenly.

"No," I said, "I don't plan to."

"I know you won't," he said, like he was talking to himself. "This land is ours, Mart. I picked it out myself and brought cattle for it all the way up from Texas. I made this land something worth holding to. I didn't put my life's work into this valley just to see a herd of strangers piece it up among them. This ranch doesn't mean much to your brother, but it's my life and nobody can take it away without shooting me down first."

In later years I often thought about Father saying that, for I believe the land *was* his life—more than his life, maybe. And yet he was not a greedy man like some homesteaders might have believed. What land he controlled he took care of, and that's more than you could say for many of the men who became nesters in Wyoming and relied on the government to provide their start and protection. Or depended on ranchers like my father for beef and supplies when broke and the weather withered their crops. I suppose things might've turned out differently if all the large cattlemen and small homesteaders had worked as hard as my father to own something. . . .

As we rode to the Two-Bar-K, Father seemed completely absorbed in his own thoughts, and I was a little afraid to interrupt whatever it was he kept turning over in his mind. The afternoon was hot—a man riding felt the heat of dry land, and a scorched wind blew into our faces from the southeast.

I was glad when we'd ridden past Stenger's and the massive rock formations along the river gave us some protection. A turkey buzzard was circling around above Split Rock on huge, tilted-up wings, flapping slowly now and then. You saw buzzards along the Rattlesnakes in summer and they were graceful enough in the air, but I remembered as a little boy seeing one up close picking the bones of a dead longhorn. Its small reddish head was long, flat, and wrinkled-looking above the big dark body perched beside the rotting TX steer. After that, seeing a buzzard made me think of something dying, and I still can't watch one without recalling that year of 1889, when a whole way of life died on the Sweetwater. . . .

Before we got to the Senator's ranch a single horseman approached us. Long before he reached us Father had told me it was Clayt Paulson on the buckskin, and something in his voice made me think he didn't like Mr. Karr's not being with him.

"Good afternoon," Clayt said when we met. "The Senator wanted badly to come with us, but a business matter came up at the last minute. He asked me to tell you that he will meet us at Volanski's if he possibly can."

"I reckon he will then," was all that Father said about it.

We rode along south for a ways and then cut over to Cottonwood Creek. Neither Father nor Paulson was in a talking mood, which was all right with me. I was wondering just what my father's relationship had been with a woman like Ella Watson. Had I grown up thinking of him as one sort of man, driving himself to build up a large ranch and cattle herd, and not seen another side of him that might hunger after a woman enough to risk ruining his reputation? Maybe being with Jenny Rodriguez in her cabin behind Stenger's had opened my eyes. Maybe in myself I was seeing something of my father's loneliness and needs . . . and I wondered if there were other ways I still hadn't seen that marked me as Martin Tyrrell's son.

Another thing I'll never forget about that ride was coming over the edge of a little draw and seeing an abandoned homesteader's shack. The man, whoever he was, had dug out a hole in the far side of the draw and built the top half of a cabin over it with old logs and warped boards. A couple of buckets with their bottoms rusted out and a tin washtub were overturned by the door, along with some rotten plowlines and a horse collar the gophers or pack rats had chewed up. Somebody must have dragged the rickety stove outside, thinking it worth carting off, and then seen it in the light and changed his mind. To one side of the shack you could see an ugly pile of rusty tin cans, rotten gunny sacks, broken bottles, a set of bedsprings that must have been quite a luxury once, joints of stovepipe, and the handles and share of a cheap plow.

We sat for a while looking at the snakeweed and sunflowers growing where the grass had been plowed up or sheeped-off all around the shack. The homesteader had started a barbed-wire fence down one side of his 160 acres and then apparently given it up, but the old wire was still hanging from crooked posts. I followed Clayt and Father when they rode over that way, where it looked like a dead horse was lying. The animal must've got into the fence the winter before and died trying to fight free of the wire. Just the skeleton and a shrunken, dry hide was left, but you could see enough of the brand to figure the horse had belonged to the Two-Bar-K.

Paulson cursed, and I realized he was extremely angry. "What sort of man would leave barbed wire strung up to kill a good horse that way? I would like to have the son of a bitch here now with his own sorry feet caught in the wire." When he turned to us I was startled by the hard yellow of his eyes—not a man's eyes but more like those of a wild animal. I didn't care for the horse getting in that wire, or the look of the abandoned homestead, either. But I couldn't feel the kind of hatred I saw in Paulson's face.

"It's too bad, Clayt," Father said. "I'd say the fellow got his punishment beforehand, trying to live out here in a shack like that."

Paulson was still staring at the skeleton. "A horse is worth more than most men I've known. He doesn't care about what kind of family you come from or what you do for a living. All a horse cares about is how you treat him. If you are careful in riding and feeding him, he will respect you and give you good service."

Father frowned as though the words pained him. "I think most men are like that too," he said quietly.

The Association detective shook his head. "I believe you are wrong, Mr. Tyrrell. A man judges you on your family, your wealth and position, your usefulness to him. I have none of these things now except the usefulness, but someday I will have them all. I will get them by doing the work that others won't dirty their hands with. It doesn't bother me, Mr. Tyrrell, for I always have lived with fear and death. And when I save enough money I will go away and raise good horses, for they will respect the worst criminal or a man who has nothing. They are far more honest than this man who dirtied the range with his foolishness and left barbed wire around where a horse could step in it."

166

"You don't need to be ashamed of your family," Father told him, as though he was speaking about something the two of them shared but didn't talk about often. "I can't name any man in Texas I would rather have had for a friend than your father. I'd give quite a bit to have him alive today."

"But he isn't alive," Clayt said without emotion. "Being a friend of the Tyrrells was expensive business for him. . . . He would have been better off carrying a six-shooter for pay or his own honor, instead of for friendship."

"I reckon he didn't think so, Clayt."

Father said nothing more as we rode on toward Green Mountain. I saw there was more to that talk about Clayt's father than what they'd mentioned, and it bothered me. So did Paulson's talk about liking a horse better than a man. I knew my father figured everyone had a right to his own opinion and wasn't going to argue about it. If Clayt really did believe what he said back at that old homestead, the talk about his willingness to kill a man seemed pretty possible. The trouble was, though, that men like Senator Karr and my father paid the money which the Association used to hire him. In a way it looked to me like that made them responsible for Paulson's actions too.

And watching Clayt Paulson and Father riding ahead of me, I had a strange feeling that they might have more in common than I'd thought. I didn't care for that feeling very much more than I cared for seeing the turkey buzzard at Split Rock. I was remembering how that bird was like the one in the dream I'd had about Mary and me when Ira first came back to the ranch before spring roundup.

Chapter 12

It was late afternoon when we left Cottonwood Creek and cut toward the mountains with Paulson leading the way. He didn't ride straight for Volanski's homestead, but instead took us around through some eroded foothills and scrub pines. Finally he seemed satisfied with where we were. He sat there smiling to himself for a while, and then he got off and tied his horse to a tree. After Father and I had done the same, Paulson took his field glasses from the saddlebags and slipped the long-barreled Winchester from its scabbard.

"I'll take you close enough to see the cabin and corrals," Clayt told us without raising his voice. "I wouldn't expect them to butcher until almost dark, but we will know when they drive a steer into the old shed they use for a barn. Once they are busy inside, I will take you down where we can surprise them."

He didn't wait for any reply but started moving

quietly off in a way that made you believe the stories about his Indian blood were true. He looked like some kind of dark shadow blending into the dry trees and chalky outcrops that were turning reddish as the dusk came on. I felt clumsy enough just watching Paulson, so I let him and Father go first while I followed, trying not to make much noise.

At last we came out behind some big rocks and below, where the sage and grass lapped a little tongue of rangeland into the mountainside, we saw Volanski's cabin. It wasn't much better than the abandoned homestead we'd passed earlier. But at least Volanski had built his shack above ground from untrimmed logs thrown up to form one room where the three of them—Paulson had said the Russian had a wife and son—must have cooked, eaten, slept, and talked over the price of fresh-butchered beef in Rawlins. A trace of smoke was drifting up from the stovepipe in the roof, and I figured they must be inside eating.

To pass the time I watched a couple of nighthawks flutter and dip on quick wings to catch insects in the sky above the cabin. You could hear them cry *speent . . . speent* as they dove and cattle bawling in the corral, which was too close to the house and made of junk wire strung around a few poorly set pine posts that looked like they were being held up by the wire. The shed with the crooked roof that Volanski used for a barn formed one side of the corral, and I remembered Clayt telling Father that the Russian had chinked the cracks in both his cabin and the milking shed with cow manure.

After what seemed a long time, a boy wearing old overalls came out the cabin door, looked over at the corral for a minute, and then took the dishpan off its peg beside the door and went back inside. When nothing else happened, Paulson grunted and we settled down to wait some more. The nighthawks had gone . . . and the rock slab behind my back was beginning to cool off. The air smelled of dry pine needles and the manure in Volanski's corral. But as the sun started down I could feel a little breeze from the west cool my face. It carried the smell of sage, and I watched it play with smoke from the cabin that stood out now against darker evening sky.

A magpie drifted over us and dropped down in lazy swoops toward a tree behind the corral. Another followed and then several more, until a bunch of them were squalling down there as though they'd found an owl to torment. . . .

Finally the man came out. He was larger than I'd expected, wearing suspenders with his overalls and a flat-looking black hat. He stood there for quite a while gazing at the mountains, and then he moved around the cabin to look off in that direction. Apparently satisfied, he walked over behind the shed and disappeared, but pretty soon the magpies stopped their racket, and you could hear him chousing the milk cows toward the corral. The boy came out too and ran over to open the gate. I saw three milk cows and a woolly old pilgrim bull enter the corral, along with about four horses and several steers, though it was getting too dark to tell for sure how many there were. Volanski and his son turned the bull back out and let the cows into the shed.

"There will be a steer or two in with those cows," Paulson told us.

After the milking had been finished, Volanski came out and gestured to his woman, who brought a lantern from the cabin. The steers began bawling, and there was a brief scuffling sound inside the shed. We heard the shed door creak and the cows moving, and it sounded to me like Volanski had turned them back out in the corral. When the door had closed again and it got quiet inside, Paulson stood up and without saying a word began to work his way down toward the homestead. Father and I followed him as best we could, for it was almost dark.

Once we got on level ground Clayt moved very quickly. He led us behind the cabin to the back of the milking shed. We could hear the three of them talking in low voices. But Paulson seemed satisfied with what he heard. He slipped on around the shed, pausing once to look at the horses bunched in the far corner of the corral. All

I could see was their eyes shining in a slit of dull light coming through a crack in the shed door, but he found out something by looking at them that seemed to please him.

Then he was over beside the door, motioning us to stay where we were. I remember wondering what would happen if Volanski had secured that door from the inside . . . but Paulson must've known about that too. He suddenly threw the door open, bringing his rifle up waist high and at full cock.

Inside stood Volanski, his wife, and the boy—not moving, like figures posing for a portrait. At their feet lay a young, half-skinned-out steer. Volanski, a butcher knife grasped tightly in one of his big hands, stared out at us with disbelief. His wife, who held the lantern, was a large dark-skinned woman, wearing an old yellow slicker to keep the blood off her dress. On the other side of the homesteader the gangly boy still held the steer's front leg back to make the carcass lie steadier while his father worked on it.

Volanski finally spoke, all the while looking from Clayt Paulson to Father and me and then back to Paulson. "What you want here?" he said hoarsely. "Who you are to come here with gun and scare us like this?"

His talking sounded cool enough, but I noticed his hand holding the knife was shaking, and you could be sure he'd heard all the details about the hanging of Watson and Averill. The woman wasn't a bit scared, though.

"You've got no right to break in here," she said coldly. "We ain't got anything worth stealing, if that's the kind of idea you've got in your minds."

Her talking like that seemed to give her husband more courage. "Who you are?" he repeated, only saying it louder this time. All the time the boy wasn't saying a thing, just looking at the rifle in Paulson's hands like he'd never seen a Winchester before.

It was Father who answered him. "I'm Martin Tyrrell and I own the TX ranch north of here. This other gentleman is an investigator for the Stock Association. I reckon you won't mind if we look at the brand on that steer you're butchering, will you?"

"You must be that murderin' Clayt Paulson," the woman said angrily to the detective. "You hung any more women lately? The Association ought to be mighty proud of paying you to help 'em murder a woman. I know you and your kind all right." Her eyes flicked over to Father and me. "And I suppose you had a hand in it, mister. Ain't you got enough to do ownin' half the land and cows in the valley without proving how brave you are by lynchin' folks that want a few acres of ground out here too?"

"Let me make the talk," Volanski told her. He

looked at Father then. "I hear of you, mister . . . you and TX brand. Your other boy I know also— not this one but older boy."

"We will take a look at that steer now," Paulson broke in. "Why don't you throw down that knife and turn the hide over where we can see it?"

"Just a minute, Clayt," my father said. "How did you happen to know Ira, Mr. Volanski?"

The homesteader shrugged and pitched the butcher knife to one side. "We make some business together. I know him awhile all right. If you want to look that steer turn him over yourself, Mr. Detective." There was a look of shrewdness in his face that I didn't much like.

"Honest folks ain't afraid of your Association," the woman taunted Father. "We got the government in Washington on our side and most of the courts in the territory too. You cattle lords had things going your way so long you forget poor folks got some rights in this country. The day ain't far off when you won't have nothin' left in Wyoming, mister, and folks like us will have a fair piece of ground like we got a right to. You and all those foreign companies got all them cattle runnin' on government land that belongs to everybody, and then you come around whenever one of your steers gets lost and try to say somebody changed its brand or butchered it. I ain't afraid of any of you. Arrest us for anything and you'll see how the court in Rawlins or

Lander ain't afraid of your murderin' Association either."

"Turn the hide over," Paulson said again to Volanski. "He ain't going to," his wife said. "None of you got a right on this place."

"I'll do it," I said, stepping into the shed. I didn't much like the woman or what she was saying. I'd heard her kind before—always talking about their rights and how other people were mistreating them. But the only things they ever had was what somebody—the government or some do-gooder—handed out to them. The next time you saw them they had nothing again, and they'd tell you how somebody had cheated them, or how they'd had a run of bad luck, or how everybody was against them. I didn't think too much of the way Paulson went about his job, but now I wanted to hear what Volanski and his big-talking wife would say when that steer turned out to be marked with a TX or = K.

The boy was glad enough to get out of the way, and neither Volanski or the woman said anything when I grabbed hold of the loose hide. That surprised me a little. I flipped it over and there was no brand on the left side where cattle belonging to Senator Karr and my father carried their marks. Feeling shaky, I grabbed a front leg to roll the steer over. The woman was grinning as Father took a hind leg to help me. The brand was a clumsy job but clear enough—a big V.

"You see," the woman laughed. "I told you not to come around botherin' honest folks. That's our brand, even if your Association won't recognize it and let us ship our steers."

Father didn't say anything as he bent over the steer and then ran his fingers over the brand to see if it might have been cut into just the hair with a sharp knife. It hadn't been.

"That steer he is mine all right," Volanski said. "You damn fellows bother me for nothing."

Clayt Paulson hadn't moved the muzzle of his Winchester away from them. "What about the other steers in the corral? Shall I look at them also, Volanski?"

"If you want to make fool, go ahead to look. All them outside is mine with same brand like this one. My family have to eat, so I butcher this cattle tonight. Sure. . . . Look at them all and be damn."

"I will before I'm done," Paulson told him. "I know a rustler when I meet one, and I would imagine that other steer you butchered this morning or late last night is still around. Wouldn't you think so, Mrs. Volanski?"

The woman looked at him with contempt, but I thought her husband was uneasy for a minute. I was watching the boy, whose eyes had glanced over in the corner of the shed beyond the pole stalls when Paulson mentioned another steer being butchered.

176

I went around there, and sure enough I found a beef wrapped in an old piece of canvas and hanging from a gambrel roped to the log center beam. The only trouble was that the hide was gone. . . . And I remembered Clayt telling about Volanski burning the brand of another butchered steer in his stove and getting the boy to bury the rest of the hide.

When I told Father what I'd found Paulson began to smile. "Should we ask your boy where the hide is, rustler? We might even find that steer's head back on the mountain somewhere. I would imagine we might find earmarks on it, even if the brand was cut from the hide and burned up."

For the first time Volanski's woman looked shaken. "You leave that boy alone, mister. We ain't done anything but fix some meat to sell and eat ourselves. I guess the Association ain't made no law against that yet."

"It depends on who the steer belongs to," the stock detective said. "By the way, Volanski, I notice you bought a new sorrel horse."

"So why is the horse your business?" Volanski answered sullenly. "I need new saddle horse so I bought one."

"Is that so?" Paulson handed me his rifle and picked up the homesteader's blood-spattered lariat, which lay coiled beside an ax near the shed door. He disappeared, and I could hear him talking gently to the horses in the corral. When he came back Paulson was leading the sorrel horse by the rope. He brought the animal right up to the door.

"That brand doesn't look much like yours," Clayt said. "Wouldn't you call that a Walking W he's marked with?"

The woman didn't like that. "We haven't had him long enough to get around to brandin' him."

Paulson took the Association's brand book from his shirt pocket and checked through it quickly. "Who did you say you bought that sorrel from? Apparently I was thinking of something else when you mentioned it."

The woman began cursing us, but Volanski must've been figuring what he was going to say. I had to admit he was shrewder than he looked at first. Especially when I heard him tell Father, "I don't know who this horse belong to before. We get him from your boy . . . Ira Tyrrell his name. He said well broke and good to ride or carry the pack, so we don't ask no questions about where he get this horse. Sure, I hear nothing bad about the boy before so I trust him."

"Where is your bill of sale?" Paulson said.

"We don't have to show it to you," answered the woman. "You ain't the sheriff around here."

"Maybe you don't have a bill of sale on that horse."

Volanski kept his eyes on Father. "I trust that

boy who sell me this sorrel horse. He look like a nice fellow, so we don't ask no questions. If somebody stole this horse, you want to ask your boy about it. I'm just dumb farmer that finally learn to keep his mouth shut, Mr. Tyrrell."

"Show us the bill of sale," Clayt Paulson told him again.

"I forget where I put it."

"Shall I ask the boy? I imagine he will remember about the bill of sale and about that other steer too."

The boy's eyes got a funny look in them, and he stepped back against the side of the shed. "Don't you touch him, mister!" Volanski's wife screamed at us. "He don't know anything we haven't told you."

"He knows that horse was stolen from the Walking W on Powder River. Isn't that so, son?"

I knew Paulson was probably running a bluff, but the boy really was scared—afraid to look at his folks or at us either. He just licked his lips and stared down at the dead steer.

"I believe we should take Volanski here to Rawlins," Paulson said to Father. "He doesn't have a bill of sale on that horse, which was reported stolen last spring."

"I told you before there ain't a chance in the world of a court in Rawlins finding him guilty," the woman said defiantly.

Paulson nodded in agreement. "That's true

enough, Mrs. Volanski. But I imagine you have heard it said that if the Association can't convict a rustler any more in the territory, at least the lawyers can break him from paying them to save his neck."

She didn't have an answer to that, for what the stock detective had said was true enough. The Association had plenty of money to fight a case, but a homesteader could be hard pressed to pay for his defense. And the lawyers in our country weren't noted for being poor.

It was Volanski who finally spoke, and you could tell a lot of the fight had been taken out of him. "Your son mixed up in it," he said to Father. "He sell me that horse like I say. You want him to have trouble?"

"I think you're lying," said Paulson. "In the morning we will let you ride that horse to Rawlins with us. Or maybe the boy will want to take us to where that other steer's head and hide are buried."

I turned to look at my father, whose face showed nothing except for those heavy lines deepened in the corners of his eyes by the poor light. When he spoke to Paulson it sounded like he wasn't aware any longer of Volanski and his family being in the shed. "No, we won't do that, Clayt," he said.

I hadn't expected him to say that either. When I glanced at Paulson, I saw that same anger in his yellowish eyes that I'd seen at the abandoned homestead on Cottonwood Creek. "You can't be serious," he said. "If we let this man go now, we can expect the rustling to be worse than ever."

"You heard me right, Clayt."

"You better turn us loose," the woman broke in. "That son of yours could get in Dutch aplenty over sellin' a stolen horse. Everybody knows he's taken to bad company since you run him off your ranch."

Father looked as if he hadn't heard her, but Volanski muttered at her to keep quiet.

"You can see already the kind of talking these two are going to do if we back off now," Paulson told Father.

"I reckon I know, Clayt."

"And I know some people who will be awfully disappointed in you."

Father's temper flared then. "I'm through arguing about it with you!"

I watched him turn from Paulson to Volanski and his wife. "You think I'm letting you go because a son of mine might get into trouble over that horse. I'm telling you different and you better listen. If I thought any good would come of trying you, Volanski, I'd be damn sure you stood up before a court and it wouldn't matter what part my son played in any horse deal. But we both know that court in Rawlins never convicts a rustler, and we both know that's just what you are."

Suddenly Father's voice became hard and flat, like I hadn't often heard him talk. The edge to his words made my scalp crawl a little, and I saw how Volanski and the woman wouldn't meet his eyes any more. "If you butcher another head of beef that belongs to me I'll ride over here and kill you myself. We won't need a lawyer or a judge, Volanski, for I've seen the kind of man you are and heard your woman talk, too. And if I hear of you selling anyone's beef in Rawlins you can expect the Association to take action against you. If they decide then to hang you by your worthless neck I'll help them. Do you understand me, Mr. Volanski?"

The homesteader stared down at the ground without answering.

"Answer me, by God!"

"I hear . . ." Volanski stammered.

"Do you believe what I said?"

Volanski glanced over at his silent wife and then nodded.

"All right," Father said. "Don't you forget . . . because I won't."

He turned abruptly and walked away through the corral. After hesitating for a minute Clayt Paulson cursed under his breath and followed. We heard Father's footsteps ahead of us in the darkness as he headed straight for the horses. He was moving so quickly that we had difficulty catching up with him. And Paulson didn't talk to him until we had ridden off the mountain and reached Cottonwood Creek.

Then he said coldly, "I think perhaps you made a mistake back there."

Father reined in his bay horse and faced Paulson. "I gathered you thought so, Clayt, but I don't intend to argue it any farther. Since Wallace didn't get there, I did what I thought best."

"I will tell him that."

"Do that. Next time he can handle Volanski himself if he isn't satisfied with my way."

"All right. I will mention that also." The stock detective started to ride off toward the Two-Bar-K.

"One other thing, Clayt."

Paulson reined the buckskin around. He was still angry, I thought, but he was controlling it well. "What's that?" he asked.

"I'm tired of hearing these stories about rustlers and horse thieves using Willow Springs Canyon," Father said. "I want you to find out the truth of the matter. I reckon you could call it a private arrangement between you and me."

"Are you serious about wanting the truth?"

"I am."

"Your son might be involved with the stealing, Mr. Tyrrell."

"He might and then he might not."

"All right." Paulson spurred his horse down into the creek bed and then we couldn't see him any more.

Father and I rode on through the sage. After a while he said, "You wanted me to take them to court, didn't you, Mart?"

"At first I did," I said, thinking hard. "When that steer turned out to be their own, I figured we didn't really have enough against them. I thought it was funny that Mr. Karr didn't come with us, too."

"I reckon he had his reasons," Father said, like he didn't want to talk about what the reasons might be. Then he added, "I've known plenty of people like Volanski and that woman. You'll hear men say that all of us were made equal in the beginning, but I find that hard to believe."

"What do you mean?" I asked him.

"I mean that no men are truly equal. Just like cows—some grow tough and able to take care of themselves, and others will give up and die when the grass is covered by a few inches of snow. The longhorns we brought up the trail were a hardy breed, and these new pilgrim cattle from Oregon don't want to get out from sight of the ranch buildings. Take a man like this Volanski. He wants to have something without working for it. The government gives him a plot of land, but he's never earned enough money before to buy any stock or even any farming tools. So he butchers somebody else's cattle to sell and keeps his belly full that way. It's not like he was branding mavericks to get a herd of his own—like some of us did to get a start. At least we knew our neighbors were doing the same thing and it balanced out."

He didn't often talk to me like that, and I remember trying to see his face better as we rode along together. But his hat was pulled down low, and all I could make out was the dark flowing line of his mustache below the forceful hook of craggy nose.

"My father used to always say, 'Blood will tell—in stock or men,' " he told me. "But I don't hold to that as much as he did. Some men from the worst kind of families believe in themselves enough and sweat enough to end up with the land or cattle they want . . . or with the woman or sons or whatever it is they think worth living for. But a man like Volanski thinks there's an easy way that don't involve a lifetime of making do for yourself. That kind of man will probably be the only kind around someday, son."

"Maybe so," I said.

And Father said, "I hope to God that Ira and Wallace Karr won't be among them."

I wondered what he would say about Ira owning a band of sheep that a one-eyed Mexican was herding on range claimed by the Two-Bar-K. You could say my brother was "making do" for himself, but I wasn't sure

Father would look at it that way. He'd probably call it a sorry thing for Ira to get into. But what Jenny had told me about my father and Ella Watson didn't make a very good story either. . . .

Chapter 13

Something happens to our country at the end of summer. The sky loses its color, and you realize suddenly that the grass is stiffening up to die. The stock feel the change too. They begin to rustle harder for feed and drift farther away from their summer range. And in the cooling nights you sometimes wake up shivering and know the summer will soon be gone. . . .

One morning I got up to find the chuck wagon over by the bunkhouse kitchen again. We were getting ready for the beef roundup, I knew, and I always felt excited by the preparations. When Father asked me to ride over and check on the starting date with Mr. Karr, I was so pleased that I stopped thinking about the troubles we'd had since spring. A long ride by myself always helped me see things more clearly, so I was feeling good by the time I unsaddled at the Two-Bar-K.

The Senator's big headquarters was quiet, and it was the Indian woman keeping house for them who took me to Mr. Karr's office. He was not working on any of the papers or ledgers spread over his polished walnut desk, but staring out the window with his white hands clasped across his stomach. Mounted heads—a buffalo and a longhorn steer—hung from the walls. They were so skillfully stuffed that they made me feel uncomfortable. Indian relics and ceremonial beadwork were displayed on the walls also, along with a sagging grizzly-bear hide and portraits of the Senator shaking hands with some Sioux chief or standing with his rifle in a group of British gentlemen and flanked by dead antelope or elk.

He was startled when I spoke to him from the doorway. "You surprised me, Martin," he said, without smiling.

I apologized and took the chair he indicated. Being here by myself made me feel clumsy for some reason. Usually Leah greeted me and put me at ease. The Senator flipped his watch chain against the buttons of his vest. His black, high-topped shoes, unpolished and shabby, I noticed, rested before him on a dusty buffalo hide. His suit was unpressed and worn at the knees. He seemed upset by something—slumped by a moodiness I hadn't seen in him before.

"Father asked me to arrange the date to meet for beef roundup," I said.

He kept staring through the flyspecked window which framed a dry square of his poorest rangeland. "I can't begin until the first of next week," he said heavily. "My Leah is getting married in Rawlins this weekend."

Leah was getting married? . . . I didn't know what to say.

"She and her mother are in Denver now to buy wedding clothes. I'll meet them day after tomorrow for the ceremony. Are you surprised, Martin?"

"I guess I am," I told him. "We hadn't heard anything about it."

"No, of course not. It was all decided rather quickly this last week. You know how the women are. Her mother wanted her to wait longer, but she and Clayt thought it best to have the wedding before we all got busy with the fall shipping."

The Senator cleared his throat. "They will live in Rawlins until Clayt finds a suitable ranch operation in the Southwest. He has been terribly treated in this agitation over Averill and that poor whore at Bothwell. If he had been involved in the affair it would be to his credit. But the yellow press in Casper has decided to ruin his reputation, along with mine. 'The *bull*ionaire king of the Rattlesnakes,' they are calling me. Clayt Paulson is my 'foaming-mouthed, vicious-tempered killer wolf.' No one points out that most of the lawless residents have left the Bothwell country since July. I would say that hanging those two troublemakers has had a desirable effect in controlling the unjust appropriation of our land and stock. . . . But the campaign of vilification goes on against us."

Karr sighed and took a dark cigar from the inside pocket of his coat. "I understand your father is having his troubles also. It must be difficult for him to be defied by his own son. I have even been told that your brother is aiding the undesirable elements along the Sweetwater."

"Ira's not helping anybody, Mr. Karr," I said carefully. "He's trying to leave everybody alone and get a start in the horse business."

"It's well known that rustlers stop at his 'horse ranch.' And I understand there were stolen animals in that bunch of horses he bought in Idaho."

I'd already heard this latest story and asked Ira about it. "He sent money for them to their owners. It was an accident that he couldn't help. He bought the horses in good faith."

Cigar smoke obscured Mr. Karr's face. He had his hands reclasped on his vest. "Really? Yet he did sell a horse branded Walking W to that thief Volanski. . . . In any case, it can't be pleasant for your father, Martin. It has been a bad year for all of us."

When he seemed to be sinking deep into his own thoughts again I said, "I better be riding back. I'll tell Father you want to begin the roundup Monday."

He didn't look at me. "Fine . . . fine." Then, as an afterthought, he added, "Tell your father I am sorry I couldn't join him last month, when the two of you went with Clayt to check on Volanski's rustling operation at Green Mountain. I was terribly busy, of course, and unable to get away until it was too late. You see, I am thinking of selling the ranch and going back into law practice. Perhaps I might have a try at the state legislature in a few years. No fool like an old one, they say."

"Father will be surprised to hear that," I said, astonished myself.

Mr. Karr waved his cigar at the animal heads on the wall. "Perhaps a man can learn a lesson from those old fellows. The good range days are past, I'm afraid. I can't go on giving my steers away year after year in Chicago. With statehood times will be different for us—we will have new industries, new railroads. I am too old to keep fighting the weather, the market, the squatters. Now my Leah is getting married, and Clayt wants to make a new start somewhere else. I have no kin to take over the ranch. . . ."

I stood up to leave. "I hate to think of another person owning the Two-Bar-K, Mr. Karr."

He coughed sadly, sprinkling ashes on himself. "It's not that I am giving up willingly. I would battle these emigrants and rustlers to the finish . . . if I saw a way to win. You understand that, don't you, son?"

I shook my head. "I'm not sure I do. You said before that we should fight for our rights here. I've heard you and Father saying that for years."

"Times change in a country. Of course I haven't decided for sure yet. However, I want to let your father know what my thoughts are. This is a hard decision to make when a man is not young any more."

I wanted to get away from the cigar smoke and the Senator's plea for sympathy. He wasn't talking like the person I had respected for so long. Although I figured he had a right to do what he wanted with his ranch, I didn't like the way he talked so easily about "new industries" and "changing times," like a politician talking to a newspaper editor.

"Come over again, Martin," he said as I was leaving. "It will be lonely here with Leah gone."

I left him slumped in his big chair with the dead cigar hanging down in one hand, his expression as fixed as those of his mounted heads or his face in the picture of him with the Sioux chief. It was like leaving a room full of ghosts. . . .

The air outside was clean and tinged with the smell of drying grass. With Leah and Mrs. Karr gone and the Two-Bar-K cowboys riding line, the ranch looked deserted and shrunken, so it was hard to remember that Karr ran more stock than anyone else in our country. He was going to sell out completely, I figured—cattle and horses, the home ranch, board corrals, line camps, and homesteads he'd bought to control the best grazing land—but the way he talked was what bothered me most.

On the ride back to the TX, that saddle he'd given me felt uncomfortable, too small somehow, and I wondered what Father would say when I told him about my talk with the Senator. Then too there was the business of Leah marrying Clayt Paulson. They didn't seem to go together very well from what I'd seen, but a man couldn't judge a thing like that unless he had more experience than me. I hoped it would work out all right for her.

I didn't take the trail beside the river but cut off through the Red Rocks instead. Riding close to Willow Springs Canyon made me think of that other time I rode over at the beginning of spring roundup. It was all different now with Jules Lamar dead, Ira gone from the TX, and the hanging of Ella Watson lying over the country like the shadow of a spring storm. The range and cattle still were the most important things in my life, but now they seemed to be embittering the people who had them. Our whole valley was stretched taut with the threat of violence. Even Father was caught up in it since Lamar was shot, and I figured he had begun to brood over his suspicion that Ira was turning against him.

Only Mary seemed a part of the Sweetwater country that I could count on not to change too much. She was at the heart of my memories about growing up on the ranch, and she belonged to the land like the antelope and longhorn cattle . . . and to my brother. . . .

Coming over a rise, Blacky suddenly whinnied, and I saw a bunch of horses being driven toward the canyon. A man rode behind them in the dust, his face protected by a red scarf. He raised one hand on sighting me, and I recognized Ira on the bay mare. When he waved me over I put Blacky scrambling down the slope in crowhops and rode in behind the horses—young geldings with a couple of old mares leading the bunch.

"I'm glad to see you, Mart," Ira said when the horses were corralled near the rock beyond Lamar's cabin.

He looked different when he pulled down the dusty scarf. His hands were hardened and very brown. He appeared stronger than before, but he was thinner-looking too, in a way that made him resemble even more the old pictures of our mother.

"I've been hoping you would stop by," he said.

I told him I was riding back from the Two-Bar-K. "Leah's getting married," I said then.

He took the news calmly, but I could tell he hadn't expected it. "Clayt Paulson?" he asked.

"Yeah, Paulson. Wedding's this weekend in

Rawlins. Mr. Karr just told me. And he's talking about selling out here after Paulson gets a ranch in New Mexico or Arizona Territory."

Ira nodded thoughtfully. "An Association detective would get along better where he wasn't known."

"Good horses," I said to change the subject.

"I'm breaking them for a man in Lander Valley. I rode over yesterday to pick them up." He saw me glance at their brands. "They're all clean, Mart. You can tell Father that."

"I never believed the talk," I said defensively.

He smiled and slapped dust off his hat. "I know that, Mart. Let's go up to the cabin. Mary has been wondering why you haven't come over more often."

We walked together on the path from the spring. Young magpies were croaking as they quarreled in the willows. I could see the flat prints of Mary's moccasins lightly marking the dust. I was thinking how good a dipper of spring water would taste.

The sun shimmered off the cabin's window-panes, making them look like glassy water, and the plank door was halfway open. Ira stopped when he saw the door. "Mary," he called. "It's Mart with me."

We heard only the magpies squalling.

"Her horse was in the corral," I said. "Maybe she's asleep."

Ira stepped inside, and when he didn't speak I

followed him. The cabin was freshly cleaned, and a partly finished quilt was stretched on a frame by the window. But Ira was staring at the big bed in the corner of the cabin. There was a long smooth bulge under the scarlet blanket. A bullet hole made a tiny tear in the wool.

My brother walked over the swept dirt floor, and he bent like an old man to touch the blanket. He pulled the edge back gently until the sleek black hair, twisted into hard braids, and light tan skin of Mary's thin face were revealed on the feather pillow. She looked like she'd fallen asleep in the sun. . . .

She's dead, I thought, seeing the blood soaking her blouse. . . . She's dead. But even as Ira reached to feel for her heartbeat she rolled her head to one side and whispered something over and over. I didn't know what it was at first. Then I listened more carefully and heard the words that Ira was hearing too: "Mart . . . oh, Mart . . ."

Ira didn't show anything, though. He was busy unbuttoning Mary's blouse to see just how bad the wound was. It was hard to tell at first, because she'd lost a lot of blood. But finally we saw the bullet had struck below her collarbone— right in line with her heart but high. The shot must have been fired through the door or open rear window, I thought. Her shoulder didn't look good, and yet it seemed to me that the bullet hadn't touched her lungs.

She moaned something unclear and then, "Mart . . . I'm sorry . . ."

My brother straightened up as if he hadn't heard her. "It's a long way to Rawlins or Lander, Mart."

I was thinking the same thing—a long way to take her and a long way to ride to bring back a doctor. "Cookie's had experience with gunshot wounds," I told him after a minute. "I can get him over here quick enough. Might be better than trying to move her. Then I can ride on to Rawlins for Doc Parker."

"Would you do that?" Ira said tightly. "Cookie and I will do whatever we can until you get back with the doctor."

"I'll get him here," I said, starting for the door.

I wanted to have a look around the outside of the cabin for tracks, but that would have to wait now. It would be easy enough to get Cookie. I'd be riding all night getting to Rawlins, but the doctor there was a friend of Father's. . . .

As I rode from the cabin, though, I was thinking about the way Mary had called out. Ira had heard it too—with maybe more to come, her being out of her head that way. And then there was also the shooting itself. I couldn't forget the look of that little hole in the blanket and then what the bullet had done to her smooth shoulder.

If I'd had time to check for sign around the cabin, I figured I would know a lot more about what had happened. Even without finding tracks

I could make a fair guess. Father had asked Paulson to keep check on Ira's activities at Willow Springs, and it wouldn't be the first time Clayt took things into his own hands. That was what the Association paid him for. He could wrap his feet in gunny sacks and move around quiet as a hungry wolf. It was possible he could have thought it was Ira or someone else in the bed. Or even that he'd known it was Mary, though I couldn't see why he would deliberately shoot her.

Something else bothered me too. I'd been trying hard to see my father's side of things and believe he'd been right in much of his disagreement with Ira. If Clayt had something to do with what had happened to Mary, Father would be responsible also . . . in a way. He'd made that deal with Paulson, and a shooting like this one was just what Ira had been afraid would happen unless my father broke with the Association's way of protecting their interests. If Clayt Paulson had shot Mary, I'd have to hold it against Father. . . .

Chapter 14

When I started out for Rawlins the clouds were building up dark over Green Mountain, and the wind was soughing in the willows by the river. It whipped down the dry grass so you could see the cattle begin to bunch together, but you couldn't hear them bawl. Then that moaning of the wind stopped. There was lightning off to the west for a while, before the first rain fell. I reached Crook's Gap in a hard rainstorm that muddied the wagon ruts until Blacky was slowed down to an awkward, sliding walk, and even wearing a slicker I got soaked through with cold rain.

It was that kind of trip there and back the next day with Doc Parker, but he fixed Mary up pretty good—though Cookie said he'd cleaned her shoulder so there wasn't anything left for Doc to do except change the dressing. I don't know, because I wasn't there while he was working. I went all around the cabin and corral looking for tracks, but it had rained some at Willow Springs too. Any footprints had been washed out by the time I got a chance to look.

Ira saw what I was up to and came out to the corral. He looked tired, which didn't surprise me, but his face showed more than just worry or not getting any sleep. For a minute I had a funny feeling that it wasn't my brother I saw walking toward me. His eyes were hard like those of a hurt hawk. But the main thing was how much older he seemed—and something flinty in the sound of his voice.

"You won't find any footprints," he said.

"I guess not after that rain. Thought I'd look to make sure, though."

"I can tell you what you would've seen if there hadn't been any rain. You can probably guess for yourself."

"Did you look around the other afternoon?" I asked him.

"Yes, I did."

I waited for him to go on, but he seemed more interested in turning something over in his mind. Finally he said, "I didn't think Father would go that far. Did you know Paulson was snooping around here, Mart?"

I nodded. "I knew . . . but I didn't think it meant much. He's always moving through the country and watching what goes on."

"He doesn't just watch. The Association can use him whenever it wants to frighten someone off the land. Or when it wants to get rid of a particular man. . . ."

"Maybe some of that's just talk," I said.

He gave me a strange, hard glance. "Grow up, Mart. Father told Paulson to watch Willow Springs, didn't he?"

"Yes," I said. "But that don't mean . . ."

"That Paulson was the one? Of course you couldn't be certain unless you actually saw him—or Mary saw him. If it was Paulson I don't think she would've seen him, though."

I took out my pocket knife and began to scrape mud off one of my boots. "How do you figure it was him then?"

"I'll tell you how, Mart. Outside the cabin, around by the back window, I found a man's tracks. At least they were the kind of tracks a man would make if he wrapped his boots in gunny sacks. He didn't get close enough to the window so anyone inside might see him clearly. Then afterwards he slipped around onto the rocks. I didn't want to leave Mary long enough to see where he came out on top, but he probably had his horse hidden back there."

"Some say Clayt Paulson has worked that way, all right," I said. "Though I suppose someone else might want to make this shooting look like Paulson's doing."

"Who?"

I didn't like the way he said that, almost like I was defending Clayt. But I didn't have any good answer either.

"You see what I mean?" Ira said. "I imagine Mary was mistaken for me when that shot was fired. Some of the cattlemen who killed Ella Watson and Averill would like to get rid of other homesteaders too—including me. But they're afraid now to come right out and try another hanging. Besides that, they want to get their money's worth from the salary they pay Paulson."

"Father wouldn't allow it," I told him, after hesitating for a moment.

"I'd like to think he wouldn't. If he told

Paulson to watch me he must have thought I was guilty of something. And if he believes that, he might have decided to let the others in the Association take steps to get me out of the way."

"He wouldn't," I said again. "I know him better than that. Besides, I was there when Father talked with Clayt Paulson about you. It sounded to me like he was having Clayt check on Willow Springs so he could put a stop to that talk about you throwing in with the stock thieves. I know him better than to believe he'd let anyone take a shot at you."

"You might not have heard the whole story, Mart. I don't think you know Father as well as you think. He'd do anything to protect what he thinks is his land, and he believes Willow Springs belongs in the TX. He once thought of me as a part of his belongings too."

I just stood there watching the coldness in Ira's blue eyes. I remembered him facing up to Father in the corral. But he'd been different in the spring—calmer and sure Father would listen to his arguments. Now I was a little afraid of the way he looked and talked.

"Is Mary going to be all right?" I asked then.

"Dr. Parker thinks so. When she's strong enough I'm going to take her to her relatives on the Reservation. She'll be safer if the trouble gets worse here."

"I feel bad about what happened to her," I said.

"Why don't you tell Father that, Mart? You can also tell him something for me. Just say I've learned who has more of the right on their side."

"What does that mean?"

"He'll know. I'm through trying not to get involved with the people that are fighting the Association. Tell him not to worry any more about whether he can trust me. He can't."

So there it was, and if I didn't like what he'd said, there wasn't much I could do about it. "Does that go for you and me too?" I asked him.

He had turned to walk back to the cabin, but he heard me all right. "Not unless you want it to," he said more gently. "You didn't have anything to say about being born a Tyrrell."

That was the only thing he'd said so far to anger me. "You're a Tyrrell too!" I shouted at him. "You never acted like one, but you've got the same blood as me. Father built that ranch for you as much as for me. You know that's true. If you hadn't left him none of this would've happened, either. Damn you, Ira!"

Whatever my brother felt then didn't show. "No, it might not have happened quite the same way, Mart. But staying on the ranch would have been worse—you can't respect a person who just drifts along with something he doesn't believe in. I think one of these days you'll see what I mean, even if Father never does."

"He'll never give up the ranch to a bunch of

foreign farmers who can't possibly make a living here."

"I didn't ask him to do that," Ira said. "I wanted him to treat them fairly and not try to hold more land than he needed. If a law's going to work it has to apply to both sides. The Association wants to make its own laws for its own benefit. You know that nothing will happen to the men who lynched Jim Averill and the Watson woman."

"They built a herd of mavericked cattle."

"How did Father get started in Texas? I believe every cattleman in this valley has branded more mavericks than Jim and Ella would ever have had in their herd. Anyway, you've heard it all argued out before. You've got to make up your own mind now."

"My mind's been made up," I told him. "Nothing's happened to change it either. You've got no proof that Paulson shot Mary."

"All right, Mart."

I was still angry enough to be unfair. "Since you promised Jules you'd take care of her, you ought to've been more careful about leaving her alone out here. I'd have—"

"You would have kept her from being shot?" he interrupted. "If you had been responsible for her? You might have, Mart. . . . I heard her call for you in the cabin when we first found her."

His saying that threw me off balance, and I

couldn't think of any way to answer. Suddenly I didn't feel angry any more—just ashamed of myself for what I'd said. "Forget that about you and her," I told him. "I hadn't any right saying it."

He stood watching me for a minute. Then he said, "You should know something about Mary and me. Like you say, I told Jules I would take care of her if anything happened to him. I wanted her to pretend we were married so nobody would make a lot of false talk or try to take Lamar's homestead away from her. I thought someday she would want to marry me, but I'm not very sure about that now. . . ."

I just stared at him, and then we both heard Cookie calling him from the cabin.

"I didn't like seeing her shot any more than you did," Ira said. "She's the only girl I've ever wanted, and I'll still marry her if she decides that's the right thing for her to do. Don't forget that, Mart."

He walked away from me quickly, and I didn't move until long after he had entered the cabin where Mary lay. . . .

Father started the fall roundup on Monday, and when the outfits in our district were all together the owners voted to begin by working the country around Devil's Gate. The roundup foreman was to be Father, which caused some grumbling among the hands who hadn't liked the way he drove them that spring. Some of the men no longer cared whether or not I heard them talk about him, but I wasn't paying much attention to them anyway.

Before I'd always enjoyed gathering cattle for shipment. This time I had to work hard to keep the time moving and keep myself from thinking too much. I had good circle horses in my string, and riding over open country all day hunting cattle usually gives a man the chance to feel at peace with the country and himself. He moves with the sun and wind, feels the muscles working in the shoulders of his horse, and knows a sense of freedom that comes from the peculiar light and space that you can still find riding north of the Sweetwater through broad slopes of grass and sage . . . sandy gullies threaded with thin, clear creeks where antelope and sage chickens water . . . high ridges of weathered granite and grass-softened swales where cattle gather in the glaring afternoon sun. . . .

But it was the nights I couldn't take. Lying in my soogans when I wasn't on night guard, I always ended up remembering how Mary had called to me in the cabin, and what Ira had said about not being sure she wanted to marry him. I could turn it all over and over in my head, without knowing any better how to feel toward her. And the more I thought and worried about Mary, the more I wondered about whether my father had been responsible in any way for her getting shot. Whether Clayt Paulson had been the one who made the tracks Ira had seen behind the cabin . . .

One night when the roundup crew had begun working the country near Stenger's, I got Slat to ride night guard for me. After supper at the chuck wagon I led Blacky away from the campfire and rode south. An hour or so later I crossed the river and hobbled my horse behind Jenny's cabin. I figured she was working at the saloon, and so I waited awhile in the cabin. Business must have been slack, because pretty soon I saw her walking down through the sage by herself. I went outside so I wouldn't frighten her.

"Martín?" she called, keeping her voice low.

"Yes," I said. "I wanted to see you for a minute."

She seemed glad I'd come. "I had hoped you would visit here again, but I knew this month you would be busy riding for the cattle."

I nodded. "That's right. I can't stay long."

"But come in," she said, "and we will talk after coffee."

I followed her inside where the dusk gave a lonesome feeling to the flour-sack curtains, old iron bed, table, and a couple of chairs, which were about all the furnishings Jenny had. She kept everything clean, though, and when the coffee had warmed she poured it for me in a thin china cup like the ones of Mother's that my father brought up to the ranch from Texas.

"Are you hungry, Martín? I think you have ridden a long way."

"I ate before I left, thanks. The coffee's good."

She poured me another cup and waited without saying much until I got finished with it. Then she made brown cigarettes for both of us, working her fingers a little too fast, like she needed something to do with her hands.

"So you came back to see me," she said in a whisper. "That is good." She put a cigarette between my lips and lit it, her eyes shining in the match flare. "I have thought of you and wondered if you would get lonely enough to visit me again. I thought, Jenny, he will not waste his time here, so forget about it. But now you are back."

She looked down at the cigarette in her fingers and smiled. "You will have a real girl friend someday, Martín. Perhaps already . . . but that does not matter now. Who knows—perhaps they will hang me and *Señor* Stenger next . . . now that the man and woman at Bothwell are dead."

Jenny crossed herself and got up to secure the door to the cabin. Then she sat down on the bed. "Come, Martín," she said.

And I went to her there—sober this time—and held her. The black hair fell over my arm when she loosened it. I can still recall that night clearly . . . both of us worried and lonesome . . . the tiny gold cross shining on her brown breast . . . and how she lay back on the bed under me, murmuring, "*Qué tal*, Martín? *Me gusta. . . . Qué tal?*"

I knew more than I had the first time, but in that moment when she clung to me with smooth, soft limbs and we were one flesh I passed some line that made me different and grown up. And lying beside her afterward, I was thinking how right Ira was when he said I needed to make up my own mind about Father and the Association. About what I wanted to do with my life too, I decided.

Jenny lay touching me lightly with one hand, her eyes half closed in the early darkness. "I think you are much like your father. Does that displease you? It is true, though. *Ai!* . . . A strange man no one can know well. You also, Martín. . . ."

I wondered what else she would tell me about him. "Why do you call him strange?" I asked her. "Can you tell me, Jenny?"

"Who knows a man like that? But there are few left like him. When he must decide whether or not to do a thing, he listens only to himself and does what he thinks is right. If he finds he is mistaken he takes the blame on his own shoulders too. I think it would be hard to live that way, Martín."

What she'd said so far squared with what I knew of my father. "Go on," I told her.

"There is not much else I can say. He desires more than most men—more of the land, the cattle, the good horses. But he wishes them for his sons. . . . He used to tell me so himself. I am sorry there is trouble among the three of you."

"But why should he insist that Ira live like he does? Maybe I don't really know what's bothering him."

The young Mexican woman sighed and rested her flat cheek against my shoulder. "Did you ask him about it, Martín?"

I thought a moment. "No," I finally said, "I guess I haven't."

"Perhaps he would tell you. Who can say? But both you and your brother cannot leave him. . . . I think that would kill him inside. You should try to help him, for he is a lonely man."

"He won't let anyone help him," I said. "He won't listen to Ira or me or nobody else. He's never wanted me around as much as he's wanted Ira, and he's sure not about to let me do anything for him."

"Can you be certain he feels this way?"

"I've seen it for almost all my life. When I was born my mother died. I robbed him of her, and Father's never forgotten it either. Ira looks a lot like her, and my father always figured Ira would take over the ranch. It's almost like he feels guilty about Mother's dying and wants to make up for it by giving Ira everything."

Jenny was shaking her head without saying anything, and I heard a coyote up toward the Rattlesnakes. Hearing one always makes you feel all alone somehow—like you don't really belong on the land at all. I remembered Ira saying once that if coyotes, wolves, antelope, deer, sage chickens, and jack rabbits could all live on the land without owning or destroying it he figured people could do the same. I guessed people weren't jack rabbits, though. . . .

I sat up on the bed and began to pull on my pants and boots. "I've got to start back for roundup camp," I told Jenny. "Thanks for listening to all my troubles this way."

"I am sorry I cannot help you."

I lowered one boot back to the floor. "Maybe you can help me."

"How is that?"

"Have you heard any talk in Stenger's place about someone shooting the Lamar girl at Willow Springs Canyon?"

I heard her breathe quickly in surprise. "No, Martín! . . . When did this happen?"

"About ten days ago. Ira asked Doc Parker to keep it quiet until he could move her away from here."

"Then she is not dead?"

"No."

"That is good. . . . Listen, Martín, and I will tell you a thing that may interest you."

Jenny lowered her voice and spoke close to my ear. "In the saloon over a week ago . . . two cowboys from the Powder River on their way back from Rawlins. They spoke of a man they had met in a bar there. Very drunk, they said, and bragging of people he had killed for the money."

"Go ahead," I said when she stopped talking to listen for sounds outside. She was really afraid, I knew, and I didn't blame her.

"One man I remember them mentioning as being killed was a cattle thief in Texas. These cowboys also said the man in Rawlins bragged of helping Ella Watson die on the rope. . . . And—I am sure of this—he mentioned just getting the money for taking care of a horse thief."

My heart was beating harder, and I felt sweat on the palms of my hands. "That's all? The cowboys didn't say any more about who the man in Rawlins was?"

"Not that I heard. . . . Oh yes, he had told them also of wrapping his boots in sacks to walk quietly and keep from leaving clear footprints. And I thought at the time that the drunk man was joking with them by telling things he had heard about . . . about . . ."

"Clayt Paulson?" I said it very low, but she flinched as if I'd slapped her.

"I did not say his name," she whispered.

"It's all right," I said. "I won't tell anyone about what you heard. You don't have to worry about that. And I think it would be best if we didn't mention what happened to Mary Lamar either."

"You can trust me." She looked up, trying to smile, and then rested her head on my shoulder so her hair fell across my back. "They say you were fond of that Lamar girl. Is it so?"

"I liked her once," I said.

"No longer?"

"She's my brother's wife." I wasn't going to shatter that lie, just in case it might still give Mary some sort of protection. But saying it wasn't easy.

"Yes," she said, "I know that. But you did not answer my question. Never mind, Martín, for it is not my business. Will you come again to see me?"

I nodded. "I will, Jenny."

I finished pulling on my boots, and when she was busy dressing herself I put some money on the table for her. She walked outside with me. I left her standing by the cabin and rolling a cigarette in the dark, while I found Blacky for the ride back to roundup camp.

It seemed cold crossing the river, though I didn't get very wet. And the sky had a dark blue hardness which went along with an edge of frost in the air to remind a person that winter was only two months away. In my mind I could imagine Clayt Paulson as he crept up behind the cabin and carefully lifted the Winchester until it pointed straight at the form lying under the scarlet blanket. . . . And I think that night leaving Stenger's was when I actually began to distrust my father.

Chapter 15

The roundup crew moved along north of the river, gathering cattle each day without anything happening. I didn't really know what I expected, but I remember being uneasy every morning as I woke to the cook's call and saw stars dying out in the pale September sky that was touched with gray as often as it was clear.

I think Father knew I was avoiding him for some reason, but he didn't mention it whenever the work accidentally brought us together. At night he sat briefly at the fire drinking coffee while the cowboys told stories or jobbed each other. Then he rode off to check the cattle being night-herded. When he got back Father never came to the fire again. A special bed tent had been brought along for any of the owners who came to the roundup. But my father would never permit it to be pitched for him, and he slept off by himself in the same soogans he'd used on the trail drives.

I didn't care what he did—at least I told myself that. When the fall work was done and I had a chance to get everything straight in my mind, I figured to tell him I was through with the TX. I'd tell him what I thought of him putting Clayt Paulson in a position to shoot Mary—or Ira, if the killer had thought he was shooting my brother. And once I'd convinced myself that Father could've been involved in what happened to Mary, I began thinking of other things he'd done too. Like visiting Ella Watson and then letting his cattlemen friends hang her . . .

One morning when we were getting close to our home range Ira rode into the camp while we were eating breakfast. Maybe Cookie and some of the hands had seen him riding up—if so, they didn't warn Father. I just looked up and saw him by the rope corral. He had a string of horses with him, and after he'd turned them into the corral he walked over to where Father and the hands were drinking coffee by the chuck wagon. Ira stopped in front of Father, who stood up slowly and drained the cup of coffee in his hands without taking his eyes from my brother.

"You wanted something?" Father asked then.

Ira was just as cool as my father. "Yes. I'm joining this roundup as a rep."

Some of the cowboys looked at each other in surprise. It was common practice for owners outside a roundup district to send a man to represent their interests at roundups in neighboring districts—and bring back any stray cattle belonging to them. We had several "reps" with the roundup now, but it was hard to see how Ira could be working for any of the cattlemen in our country.

Father threw coffee grounds from his tin cup and waited while the hands stood up too and took their cups and plates over to the washpan. "What brand are you representing?" he said, as though he was talking to a complete stranger.

"Mr. Lamar's brand," Ira told him. "The JL. I believe it has been registered correctly and approved by the Association."

I watched Father closely and wondered what he might be thinking. But before he spoke Roan Meyers came over to where the three of us were standing together.

"Since Senator Karr isn't here I want to say something," Meyers told us. "Mr. Karr mentioned he wrote to the Association about your son's sellin' a stolen horse to that rustler Volanski. I know the Senator would raise hell if I stood by and let someone like that rep on this roundup. I'm sayin' now that he won't like it even a little bit."

Father turned on him. "I reckon that's plain enough, Roan. Maybe next time the Senator will be here to speak for himself."

Instead of letting it go at that, Meyers pushed

his hat back so his red hair showed. "I figure if we let him on this roundup there's others who'll think they got a right to come along too. For all I know the Association has blackballed him by now. 'Course you're the foreman here." Meyers looked over pointedly at Ira. "I say a man who'll steal a horse will steal anything."

Ira didn't seem angered. "What do you say about a man who murders another man, Roan?"

"What the hell does that mean?"

"I think it's perfectly clear to everyone else," Ira said.

Meyer's face became redder, and he hitched up his gun belt. "If you want some trouble, sonny, I'm the one who can give it to you."

"I thought old men like Jules Lamar were your specialty," said Ira.

I noticed then that my brother wasn't wearing a six-shooter, though he probably had that old .38-55 Ballard in a saddle scabbard. It was just like him not to worry about it. Whether he had a gun with him or was unarmed, he usually talked about the same, so like a lot of things he did you could say it was brave or foolish, depending on the way you looked at it.

His voice grating and mean, Meyers said, "You heard wrong, sonny. My specialty is half-baked horse thieves with big mouths like yourself."

"I reckon that's enough from both of you," Father cut in. "Like you said before, Roan, I'm in charge of this roundup. If I need any help I'll ask you for it."

"That's plain," Karr's foreman grunted, "but I'm having enough trouble with some of the hands like it is. About half of them are itchin' to get blackballed so they can start rustling cows from us like a lot of their friends are doing. Lettin' this nester-lover rep is likely to give them the idea they can get away with stealing too. Senator Karr won't go for it and the Association won't neither."

Meyers walked off, his heavy body moving defiantly. Then he turned around and told Father, "He's your boy, Mr. Tyrrell, but I won't take anything off him if he crosses me. I've always got along fine with you. This horse thief and his rustler friends are a different story."

"Get the men started, Roan," said Father.

When Meyers shouted angrily at the cowboys to catch their horses Father turned back to Ira. "You've got a right to work with this roundup just like anyone else repping for a legal brand. There's one thing I want to get straight first."

"All right," Ira said.

"Did you sell a stolen horse to a squatter named Volanski?"

My brother shook his head.

"Why didn't he have a bill of sale?" Father asked.

"I gave him one," Ira said. "I bought that horse

with a couple more from a man in Lander Valley. I received bills of sale from him, and I gave Volanski one when I sold the horse again. If he told you he didn't have one he was lying for some reason."

I figured Ira was telling the truth, and Father must've known it too. It looked to me like Volanski had used Ira's name and that talk about not having a bill of sale to get himself out of a tight spot. The horse might've been stolen from the Powder River country like Paulson claimed, but Ira wouldn't have known that.

If Father was either angered or pleased at what my brother had said, he didn't show it. "You're smart enough to know the kind of men you're dealing with," Father told him. "As far as your repping here goes, that's up to you. I reckon it's plain that you'll stir up some trouble for me and the other men here, but I guess you know that already. Don't look to me for any help if you get into a jackpot."

"I know better than that," Ira said in a way that wasn't accusing or friendly either.

"You should. A man that keeps stirring up trouble usually gets plenty of it." My father walked away then without waiting to hear what Ira might answer. Slat Honeywell had roped out a horse for him, and Father began to saddle the animal.

Ira spoke to me and then started for his own

horse. I stopped him a minute. "What, Mart?" he asked, smiling.

"Meyers meant it when he said the cowboys were touchy," I told him. "They didn't like the hangings at Bothwell, and Jack Stenger's been stirring up trouble too."

"I imagine so," he said. "I didn't like the hangings either."

"Roan Meyers is dead serious," I went on, "and from what I hear you're not very popular with anybody in the valley."

He nodded, still smiling. "I've heard that. Thanks for reminding me, Mart."

"It's none of my business," I said. "But I wanted to be sure you knew how the talk was going. Then there's this deal of your owning some sheep too. I don't think that story has been spread around yet—and it won't be me that lets it out—but I guess you can expect the word to get around someday."

Ira's expression didn't change. "I wasn't particularly trying to hide it. I met Mr. Rodriguez last summer in Lander, and we discussed the whole thing then. He had the experience and I had some money I'd saved up. It seems to me we have as much right to graze sheep out here as the Association members have to turn loose their cattle. They don't own the land any more than I or Pete Rodriguez do."

When I didn't say anything more he asked,

"Was there something else you wanted to talk about?"

There was, but I didn't much want to bring it up. Ira must've guessed what I was thinking. "Mary's going to be all right," he said. "I received a letter from her the last time I went into Rawlins. She won't be able to move around much for quite a while, but she's not in any danger now."

I said, "That's good. Thanks for telling me."

"Maybe you'll be able to see her when the roundup is finished."

"Maybe," I said, trying to keep my voice even. "Did you learn anything else about who did it?"

He shook his head. "Not really. Of course you hear some talk about it. I think the whole thing will come out in the open one of these days."

"I imagine so," I said, remembering what Jenny had said about the drunk man bragging in Rawlins. "Is that why you came here?"

His face was completely serious now. "No . . . I'm going to cut out some of Mr. Lamar's steers and ship them for Mary. I'm here because I have a right to be here. It's that simple, Mart."

I guess it was simple to him, though it looked to me like he really was asking for trouble. You could see the cowboys watching him while they saddled up. They didn't trust him any more than Roan Meyers or the Senator did. And you couldn't call Volanski or Clayt Paulson friends of his either. . . .

As I caught my own horse that morning I tried to tell myself what Ira did wasn't any of my business. But somehow I couldn't keep from thinking that he was my brother . . . and admitting that he and several other smaller ranchers had a right to round up with the big outfits. When I watched Father eating by himself after the day's circle was over, I wondered if he was thinking about Ira too. Nothing showed in his weathered face. But watching him ride off to check the beef herd, I had a feeling Ira had hurt him somehow by coming to the roundup. It was the sort of open defiance that everyone on the Sweetwater would be talking about.

And maybe, I decided later, my father already realized he was being beaten by a force he couldn't bring himself to attack directly. Indian raids, cattle stampedes coming north with the trail herds, the blizzards that threatened his stock each winter, even the rustlers branding his calves in isolated sagebrush gullies—all those threats he'd managed to hold back by the strength of his body and will. But my brother was striking his pride, and I didn't think Father would hit back against his own son. Unless he had told Paulson to scare Ira out of the country by shooting at him or Mary Lamar.

I didn't want to believe Father had done that, but in my own mind I couldn't be sure any more. . . .

For a couple of days the work went ahead without a hitch. At least there was no trouble out in the open where we could see it. Ira rode in the same circle with me, though we didn't have a chance to talk much. He cut each day's gather for steers branded JL, but you had to admit he did his share of the other work too. Even so, on the third day Ira'd been with roundup I heard Roan Meyers complain again to Father that he was having difficulty controlling the cowboys.

"Are you telling me you can't handle a roundup crew?" my father asked him.

"Maybe it's comin' to that," said Meyers. "The boys are restless as all hell and I figure something's going to blow up. Just this noon I rode over some country the crew had worked this morning. Found several late Two-Bar-K calves in a little draw. Somebody had hobbled them there, figuring to come back later on the sly and do some private brandin'. Next spring they'd be in some rustler's herd, and nobody could prove a thing."

"Who might've been involved, Roan?"

We had split into two groups that morning with Meyers in charge of men working north of the chuck wagon and Father bossing the cowboys riding to the south. Ira and I had both been in Meyers' circle, so I could see what he was leading up to.

"There was two or three riders, judgin' from

the horse tracks," Karr's foreman said. "I hate to say it, but your older boy was close to that country this morning. I'm not suggesting that proves anything—just shows the kind of thing we're lettin' ourselves in for."

Father turned to me. "Were you riding with the JL rep this morning, son?"

"Yes," I said.

"Were you in sight of each other?"

"Off and on. We weren't separated long enough for him to rope and hobble several head of calves."

Father glanced hard at Meyers and then back at me. "Was anyone else riding with him?"

I shook my head. "Whitey Pence and some men from the Senator's outfit were working the other side of him, I think. Ira wasn't ever very close to them. Anway, he and Whitey never liked each other well enough to go in together on stealing calves."

"Well, I wasn't accusin' anybody," Meyers said flatly. "I thought it was something you ought to know about."

He pushed his shirt into his pants, making his paunch look a little smaller. I thought he seemed pleased with himself about something, and I was right.

He said, "Another thing you ought to know, Mr. Tyrrell. Some of the boys was telling me they run into a shotgun roundup crew workin' west of here. Naturally they figured it for Finn Rankin, Seth Daniels, and the rest of the Antelope Creek saddle bums. Some of our boys thinks it's quite a joke to see the rustlers roundin' up right in the open that way. A few of them are taking bets that Rankin will force us to let him join our roundup to keep from havin' the stock lose flesh being worked over twice."

I saw Father stare at Meyers as though the big redhead had become unpleasant to look at. "Roan, you sound afraid of them." That was all he said, but from the way Meyers' eyes went hard, I guessed my father had made it plain enough. . . .

In the morning we woke up cold and wet—an early storm had laid down three or four inches of snow over the range, and flakes were still falling from a dark, wet-looking sky. After the hands finished a soggy breakfast they stayed around the fire in their slickers and whatever heavy shirts or jackets they'd thought to bring. Being cold and idle, the cowboys began to play monte and argue with each other, their breath smoky when they swore at the cards. Father had the guard holding the beef herd changed every two hours. Even so, by noon many of the hands, especially the younger ones, began to talk sullenly of the weather, the money they had lost gambling, or—since Father was not at the fire—the injustices of the various cattle companies they worked for.

Whitey Pence was one of those most insistent that a man was a damn fool to work for wages when, with just a little luck, he could have land and cattle of his own.

"Like those boys on Antelope Creek or Hole-in-the-Wall," Whitey said. "Now ain't it sweet to see Rankin and Daniels havin' a roundup of their own? Times has changed the last couple of years, I'd say!"

Late in the afternoon a patch of sky cleared off above the Wind River Mountains to the west, and the sun hung there half in the haze like the cancered eye of a giant bull. The snow had stopped finally, but there wasn't time to make a circle. And as Cookie began banging his pans around to start supper, Finn Rankin's shotgun roundup crew rode up from the river with their wagon and horse herd.

Father, who'd just got back from checking the cattle, must have seen them already, for he called Meyers and Slat Honeywell and then rode with the two men to meet the riders. I hadn't been invited, but I went along behind Slat anyway. I had an old Colt I'd traded from one of our cowboys, but it was rolled up in my soogans. Cookie grabbed hold of me, though, when I walked past the chuck wagon. He reached below the wagon seat and thrust a short-barreled shotgun into my hands.

"See if there's any sage chickens where the hell

ever you're going, Mart. It's got buckshot in it, so don't be shootin' no birds close up like a damn fool."

The shotgun seemed very heavy under my arm as I walked toward the riders. I was sure the ten or so cowboys with Finn Rankin would be staring right at me and that scatter-gun, but when we got close to them I realized they were so heavily armed themselves that I wasn't attracting much attention. That suited me fine.

Rankin looked small up on a rangy dun horse that had about half a dozen brands on its shoulder and hip. He'd always liked mounts that were about three-quarters bronco and could be counted on to buck when saddled on a cool morning. The dun looked snorty enough, moving its feet all the time and trying to shy at Rankin's rattletrap grub wagon, Father's bay, and the four of us coming out through sage and half-melted snow.

"Weather ain't much for roundup," Rankin said when Father reined up a little ways from the wagon.

"It could be worse, Finn."

"Like two-three years ago along in the winter," Rankin agreed. "Caddle are a sight better now than they was then. That winter they was just lookin' for a excuse to lay down in the snow and die."

"That's so," Father said quietly.

226

Some people might have misjudged Finn Rankin—who was a small man with freckled hands and face like those of a boy—but my father knew better. The sandy-haired cowboy was close to forty, quick-tempered, and completely unafraid in any situation. What made him dangerous was the fact that he sometimes made rash judgments, and then his temper usually prodded him into backing them up against anybody. Under my father he'd made a good foreman, though. I guess Father had known how to handle the Texan, until Finn got into that argument with Ira on roundup.

Now I watched Rankin squint up his eyes thoughtfully, although there wasn't enough sunlight to bother him. The other cowboys weren't saying a thing. I figured they'd decided earlier that only Rankin was going to talk. Bearded and long-haired, a little arrogant like Texas cowboys sometimes were in a bind, they were just waiting for the cards to be dealt.

"Guess you heard we got a roundup outfit of our own now," Finn said. Then he grinned without much humor showing in it. "Had to make a pool crew with these boys, since people wasn't friendly about our workin' caddle with the Ass-ociation."

Father nodded. "I see that. I'd say you had a fine outfit, Finn, though it's getting a little late in the fall to be gathering steers."

"Well, that's so," agreed Rankin, "but we figured somebody might let us join this roundup. Most of our caddle are runnin' from here to Beaver Rim and maybe south past Green Mountain. Since that's the country you'll be workin' now, we thought to make things easier by throwin' in with you."

When Rankin was finished, my father waited a little, like he might really be thinking it over. Then he said, "I reckon not, Finn."

The Texan probably wasn't surprised, but he pretended to be. "Why, think of all them pounds of beef saved by the caddle just being worked once. When I rode for the TX you always told me a smart cowman never let his caddle move but at a slow walk and never worked a herd more than once a season."

"No cattle belonging to you or your friends have been in the country we've worked," Father told him. "You can ask the crew if you don't believe me. If you plan to work those cattle again you've got a job that'll take more men than you have here. As far as joining this roundup to work your part of the district goes, I can't allow it. I might like to personally, but your brands are still illegal. . . ."

I watched him pause and take in all Rankin's bunch with a sweep of his brooding eyes. "Besides that, Finn," he went on, "you and I both know all your cattle are down on Antelope

Creek, where your boys can find them in a couple of days."

Rankin's face flushed angrily, and he pulled too hard on the dun's bit getting him quieted down. The horse tossed his head like he might buck if he could get a little slack in the reins, which probably would've pleased Finn any other time. He cursed the horse briefly and finally got him settled down, though the dun kept his ears laid back.

"Where a man's caddle run is his business," Rankin flared. "Most of this valley's still open range, and we got the same rights as anybody."

"Then round up yourself." Father kept his voice even. "You're running a bluff that won't work. I've no quarrel with you or your friends, Finn, but I won't be run over either. You're not joining this roundup."

One of the Texans muttered something I couldn't make out, and then Rankin said, "Maybe everybody ain't had their say yet, Mr. Tyrrell."

I saw where he was looking, and I turned enough to see that most of the cowboys had left the fire and started walking toward us. They didn't come too close—just far enough to make it plain they were butting in. Most of them were from the Two-Bar-K or the other outfits, I noticed, but Whitey Pence was there, right in front with a couple of the younger TX hands who were friends of his.

Father guessed what was going on without looking around. "Tell those men to go back to the wagon," he said to Roan Meyers. "If I want them to do something I'll ask them quick enough."

But before Meyers could say anything Whitey Pence spoke up. "We want to know whether you figure to let these fellows round up their stock with us, Mr. Tyrrell."

"I don't intend to, Whitey," said my father. "And I don't intend to argue it with you men either. If you value your jobs, you boys will go back to the chuck wagon and get ready for supper."

I saw some of the cowboys hesitate like they were going to listen to him, but Whitey shook his head. "Some of the boys been talkin' together and figure Finn's got a right to be here if your older boy's going to rep with us."

The Texans with Rankin began to grin at each other, for you could go a long ways in the cattle country before hearing cowboys openly defy an owner like that. I knew they wouldn't be doing it now if Ira hadn't been allowed on roundup—and Ella Watson and Jim Averill hadn't been lynched a couple of months before.

"I told you the boys was restless," Meyers said. "I'll go try to work something out with them, if you want me to. If they should quit the roundup now we'd be in a hell of a shape handlin' that beef herd."

"You won't work anything out, Roan," Father replied. He half turned in his saddle so he could watch Rankin and our roundup crew at the same time. I remember smelling wet saddle leather and the damp, musty odor of wet horses as I waited with the shotgun cramping my arm. Over by the chuck wagon Cookie's fire of sodden wood made heavy, powder-colored smoke. I thought I saw Ira standing there beside the cook.

"You boys have about one minute to do like I told you," my father called to the hands. "After that you'll be looking for work somewhere besides Wyoming Territory."

When the men didn't move Rankin laughed. "They don't give a good god damn for working the big outfits no more, Mr. Tyrrell."

But Slat Honeywell shouted, "You heard the boss, Whitey. Get the hell back to the wagon!"

The old cowboy meant it, too. I saw several men tug sheepishly at their hats and start to walk away. Whitey cursed at them, and when the men stopped he looked more cocky.

"Seems to me you ain't got too much choice," he blustered to Father. "It's damn late in the season, and you need a full crew to finish gatherin' and drive a herd of beef clean to Rock Creek. We ain't being unreasonable—most of us worked with Finn and these other boys, and we figure they ought to get a fair shake. After all, Mr. Tyrrell, you done let Ira on roundup. We don't want to have to quit you at a bad time, but it ain't right to favor your own son and then give Finn here a screwin'."

I think my father must've known then that he was going to lose control of his roundup crew. It wasn't really a question of whether he was going to give in to their demands and let Rankin round up with us. I knew he hadn't even considered that. But if the hands did ride out of camp now and leave us with the fall's work unfinished it would be the first time Father had ever completely lost the respect and loyalty of cowboys working under him. He was a proud man who wouldn't show the hurt to anyone—but I knew his pride would be scarred in the same way barbed wire left its jagged mark on the forelegs of horses that stepped in it.

And I knew people would say, as they must have said when hearing about Volanski not being taken to trial, that my father was protecting his nester-loving son. I had reason not to believe it, after Mary's getting shot, but that's how the talk would run. Hearing Whitey going against him that way, I couldn't help feeling that Father deserved to lose some of his pride. I didn't figure Whitey Pence or Finn Rankin were the ones to give him a taking down, though.

While I was thinking that, Father's voice, edged with contempt, lashed out at Whitey and the cowboys with him. "I reckon you've talked enough, Whitey—you're finished at the TX. Any of you other men who start walking for the wagon now have still got jobs."

Three of our cowboys and a couple of men from different outfits turned and walked off. The others jeered and hoorawed them some, saying Father was bluffing and besides their bosses wouldn't let them be fired anyhow.

"All right," my father said to Whitey and the hands standing behind him. "You boys don't need to wait for supper before pulling out. I'll see that Wallace Karr and the other owners you've been working for know just what went on here. I don't reckon they'll trust you now any more than I would, especially since their beef is only part gathered."

Whitey Pence started to talk back, but Father cut him off. "You hard of hearing?" he called. "I want you boys to ride. Now!"

I watched them mutter angrily and hitch at their gun belts, then begin to move in a group toward the camp. You could figure them to talk big and bluster some . . . that might be as far as it went. I noticed that Slat was keeping his eye on them.

"Well, Finn," Father went on, "I'm sorry to disappoint you. I guess everybody's had their little say now, and you aren't rounding up with us."

"You ain't got them caddle delivered yet,"

Rankin said tightly. "I wouldn't tally up the score so soon." He pulled the dun around sharply and spurred him hard. The other Antelope Creek ranchers stared at us for a minute, and then Seth Daniels, who was driving their wagon, started the team around. Finally they all rode off behind Finn, the old wagon creaking and their horses kicking up little flecks of the damp, sandy ground.

Chapter 16

That same evening Father sent me back to the TX. And the next morning I returned with six men who had been cutting wild hay along the river for horses we kept up during the winter. The outfits in our district still didn't have enough hands to keep on gathering cattle, but at least we could handle the beef herd. With the weather looking bad, we didn't have time to waste either.

My brother Ira stayed on, though I noticed that nobody thanked him for doing it. As for my father, he left to talk with the other owners and try to hire more cowboys.

Roan Meyers was in charge while he was gone, and at first things went well enough. Maybe we were so shorthanded that even Meyers was too busy to think about anything except keeping the cattle moving. For the first few days Father was gone, anyway . . . or maybe he'd just figured to wait until we got the beef herd settled down on the trail to Rock Creek. However it was, Roan left Ira alone until one evening when we had bedded down the cattle close to Crook's Gap.

All the hands that weren't on first guard had staked out their night horses and got together around the fire. Ira was there—drinking a cup of coffee and minding his own business like he'd been doing since he came to the roundup. The men were tired from making a long drive that day. They mostly sat smoking cigarettes while they stared at the hot, soughing fire that burned too fast to be comfortable.

After a while Meyers stood up and walked toward the chuck wagon. In passing behind Ira, he lurched and pretended to stumble, his knee hitting my brother's shoulder. The hot coffee in Ira's cup sloshed out over his pants, but he sat still, waiting to see what Meyers would say. Most of the hands kept quiet and watched the two figures—one heavy and standing big against the night, the other much smaller and sitting apart from the crew so he seemed even more alone.

"Damned near tripped me up," Roan finally said, smiling a little at someone across the fire. "You trying to break a man's leg, Tyrrell?"

Ira slowly turned his cup over and let the last of the coffee run out onto the ground.

"I believe he's gettin' deaf since he started sellin' stolen horses to all the Russian honyockers," Meyers went on. "Naturally I'd have trouble hearing too, if I figured people was talkin' about what a big hoss thief I was."

One of Karr's cowboys who had stayed with the roundup laughed from across the fire. "Hell, Roan, he's always been hard of hearing when his daddy's not around to protect him!"

"Maybe so, but even his daddy's got a bellyful of him and his rustling friends. Don't really blame Mr. Tyrrell, though, when you consider his son here took up the stealing game right where Old Man Lamar left off. 'Course if that half-breed girl of Lamar's was bunkin' with me I might become quite a *rustler* myself. . . ."

Again the Two-Bar-K cowboy laughed. "Damned if you wouldn't, Roan! Bet you'd swing a bigger loop than the Tyrrell boy, too."

I saw Ira's hat move slightly as he began to watch Mr. Karr's foreman from the corner of one eye. I didn't want to see a fight, but I knew my brother wasn't afraid if it came to one, even though Meyers and some of the others might figure his self-control to be fear. Ira had toughened up a lot since he got back from school in the spring, and lately he'd been breaking horses and riding every day. He'd always been able to move quickly and handle himself well— as I'd learned the hard way a few years back when I badgered him all during roundup, until finally one sultry August afternoon he went down by the river with me and bloodied my face. Even so, allowing him quite a bit for determination, I couldn't give him much chance against a man like Roan Meyers.

I recall staring at my brother as he sat quietly, like he was thinking about something a long ways off from that roundup camp, and then the wind shifted so the wood smoke stung my eyes. I had to blink several times, and when I looked at Ira again he was standing erect and facing the foreman.

The only noise was the snap and whining cry of the fire. And then I heard Ira say, "All right, Roan."

Meyers must have figured to finish the fight quickly—and I knew he had a reputation for being a tough customer in the saloons of Rawlins and Rock Creek. Most of the cowboys thought fighting with their hands was beneath them. Instead they carried guns, for as Slat Honeywell once told me, "If men was intended to fight like coyotes, the Lord would've given them long teeth and claws." But Karr's foreman was heavy enough to think he could handle most men with his fists, though people said he was careful not to pick a fight he might lose. . . .

Roan approached my brother in a way that forced Ira to stand with his back to the campfire. When he was in close, Meyers raised his fists and came at Ira slowly but directly, watching for the one good chance he apparently figured to get. The hands stood back at the edge of the firelight. Under big hats their faces were pocked with shadow, like glowing skulls. I knew none of them—not even Slat—would interfere in the fight, and I didn't see how I could either.

The first few times Meyers swung, my brother ducked or stepped back, his hat slipping off into the fire, where it began to burn like some trapped brown animal. But then, despite his quickness, Ira had to move close to Roan in getting away from the flames. Karr's foreman was waiting for this, and he made my brother stumble with a clumsy, hooking punch just above the eye. I could see the red mark—just below where the pale white of his forehead had been protected from the sun by his hat. Across the mark was a little line of blood working out from the split skin.

Ira was moving backward away from the fire, and when Meyers rushed after him, off balance in his hurry to end the fight, my brother struck him in the mouth with straight blows of his left arm. The punches were quick and graceful all right, but the bigger man just shook his head and pushed Ira up against the chuck wagon. Although he left his face unprotected, Roan was brawling the way he liked now, in close and swinging his big fists repeatedly into Ira's body.

Whatever my feeling had once been about Ira

and Mary, I didn't want to see my brother beaten that way, and watching it made me feel sick myself. From the way Ira was bracing himself against the wagon—bleeding from one eye and his high-bridged Tyrrell nose—I guessed the fight was about over.

Then I saw Meyers' right arm swing heavily around and Ira swaying where he stood tiredly against the chuck wagon. The blow would have finished the fight if it had landed on the side of my brother's head, like Roan figured. But Ira still had enough of his reflexes left to drop his head and shoulders so the fist grazed his skull— and smashed into the worn gray boards on the side of Father's wagon. Meyers swore and rushed at Ira again with the useless hand limp before him like the wounded paw of an attacking bear.

Ira hit him twice, moving quickly away each time so that the heavier man couldn't grasp him with his good arm. When Ira struck him again Meyers was caught off balance and half slipped, half fell, his head hitting against the wagon's front wheel. He lay there, staring at Ira as blood leaked down from a gash laid open on his head.

I turned to look at my brother, hearing his heavy breathing, and that was when Cookie shouted a warning at Ira. I saw Roan grasping clumsily at his six-shooter with his left hand.

Maybe he figured to use it as a club, though I wouldn't have trusted him not to shoot once he got the Colt into his hand.

Ira waited a moment, his hands still before him like he'd been expecting Meyers to get back up and continue the fight. Then I saw Ira move to the side, swinging himself up with one foot on the wagon tongue. He was reaching under the seat. And when Meyers tried to get up with the six-shooter in his good hand, he saw my brother pointing Cookie's sawed-off shotgun straight at his chest.

"Put it down, Roan," Ira said, still breathing hard.

Mr. Karr's foreman clutched the six-shooter tighter for a moment and then got control of himself. Scowling, he leaned down and let the Colt slip through his fingers onto the ground.

"Now tell these men you lied about my selling a stolen horse to Volanski."

Meyers looked around at the hands, like he was trying to judge their temper, but even the cowboy who'd backed him up before was silent now. Roan wiped sweat from his forehead and arrogantly stuffed his shirttail down into his pants. It was obvious that he was stalling. . . .

"I'm waiting," Ira said, holding the stubby, ugly Parker steady in both hands. A shotgun loaded with buckshot wasn't very pleasant to stare at from the wrong end. You could tell that

240

by watching Meyers try to figure an out from a jackpot he'd never counted on getting into.

Finally, when Roan saw nobody else was going to take his part, he muttered, "You got it your way. The story I heard about that horse had it stolen, but there wasn't no proof."

I was surprised my brother seemed satisfied with such mealymouthed talk. Anyhow, he nodded curtly—without lowering the shotgun. "It was the same way with those Two-Bar-K calves you found hobbled and complained to Mr. Tyrrell about, wasn't it?"

"I was making a guess about who done it," admitted Roan Meyers sullenly.

Ira smiled, and I had the feeling he wasn't finished with Meyers yet. "I'm going to let you go in just a minute, Roan. After you explain one thing more."

I glanced at Meyers. His speckled face showed nothing, but he was standing motionless now instead of fiddling around with his shirt and belt. And when I looked back at my brother he was changed—unsmiling, cold-eyed, and appearing quite capable of pulling the triggers of Cookie's shotgun.

"Were you really the one who killed Jules Lamar?" he said.

Meyers was slow to answer . . . though he'd been eager enough to brag about doing the shooting when it happened. Ira raised the muzzle of the Parker until it pointed at the foreman's thick Adam's apple, and I saw Roan lick his lips and swallow once hard.

"I don't think many people would blame me for shooting you," Ira told him. "Not after you pulled a gun on me that way. I've never killed a man, Roan. But Mr. Lamar was the best friend I ever had. Did you shoot him?"

"He was a rustler, like I always said."

"So were you once, Roan. Did you shoot him?"

"I ain't got any reason to lie about it . . ."

"I'll only ask you once more. Did you kill Mr. Lamar, Roan?"

Meyers hesitated, sweat on his face glistening in the firelight, until he saw my brother's slender fingers tighten on the shotgun's walnut grip. His throat jumped and his mouth worked like the word was hard to get out.

"No . . ."

You could see the hands hadn't expected that, but Ira said, "I thought perhaps you didn't. Was it Clayt Paulson?"

"I don't know."

"You know, Roan. It was Paulson, wasn't it?"

"All right, it was Paulson. He found the old man stealing and took care of him. I came along after it was over, and we figured it was best to keep Clayt's name out of it."

"You mean Paulson figured that was best," Ira said.

"All right. He had the say-so about it. I figured that was the Association's business, not mine. Ain't I already said the old man was a rustler? On a thing like that I just follow orders."

"Karr's or Paulson's?"

Meyers saw he was slipping onto boggy ground. "The Association's orders, like I said."

My brother let that pass. "You didn't actually see Mr. Lamar rope that calf or tie it down, did you?"

"I didn't need to. It was plain enough when I got there and Paulson had finished with him."

"Except that Paulson could've framed the old man for all you or anybody else knows." Ira climbed down from the wagon seat. He made Meyers step back from where the six-shooter lay on the ground.

Apparently he'd heard all he wanted, for he gave Roan's Colt to Cookie and asked me to bring his night horse. "Will you take care of shipping those steers of Mr. Lamar's with the beef herd?" he asked me when I'd brought the horse to the wagon.

I said I would, and then he handed me the sawed-off shotgun before he rode away from the roundup camp. Roan Meyers stared after him through the campfire smoke and then stalked off without speaking to any of us. . . .

When my father rode back to the herd with several new hands, nobody told him about the fight. He saw that something had happened, though, and I wondered if he would ask Meyers where Ira was. I doubted it. He seemed concerned only about getting the cattle to Rock Creek for shipment. Judging from what one of the new hands said, most of the ranch owners blamed Father's trouble with the cowboys on his letting Ira on roundup. You had to say the owners were halfway right, even though you could figure the same cowboys would have been sympathetic toward the Antelope Creek outfit whether Ira was there or not.

Anyway, my father must have been disappointed and shamed, for I learned later that none of the other cattlemen had fired the hands he sent back from the roundup. . . .

I was wrong, too, about his not being concerned with what had happened to Ira. He rode out one night to where I was holding the horse herd and asked me why my brother had left. I told him the story, even the part about Jules Lamar. When I'd finished he nodded curtly and rode off straight toward camp, though I wasn't surprised the next day that nothing seemed to have passed between him and Roan Meyers. A week later we reached Rock Creek and held the cattle there a few days until we could ship them on the Union Pacific.

Father and some of the foremen had to remain in town for a short while after the hands started back with the chuck wagon and horse herd. I stayed behind with my father, and we boarded at the Wyoming House hotel. On the last night I went with him to one of the three saloons that were crowded all during the shipping season.

I remember that there was a piano player at work in one corner with a funny little round hat pushed down over his eyes, several card games with the men's faces hazy in drifting cigar smoke, a yellowish picture of Lily Langtry in a tarnished gold frame hanging crookedly over the whiskey bottles. There was a smell of sawdust from the floor mixed with odor of raw whiskey and sweaty clothes the cowboys wore at the end of roundup . . . and the sound of silver on the smooth bar or whiskey sloshing into a glass.

And Roan Meyers was drinking at the other end of the bar from where I'd been standing with Father. The next thing I knew he was walking down toward Karr's foreman. Father spoke softly, but through the bar noise I could hear most of what was said.

"I understand you and my oldest son had a misunderstanding," my father told him.

From the way Meyers stared at Father before answering I guessed he hadn't expected the fight would be mentioned just then. "Your boy called me a liar," he said at last, taking a swallow of whiskey.

"Why did he say that, Roan?"

Meyers shrugged his heavy shoulders. "Got some crazy idea that old wolfer wasn't a rustler at all. We got into a fight over it and the boy threatened me with a shotgun. Finally he got scared and high-tailed out of camp."

"You didn't pick a quarrel with him?" asked Father. Meyers glanced narrowly down at me and then back at my father. "Hell no, I didn't," he said loudly.

"You are a liar, Roan," Father said.

The foreman stared at him, his scarred right hand tightening around the whiskey glass until the knuckles turned white. My father stood there waiting, and in the light from kerosene lamps behind the bar I noticed gray flecks in his untrimmed mustache and the hair on the back of his head. He was nearing sixty, and Roan Meyers was probably twenty years younger than him. I kept waiting for Roan to let go of the glass. I didn't really know what might happen when he did face Father . . . and I never found out.

Meyers said nothing—not a word—and finally Father nodded as if to himself. He turned from the Senator's foreman and walked away toward the open door of the saloon. I followed him, turning back once and seeing Roan staring down at the glass in his cramped hand.

Outside in the rocky street I looked at Father. I felt cold all over, and I wanted him to talk to me about Ira and the thing that had happened with

Roan Meyers in the saloon. Instead he acted like he was angry with me. . . . Riding to catch up with the chuck wagon the next morning, I felt like he wasn't my father at all, and I began to wonder if I'd really heard him call Meyers a liar in the saloon.

Chapter 17

There was a soft snow in late October, right after we got back from shipping the cattle at Rock Creek, and then came clear days with the willows yellow and dying along the river below sky off-blue as the eyes of a wild albino mare. The weather made you want to be out and doing something before the hard snows, but mostly we just had to wait for the monotonous winter work to begin. I helped pull shoes off the saddle stock and turn them out on winter range. The extra men hired in the spring drew pay and left for Rawlins or Lander to celebrate away their wages and hole in somewhere until green-up.

On several evenings I sat by myself in the lean-to and tried to write a letter to Mary Lamar. The first few lines, where I told her I hoped she was feeling well, always went all right. But then I would think of her riding away with Ira, after Mr. Lamar was buried, and write some fool thing that was mean or sounded like I was sorry for myself. Always I ended up crumpling the sheet, burning it—angry mostly with myself—and later lying awake all night thinking of things I wanted to say to her.

Once I went with Cookie and the buckboard to Lander. When he got delayed a couple of days waiting for a farmer to deliver our winter's supply of potatoes, I borrowed a saddle and rode one of the team horses to where Mary's relatives lived on the Reservation.

They had an old cabin on the Little Wind River, which was more than you could say for most of the Arapahoes, though part of the family lived nearby in shabby tents. A dozen pinto-colored dogs ran out barking and yapping as I rode up, and several dirty Indian kids peered at me from the tents and a pile of rotting poles where they were playing. An old woman wrapped in part of a blanket came out and shouted something I didn't understand to either me or the dogs. She wasn't much more friendly than the mongrels, but when I said Mary's name several times she brightened up a little and took me inside.

Mary was there all right, sitting in what had once been a white man's rocking chair. She looked awfully small and tired. And something else I remember noticing was how the color looked washed out from the brown-tinted skin where it smoothed over her thin cheeks. I couldn't yet put a name to what was making her look so beautiful and strange, but for years afterward, when anyone talked of consumption, I thought of Mary's face as it looked that morning on the Reservation.

"I hoped someone from the Sweetwater would come," she told me.

It wasn't quite what I wanted to hear, but I was so glad to see her that nothing else mattered too much. "You're looking pretty healthy," I said, though it wasn't really true. "I guess you'll be back taking care of your dad's cattle soon. I imagine Ira's keeping a close eye on the place until you get back, though."

"Your brother brought money last week from the cattle he shipped for me," she said.

I told myself that was natural enough, but it still took the edge off things. "He did a good job of cutting out the steers to sell. A little money comes in handy now and then, they tell me."

"When I'm strong again I must pay for the doctor, Martin," she said, laughing the way I'd remembered so well.

"He'd probably settle for a side or two of beef. . . . I wouldn't worry about it." I knew my father—feeling guilty maybe—had already paid Doc Parker, but I didn't figure this was the time to tell her.

"Next chance I get I'll mention it," I went on. "You've got a dry cow out there that's plenty fat and hasn't had a calf the last few springs."

She seemed to think that was a good idea. "You

must tell him I'll pay money if he doesn't need the beef."

I promised I'd do that.

"I don't think I'll be coming back to Willow Springs," she said then.

"There's no hurry," I said awkwardly. "Next spring you'll be good as new."

Saying that hurt her somehow, I saw, but by then it was too late. She lowered her head, the shadows around her eyes making them look large and feverish. "Not new, Martin. . . . I've been to the doctor in Lander, and the place where the bullet hit me has healed. But he said it had made my body weak . . . that I have the lung sickness now and must do nothing for a while. . . ."

I'd heard the word "consumption" mentioned a few times, and the Arapahoes and Shoshones on the Reservation, not fed very well and crowded together in poor tents and leaky old cabins, lived with it like a gaunt neighbor. But that kind of sickness hadn't meant much to me until I saw it haunting Mary's face. . . . And when I thought of the person that had shot her, I felt myself all tied up with a kind of hate I hadn't known before.

"Does Ira know about this?" I finally said.

"No. I don't want him to know."

I thought that over. "Why not?" I asked.

She looked up at me steadily. "Since my father was killed, Ira has felt responsible for me. He shouldn't feel that way any longer, Martin."

When I didn't answer, Mary touched my arm with her light brown hand. "Your brother doesn't belong on a little homestead. He admired my father and the free sort of life he'd led in the mountains . . . but Ira wouldn't be satisfied if he went for long without using his schooling. Once he told me he was interested in the old trappers and pioneers because they were starting out fresh and trying to shape a world that better suited them. He said it was like a rattlesnake shedding its old skin and starting over. . . ."

I tried not to notice the way she had to work at getting her breath back. "That's how Ira is different from your father and even you, Martin," she said then. "Different from me also, I think. . . . He wants to see people shape their thinking to fit the way things have changed since your father came to Wyoming. I know Ira would waste his life if he didn't try to be something more than a small rancher. . . . You know it too."

I still couldn't say anything, though I guessed she was right about Ira. I figured a lot of the old ideas and ways suited me and the country well enough, and I was glad she'd told me she felt the same. But she hadn't said anything very plain about herself and Ira . . . and what she thought about me was even harder to guess, although I still remembered how she'd called my name after being shot. I stared around at the dirty floor and cracking walls of that Indian cabin and tried to figure it all out. There was her being sick to worry about, too.

"Why don't you come out to the TX for a while?" I asked her. "You could rest up and eat plenty of Cookie's grub, not that it's anything to shout about. We could get Doc Parker to come out once in a while to make sure you were doing all right."

She shook her head, smiling still but looking thin and shadowy as an old Arapahoe grandmother under the big blanket. "Thank you, Martin, but I can't do that. Ira is seeing that I get everything I need here. Please don't tell him about the lung sickness, though. The doctor says I'll get well soon if I'm careful, and I want your brother to leave Willow Springs before anything happens to him."

"Maybe Ira won't leave that homestead, or you either," I said, looking down where her hand still rested on my shirt sleeve.

"I think he will when people stop trying to force him away. I hope he will. . . ."

When Mary took her hand away I stood up, still feeling her touch on my arm like I'd been burned there. Then I knew what I'd wanted to say when I first decided to ride over from Lander—what I still wanted to tell her, though it was harder now.

"I want you to marry me," I said. "Not because of what's happened to you or anything like that . . .

but I'm not a dumb kid any more who doesn't know what he wants."

"I never thought so," said Mary, not looking at me.

"I was once, but I've grown up a lot since last spring." Then I couldn't think of anything else to tell her. "Let me know when you decide," I finished clumsily. "I'll be out at the ranch."

She did look at me then. "I don't know. Once I would've answered you very quickly . . ."

"I don't want a quick answer," I told her. "I guess I'm some smarter than I used to be— probably damn little. I meant what I said, though. You can find me easy enough if you want me or need anything."

I headed for the door, so she wouldn't have to say something she didn't mean. "Take care of yourself, Mary," I called back.

I heard her turn in the old chair, her voice very low, calling, "Good-by, Martin . . ." And then I was outside with the dogs growling around my heels and Indian kids tumbling off my horse. They'd been sneaking a ride while I was busy making a fool of myself in the cabin. . . .

After I got back to the TX, I worked hard each day at whatever needed doing. When there was nothing else to keep me from thinking about Mary, I rode . . . checking winter supplies at the line camps, going with Cookie to stock up on grub in Rawlins, hunting deer for several days alone in the Green Mountain country above Crook's Gap.

I didn't especially want to talk with anyone, but I heard things from Cookie and the cowboys I'd run into on the range. The grand jury had already met in Rawlins and dismissed charges against the Association members who'd been in on the lynching at Bothwell. Rumor said the dismissal came because all the witnesses against the cattlemen had been bribed, scared out of the country, or killed—you could take your pick of the stories. Feeling was running high against the Association, but that seemed to make the cattlemen more determined than ever to drive everyone off their rangeland. They were doing a lot of talking now about how all the nesters were rustling their stock and how something would have to be done to stop them. I figured the rustler talk had some truth to it, but I knew ranchers like Wallace Karr could use it as an excuse to run off any homesteader.

Maybe that's why I was surprised by the quick way Mr. Karr leased his ranch to a Scotch cattle company after shipping time, though some people said he'd been in debt to them so long they'd practically owned the Two-Bar-K for years anyway. Apparently he was still going to run a few cattle on the Sweetwater for another year or two. So maybe his plan to sell out wasn't really a matter of saving his own skin now the

254

big ranchers were hard pressed. The Senator was opening a law office in Rawlins at the first of the year—at least that's how the story went.

Someone had told Karr about Roan Meyers admitting to my brother that Paulson had been the one who shot down Mr. Lamar, but he'd just shrugged it off with the remark that "a thief was still a thief no matter who ended his career." I wasn't so sure, and I heard some talk about Leah being pretty upset when she learned her husband had done the killing.

Father said nothing about what Clayt Paulson had done. He didn't talk about Mr. Karr leasing the Two-Bar-K either—he just never mentioned the Senator's name after that. But then my father had been moody and quiet since Ira left the ranch and the hangings occurred at Bothwell. I wouldn't have thought a man could change so much in a few months. He carried himself as tall as ever, but his eyes and mouth were lifeless and hard. He always smelled of liquor now, and the drinking darkened the hollows around his eyes even more, so he seemed to be staring at you from far away—and seeing something else.

Maybe, I thought then, he was troubled by the stories about Ira that eventually drifted back to him at the ranch. Someone claimed to have seen my brother moving strange horses through the country at night. There was talk of rustlers using his cabin on their way to Jackson's Hole or back to Hole-in-the-Wall. And one of Finn Rankin's bunch was telling everyone he'd seen Ira that summer, driving a Two-Bar-K mare and her slick yearling colt toward Willow Springs Canyon. It was peculiar the man hadn't mentioned this when it happened, but the story went well with the others being told along the river. I passed it off as a try at slander by the ex-cowboys and shirttail ranchers that hung around Stenger's talking of a fight to even up for Ella and Jim Averill. . . .

It was near the end of my deer-hunting trip before anything came up except the talk. And then what happened didn't seem to have much to do with Ira or my father. At least it didn't seem to at first.

I'd camped for the night at the head of a grassy swale, where a little spring made a thread of green through drying tan grass. I hadn't shot a deer, and maybe that wasn't what I wanted from those days by myself. Somehow I needed to decide a few things in my own mind. Like what I should do to get Ira and my father together again before something serious pushed them into fighting each other—something like what had already happened to Mary. I wanted to think Father had nothing to do with that directly, but he hadn't done anything to defend Ira's reputation. . . . To someone like Clayt Paulson that could have been invitation enough to take a shot at what appeared to be my brother. . . .

I had staked my pack mare and hobbled Blacky. The horses began cropping grass while I shot a sage chicken behind the spring, fried it over my fire, and settled down with a smoke to watch the evening come on cool and gray into the broad Sweetwater Valley. Later, when the fire died down and I was having trouble keeping my eyes open, the snort of spooking horses jerked me wide awake. Even as I chambered a shell in the .38-55 Winchester I'd borrowed from Father, a man's figure swelled up over the edge of the swale in the dusk, a voice shouting in Spanish as the shape crumpled down and jerked toward me in a broken crawl.

"Who is it?" I called before I moved.

The answer was weak. "*Amigo* . . . It is Pete Rodriguez. . . . I need help. They have tried to murder me. . . ."

I recognized the voice well enough, and I went quickly to him. His clothes were ragged and dirtier than ever. There were purplish bruises on his face, and a patch of dried blood over a tangle of hair on the side of his head. He was frightened until I got close enough for him to recognize me.

"*Señor* Tyrrell's son? . . . I thought it might be one of the men who—" His good eye stared blankly at me, and then he sighed without finishing the sentence. "Even so, I had no choice but to keep moving toward your campfire. I thank God it was you here."

I helped him limp over to the fire and poured a cup of coffee. He held it in both hands, as though he was drawing warmth from the hot metal, and shivered from time to time despite the sheepskin coat I wrapped around him. I threw more dead sage on the fire and then sat down to let him rest a little.

"The sheep they are gone," he whispered into his coffee cup at last.

"Do you want to tell me what happened?" I asked.

He gave no sign of hearing me, but all at once he began to talk nervously without looking at me. "With the sheep I was coming toward the river from Red Desert. This close to winter I did not want to be caught by the bad storm. One night ago I had finished eating after bedding down the sheep. Several *hombres* rode into my camp and stopped by the wagon. My dogs barked at the horses until I made them remain quiet. A dog is smarter than a foolish *Mexicano* who has spent his life with the sheep."

When he stopped and sank back into his own thoughts I asked, "Did you recognize any of the men?"

He shivered again. "No . . . no. They were the cowboys with their faces covered, but I did not notice that in time. Two of them pointed the guns at me. The others began to shoot . . . to shoot the sheep and dogs before me. I hear it still in my ears—the shots echoing and my *paisanos* dying before my sight."

"But why did they do it? Were you on land owned by a rancher?"

"I have heard they claim it all," he said dully, "but I was on the land of the government. I think it was another thing, for they bound my hands and asked many questions. Did I own the sheep? How did I have the money to buy so many ewes for myself? Perhaps it was someone else who bought them for me. . . ."

When Rodriguez hesitated I said, "I know my brother gave you the money to buy them."

"So? . . . These men thought it also, for they did not like false answers to the questions."

I guessed the marks on his face were a part of their dislike, and I asked him whether he'd told them the truth about the sheep.

He was afraid to admit it, but maybe he was more afraid to lie to me. "Tell them? *Si*, I tell them finally. If not they kill me, but your brother will understand. No? . . . I must tell them. And now I have nothing—no wagon or horses, no fine dogs to help with sheep. All gone. . . ."

When he finished talking I hid my bedroll, along with what camp supplies were left, where I could find them later. Then I got up the horses and saddled the pack mare for the Mexican. Riding Blacky bareback, I headed down for Stenger's as fast as was safe in the dark. I was worried that the herder might be too weak to ride, but once we got started he grasped the horn in both hands and rode humped over yet apparently secure. Even so, I wouldn't care about riding over that country again with a hurt man on a pitch-dark night.

At Stenger's I made a big circle and came up to Jenny's cabin from behind. I didn't know who might be in the saloon, but there was no reason to take a chance, even though Jack Stenger had been friendly enough to rustlers and sheepmen. Jenny heard us ride up and called out softly before opening the cabin door.

"Who is there?" She sounded frightened.

"Mart," I told her without raising my voice. "Are you by yourself?"

The door opened enough for her to see out. "Yes, there is no one here. . . ."

I led the pack mare up close to the cabin. "Listen, Jenny. Your father's been hurt. Not seriously, but I brought him down so you could take care of him."

She slipped from the cabin, wrapped in a blanket like an Indian, and helped the old man down from the saddle and inside to the bed. I waited at the door until she'd made him comfortable. I heard him stammer wildly to her about the attack—his dogs and the slaughter of sheep.

"Are you sure he is not badly hurt?" asked

Jenny when she'd done what she could for him.

"I don't think so. He's played out from taking a beating, but mostly he saw too many bad things happen. He needs a lot of sleep."

Jenny looked in the direction of Stenger's saloon—she really was scared, just like after the Watson woman had been hung—and pulled me inside the door. "I know one who helped in this meanness with the sheep," she whispered. "He was here drinking not long ago with Stenger. At first I had no thought they could be talking of a sheepherder . . . of my father."

"Does Stenger know he's your father?" I asked.

"No, I think not. . . ."

I nodded, hearing the old man moan something in his sleep. "Who was the man, Jenny? The one talking with Jack Stenger."

Her eyes became slitlike for an instant before she answered. "You know him. They call him Whitey."

"Whitey Pence?"

"Yes. He came here with you that first time."

"Are you certain it was Whitey?"

"I was there, Martín. He said, 'Well, Jack, that's what I call killing two birds with one stone.' They had the drink together. Then this Whitey said, 'Rankin thought there was something funny about the way those sheep never grazed north of the river on TX range. So he had a talk with Karr about it, and they decided to bury the hatchet and make up a party to visit the herder. I went along and we found out the sheep were bought by Tyrrell's oldest boy. Now Finn and Karr have thrown in together to get rid of him and the squatter Volanski.' They talked of some 'deal,' Martín, but I did not understand clearly."

"That's all you heard?" That much was enough to worry over for a long time, but I hoped I could find out more.

"Stenger remembered I was there then," Jenny told me. "Whitey had two or three more drinks and rode off. To the TX, he said. All one hears now is talk of thieves and hangings. Then the bad things happen—like this with my father. What shall I do to protect him?"

"Can you keep Stenger from knowing he's here?"

"I think so, but only for a short time."

"That will help," I said. "Maybe the men who hurt him only wanted to frighten away a sheepherder, but I wouldn't talk to anyone about what happened. As soon as he rests up, you tell him to ride your horse to Lander. I'm sure my brother will help take care of him after that."

Jenny nodded silently and then leaned against me, letting the blanket fall as she slipped her cool arms around my neck. "I will do as you say, Martín. Thank you for helping." She slid her lips across my cheek to meet my mouth. "*Adios,*

Martín," she called as I left the cabin. "Until *mañana. . . .*"

I guess neither of us knew how far off that tomorrow might be. . . .

I can't remember the ranch ever being as quiet as it was that night when I rode in. A lamp was burning in the bunkhouse, but I heard no laughter or talk from the men inside. The big house was dark and silent. I decided Father had gone away on one of his trips again. Or was it, I thought next, that he'd been with Whitey and the men who raided Rodriguez' sheep camp? When I recalled what Jenny had said about Whitey's talk with Stenger, I felt better. They'd mentioned Mr. Karr and Finn Rankin but not my father.

After I walked in the house I stood inside the door waiting for my eyes to get used to the blackness. I'd started for the table, where one lamp was always placed, before Father spoke to me. He formed a huge shadow at the end of the table, but his voice sounded low and unsteady, like his throat hurt him to talk. Then I heard the clink of a bottle against glass. It was a sound I'd become familiar with since Ira left the ranch.

"I didn't know anyone was here," I said. "Do you want the lamp lit?"

He emptied half his glass before answering. "Don't need any light here, boy. I can see things well enough without burning kerosene. . . ."

I lit the lamp anyway and stood watching him.

He didn't seem much like the man I'd known all my life. Maybe I'd never seen him uncertain about anything before. Or, thinking back on that night, maybe I hadn't realized until the last few months that my father was almost an old man. I'd thought the Senator was aging, for he was obviously near sixty. But my own father always had seemed to walk as tall and straight as when I was a small boy waiting for him to unsaddle and come to the house after he'd returned from trailing a beef herd to the railroad. He looked old now, though, slumped down close to his whiskey glass on the table, as if his back was hurt from lifting too much or shoeing too many horses in a day.

Finally he raised his head and gazed oddly at me, like he'd just noticed my being there. "Back from your hunt? I didn't expect you . . . tonight."

"I came down early," I said, wondering if I should tell him about the sheep.

"I didn't look for you to find me this way." I guessed it was as close as he would come to an apology. He hesitated and stared past me at the open doorway. "Today's your birthday, Mart."

So that was it. I hadn't even thought about what day it was until I heard him say the words. "I guess it is," I said. "I've never cared too much about remembering it."

Father knew what I meant. "What happened to

your mother couldn't be helped by you. I wasn't thinking about it being a thing to blame you for."

"You weren't thinking it, but I was," I said abruptly. "A thing can be plain enough whether you think it or not. She died bearing me, and you'll never forget it. Ira didn't kill her, but I did. He's the same kind of person she was—he even looks like her. And that's why you can't stand it when my brother won't take the ranch you built up for him."

I hadn't stood up to him that way before. He straightened in his chair and his eyes did see me now. All at once the strength came back into his face as his fist crashed down on the table.

"No!" he shouted. "That's not so."

I wanted to believe him; but I couldn't. "Why have you been so upset since he left us? Why are you sitting here alone with a whiskey bottle if what I say isn't true?"

For a moment he didn't even try to answer me. Then he made a sudden sweep with his arm, smashing the half-filled glass and the bottle into pieces against the wall. "Why?" he repeated dully. "Why? . . ."

"You see," I said. "Anybody can tell how you feel about Ira. I don't mind it much any more, but it looks like you don't care what happens to the ranch. You're almost never here. There's talk in the valley against you now, as well as against Ira."

His voice stayed in a monotone, and his eyes were just sockets of shadow. "What would you have me do? I wouldn't turn against my own son whether he was guilty of rustling or not."

"You do believe what they're saying about him, then?"

Father didn't move, but I heard him breathing heavily. "Some of it. He's had dealings with squatters like Volanski. He's bought horses from men that deal with rustlers—let them use his cabin and corrals. Maybe it's gone farther than that now . . . I wouldn't know for sure."

I'd said too much already to keep quiet. "Clayt Paulson must've thought you were sure about one rustler when he shot Jules Lamar."

He noticed the bitterness in what I said. "You're wrong," he said tiredly. "I made it clear to Paulson and the Association that he was to do nothing except keep watch on our cattle and horses. If he did catch Jules mavericking a calf and shot him like Meyers said, it was none of my doing."

"But you did approve of his work."

"Yes, by God! And I still approve of protecting our stock."

"Even if it means hanging women and murdering a girl?"

I thought he flinched, but I could have been mistaken. "I reckon you're talking about Ella Watson and the Lamar girl," he said. "I don't know who tried to kill the girl, and I had no part in hanging the woman."

He sat silent while I watched the whiskey he'd spilled spread out on the floor and stain into the rough wood. I remember thinking how little I really knew about my father or about what his life was like. All I'd seen was the appearance he gave of being one sort of man. I'd admired what I thought him to be, but now I was seeing something unfamiliar that must have always been a part of him too. I didn't want to see him uncertain and drunk like some wino sheepherder in a Lander saloon. Not wanting it didn't make him different, though.

Then I realized he was staring at me, and I had to look at him again. "You wanted to say something to me?" he asked. "I'm listening now."

"You won't like it," I said.

"Say it, Mart!" he thundered in his old way. "I didn't raise you to hedge a bad thing."

"All right. Last year my brother bought some sheep for a Mexican named Pete Rodriguez. I guess Ira saw nothing the matter with sheep being grazed on government land, even if it was claimed by the cattlemen. Anyway, this herder Rodriguez had his band over near the Red Desert. A bunch of masked men caught him there. His sheep and dogs were shot, his wagon burned, and he was beaten. I just got back from taking him to his daughter at Stenger's."

I expected him to ask who the men were, but he didn't. He looked as if he'd known about the whole thing already.

"I'm pretty sure Whitey Pence was with the bunch that hurt the Mexican," I told him.

Father said, "I know that. Whitey came for his back wages tonight and tried to blackmail me. I almost killed him for it."

"He must've thought Ira's owning sheep was awfully serious."

"I reckon it wasn't just the sheep." He stood up slowly into the lamplight. His shadow darkened the log wall beyond the table. His brooding face for once seemed pale behind the heavy mustache. A splash of whiskey on his white shirt was exposed by the unbuttoned vest he wore.

When Father spoke again his voice was unsteady. "Listen to me, Mart. You should know what . . . what this is all about. You listening to me?"

I sat down by the cold fireplace and suddenly felt the tiredness from the long ride in my body and head.

"The Association members are planning to move against men suspected of being cattle or horse thieves," my father said. "Ira's one of the men they'll be looking for."

"I'm not too surprised. They must figure that calling people thieves and then running them out of the country is one way to keep all the range for themselves. But those cowmen don't think you'll help them, do they?"

"I reckon they're going to find out for sure tomorrow."

I began to understand a little better. "You mean the Association ranchers are going to ask your help in hunting down suspected rustlers?"

"According to Pence, that's the plan."

"What was Whitey trying to pull?" I asked. "I can't see where he fits in."

Father looked down at the broken whiskey bottle as if he hadn't noticed it before. Then he walked to the fireplace and kicked at the cold, burned-out wood with his boot toe. "Whitey knows a thing he thinks would ruin me with the Association. Since I wouldn't be blackmailed, he's filling someone's ear with it right now."

"You mean Ira's sheep deal with Rodriguez?"

He shook his head, still concentrating on the dead fire. "That won't help . . . but he's got something else in mind." Then my father turned back to face me. "You might as well hear this from me. I used to be a friend of Ella Watson's. You're grown up enough to know what I mean. Whitey Pence found out about it, but at the time he was afraid to talk against me. After the hangings at Bothwell he probably decided I'd be worried enough to pay him to keep quiet."

"So Whitey threatened to tell the Association about you and Ella Watson," I said dully.

"That's right. I reckon he can tell them now and be damned."

"So it's true about you and her. . . ."

He didn't answer for a while. "A man gets lonely out here," he finally told me. "I didn't see her too often, but Whitey must've been snooping around once when I didn't know it. My visits to Ella's place are none of the Association's business, though they won't see it that way."

I thought he was awfully calm about the whole thing. Ella Watson had put a homestead right in the front yard of the cattlemen and, it was said, encouraged the cowboys to rustle calves for her herd. If the Association cattlemen along the Sweetwater put together his sleeping with her and then refusing to go along with lynching her, my father would be distrusted . . . even hated. Men bigger than him had been blacklisted for not being sympathetic with certain policies of the Stock Association. And if he wasn't co-operative in running his own son from the valley—if that was as far as the rustler hunt went—Father could be thrown out of the Association. In Wyoming of the late eighties, that was saying he wouldn't be able to market his cattle. He'd go broke inside a year.

I felt uncomfortable in the chair but didn't move. Neither of us spoke. A coyote was yapping on the bluff above the river, and my father's breath began to cloud in the cold air of our empty house.

"Was she pretty?" I asked at last.

"Who?" He raised his head. "The Watson woman?"

I nodded.

"I reckon not."

"Prettier than Mother?" I asked it partly out of meanness.

"Your mother wasn't real pretty, Mart. She was all I ever wanted, though, except for cattle and good horses . . . a ranch for you and Ira. Her father ran a mercantile store in San Antone. She was smart and quiet. And when we first married she was as slender as . . ." He didn't say any more out loud, finishing whatever he was thinking in his own mind.

"I just wondered if you felt right about this Ella Watson thing." I saw I was moving toward boggy ground and didn't much care.

Father stiffened a little. "What are you getting at, son?"

"You told me you were friends with her," I said. "Didn't you know what was being planned for her? Didn't the Association talk over the hanging before it happened?"

"There's always talk about how a thick-skinned pair like her and Averill ought to be strung up to get them out of the way and keep rustlers and other homesteaders in line. But most of the talk was about just scaring them out of the country."

"You couldn't have warned her what was shaping up?"

"She'd been warned and threatened several times," he said. "Neither she or the man paid any heed. She wouldn't have listened to me."

I still wasn't satisfied. "Did you try to warn her?"

"No."

"If you'd known when they were planning to hang her, would you have told her?"

The lines in his forehead deepened when I said that, his mouth tightened with a jerk, and I guessed I'd touched one of the reasons why he'd been drinking so heavily. "You've no call to ask me that," he said. "I wasn't one who talked against her."

"But maybe you didn't try to stop the men who did talk against her."

"I told them it wasn't right," he shouted angrily. "They lived close to her place. They were the ones Averill's abusive letters to the papers were hurting. They were the ones seeing their cowboys turned against them and encouraged to rustling by the woman. They were the ones losing their best rangeland to thieves and shiftless honyockers. It wasn't my place to stop those ranchers from protecting themselves, but I told them I couldn't be a party to it!"

"So you stayed in Cheyenne while they hung her?"

Father turned on me, but he wasn't shouting now. "There's some things I won't meddle in.

272

Blame me for what happened if you want to. Ira would, and you're talking like him now. If you think I wanted her murdered that way . . . if you think I haven't been thinking about her ever since . . ."

Then he was walking away from me into his office, and when he came back he had another whiskey bottle in his hand. He didn't have much control of himself or his voice. "Leave me be, Mart," he muttered when he was seated at the table again.

"I'm going," I said. "But I see now Ira was right. We've been breeding a scab on our nose out here. I can't say you haven't done what *you* thought was right. It's just that you and Mr. Karr won't admit a lot of the trouble is your own fault. You did some shifty things to get cattle and hold your land. But now you've got to make your own laws to keep other people from getting started the same way."

"What would you have me do!" he roared, crashing the bottom of the half-raised bottle back against the table. "I've lived by my lights and that's all a man can do. Ira pulled out on me and you . . ."

"Killed her," I shouted back. "Go ahead and say it for once! If it wasn't for me, she'd be here on the ranch with you now."

He stared at the bottle and then slowly raised it for a drink. "Leave me be," he said in a whisper.

"I won't bother you any more," I told him, feeling a terrible tightness in my throat. "I don't belong here any more than Ira did. The ranch can go to hell for all I care. You'll figure out a way to make the Association trust you again. They owe you something for helping pay Paulson and closing your eyes while people got shot and hung."

"Leave me be," he said again, without looking at me.

So I left him then in the same position as when I'd come in. From the lean-to where I lay open-eyed and hating myself, I heard the sound of the bottle whenever it was lowered back to the table. That was all. Finally I didn't hear that any more, but when I dozed off restlessly near dawn I knew my father still hadn't moved from the table.

Chapter 18

The morning was gray and cold when I woke up. I dressed warmly and went to the bunkhouse kitchen for breakfast. The hands had already finished eating, and Cookie only grunted when I served myself leftover fried potatoes, cold bacon, canned prunes, and coffee. He stayed busy with the dirty dishes or fussed with the stove until I'd finished.

Nothing tasted good, and I left as soon as I could. First I checked to be sure that Blacky had been fed in the corral. A chunky sorrel that Ira had broken for me was up from the horse pasture, leaning over the corral poles and whickering so I might notice and give him some hay. Instead, because he was stout enough to pack, I turned him in with Blacky. Then I picked a packsaddle and a set of rawhide panniers from the shed. Alongside them I piled my saddle, blanket, bridle, rifle scabbard, and a halter for the pack horse. I can recall how hard it was to leave the familiar-smelling saddle shed and walk back to the lean-to beside the silent house. . . .

It's funny the things you think of when you've quarreled with a person close to you—a brother, a girl, or your father. I kept wondering if Father was sick or hurt some way, but I couldn't make myself go in and face him again. All I had left to do was pack the things I would need until I found a job. Even so, I kept waiting around and wasting time without quite knowing why. I don't owe him anything, I kept thinking. I don't owe him a damn thing more than Ira did. . . .

Once I did start getting my gear together, the morning was half gone. I folded a bedroll and cleaned the beat-up six-shooter I'd had on roundup. After digging around in an old powder box, I found the shells for it. Then I packed some clothes in a canvas war bag. Father's Winchester I figured to leave, since I wasn't going to let him pay me off like he had done with Ira. I'd call the packsaddle an even enough swap, considering my father had taught me most of what I knew about working cattle and horses—among other things.

I'd just finished carrying my bedroll out to the saddle shed when the men rode into sight below the river crossing. Their horses had trouble on the thin ice. I could hear faint curses as some of the riders had to get off and lead the slipping, spraddle-legged animals across. Other horses balked and then skidded wildly when spurred jumping onto the ice. I counted fourteen men in the group before they bunched up again and were hidden by clumps of dead, colorless willows bordering the Sweetwater.

Glancing back at the house, I thought I saw a shadow inside the window of Father's office, but then I wasn't sure that I hadn't imagined seeing something. It didn't take much imagination, though, to figure out who those riders were. The last horse to cross the ice had looked to be Clayt Paulson's big buckskin.

When the men passed our corral I was far enough inside the shed that they didn't notice me. I recognized several of the riders. Besides Paulson, who wore a heavy buffalo-hide overcoat, there was Moses Ethridge, thin and stiff-looking on the gray Texas stud he'd ridden up on a trail drive in the eighties . . . the two Thompson brothers, short-coupled, sharp-featured Southerners who favored gaited horses and had been known to fight anyone who laughed about it . . . the young Englishman named Bobby Dutton, who ranched northeast of Bothwell but spent most of his time drinking brandy at the Cheyenne Club. These men, along with Roan Meyers, were said to have been involved one way or another in hanging Ella Watson.

Mr. Karr rode unsmiling beside Dutton, but what gave me a jar was to see Finn Rankin, with Seth Daniels and three other ex-cowboys homesteading on Antelope Creek, laughing at something he'd said to Clayt Paulson. It was hard to figure what they might have in common to joke about. Riding sullenly behind them was Whitey Pence and several other ranchers from the valley. And the man they herded along as a poor-looking prisoner was the honyocker Volanski.

Ordinarily none of these men would have ridden their horses so close to our house. This morning they rode right up in front. I heard horses snorting and their hoofs scraping cold ground as the men argued among themselves about who should speak for the group. Then the voices stopped abruptly, and at the same time I saw my father appear in the doorway.

For a moment no one spoke. A few of the men seemed embarrassed about being there.

Father stepped outside. I thought it impossible that I could be watching the same man who had sat drinking by himself all night in an empty house. He was freshly shaven and wore a clean white shirt with the vest and pants of a dark suit. He was unarmed.

"Men," he said clearly.

It was Moses Ethridge, his long nose red from the ride, who finally answered. "I guess you can tell this ain't a social visit, Martin."

"Well, I reckon not," Father said. "You gentlemen wouldn't bother to ride up to my front porch for a social visit."

He knew how to handle them, I thought. He kept his voice even and was making the riders feel uneasy in stating their business. Most of them, as he guessed, probably felt guilty about the way they had ridden up to the front door and waited for him to come out. But he must have realized, also, the depth of feeling against him and Ira both which was shown by their acting that way.

When Father said nothing more Moses Ethridge had to speak up again. "You probably been hearing the talk." He cleared his throat and spit tobacco juice past his stirrup. "We been figuring to stop the thieving of our cattle and saddle stock. The Association's for it, and we figure you might be for it too. We already picked up one troublemaker on the way over."

I looked over at Volanski, who was slouched awkwardly in his saddle as he stared down at his tied hands. He seemed too scared to really know what was going on, though he must've recognized Father from that night we'd visited his homestead at Green Mountain. He probably also remembered my father's threat to kill him if he butchered any more of our cattle.

Paulson's horse tossed his head restlessly and danced around in a half circle, until Clayt reined him back beside Senator Karr. "The Association members put it to a vote. You weren't there, so the others decided to talk with you before doing anything."

Father looked sharply at the detective. "You started voting in the Association, Clayt? Sounds as though you've been promoted since the last meeting I went to."

"It could be." Paulson smiled coldly. "Some go up and some go down."

"Meaning what, Clayt?" asked Father.

Before Paulson had a chance to answer Mr. Karr interrupted. His voice, I noticed, had a false sincerity that I'd first heard before roundup, when he told me he was thinking about selling the Two-Bar-K. "I see no cause for harsh words among ourselves," he said. "After all, Martin here has always agreed that we must protect our interests. We've all heard him express his views on that."

My father shifted his glance to the Senator for a moment. "Our interests, you say, Wallace?" His voice hardened. "I'd say there's some difference between my interests and yours. Wouldn't you?"

I thought Karr's face flushed. "These men know where I stand on the question of stealing. You should know also, Martin."

"I've been learning," Father said. "I know a man who offered Lamar's daughter quite a little money for a certain piece of land with good water on it. Funny thing to happen after your foreman shot—or said he shot—her father. Wouldn't you say so, Wallace?"

I'd heard the same thing from Ira, and I thought Mr. Karr might try to deny it. Instead he shrugged and glanced at the other men for support. "That was only a business matter. My ranch was close to Willow Springs also, and it would have been a shame if no one had offered the girl a decent price. I had no idea of certain . . . ah, arrangements . . . you had made with the old man."

Bobby Dutton laughed. "Really now, we didn't ride all this way into a snow squall to discuss business ethics, you know. Let's get to the point and be on our way."

"I believe we were talking on the point," Father answered. "But I'm willing to hear what you've all come to say. You going to do the talking, Bobby?"

After looking over at Mr. Karr, the Englishman shook his head and slipped his bridle reins from one gloved hand to the other. "Really, I think Mr. Ethridge or Senator Karr should have the floor. Youth giving way to experience, you know."

I'd heard stories about Bobby Dutton, whose father had sent him to America after a scandal involving someone's wife in England, but this was the first time he had come to our ranch. The cowboys said he received money each month from his father, and they called him a "remittance man." He managed a large outfit which was financed by a group of rich Britishers who didn't know the difference between a coyote and a lapdog. Dutton had a reputation for not knowing much more than the directors of the cattle company he worked for. But Father always said he spoke up at the Association meeting as if he'd personally sired the first calf crop in Wyoming. Watching him smile and make a little mock bow in Karr's direction, I could begin to see why my father said it was Dutton's own fault that his cowboys couldn't stand to work for him longer than a year or so.

Moses Ethridge spat again. "Go ahead with it, Senator. We ain't got much time as it is." The Thompsons grunted in agreement, while Finn Rankin shifted his weight in the saddle and kept watching Father. I couldn't tell from his face what he might be thinking. Or Paulson either, though I could make a fair guess.

"All right then," I heard Karr say. "It's really quite simple. The time is past due for taking further action to protect ourselves. So far nothing has served to stop the stealing of horses and illegal branding of mavericks." He gestured toward Finn Rankin with one stiff arm. "Rankin here has lost several head of saddle stock this spring, and Bobby Dutton's calf crop was only three quarters of what it should have been with an open winter last year—"

"Bobby's hands usually mark about a fourth of his calves with their own brands," Father said. "I reckon Bobby would admit that himself."

"I say now," cried the Englishman. "I'm really not that much of a fool, you know. And I've lost horses too."

"That's true enough," said Father. "Five of your mares have been running east of Longs Creek since last summer. I guess some people would call them strays."

Mr. Karr moved his horse up to the front of the riders. "We all know there have been losses, Martin. Of course we might argue over some of the details, but there isn't time for that. Clayt has learned positively that rustlers are using Willow Springs as a camp while moving stolen stock. After Bill Donohue was run out of the Powder River country by the Association, he stayed with your son for several days. There is a good chance of finding Donohue there today, too."

"You will find him there," Paulson broke in. "I haven't been asleep the last few weeks."

"I reckon not," Father said, still looking at Karr. "And what steps did you have in mind to take if you find him and Ira at Willow Springs?"

Moses Ethridge wiped his nose viciously with his glove. "Association's had Donohue blackballed for quite a while. Wouldn't be no great loss whatever happened to him."

"And Ira?"

"They'll both have a chance to prove their innocence," Mr. Karr said formally. "The main thing is to stop the loss of our property. If we fail to take steps now, the thieves and their nester friends will steal all we have. It is as simple as that."

"What if I don't go along with it?" asked Father.

I knew what the answer would have been a year ago, but I could tell by the men's faces that Father wasn't going to stop them that way now. I figured Ira's defiance was the main reason my father had lost his influence with these men. But as it turned out I wasn't entirely right.

"We will go without you," Karr said. "That might be the best plan anyway, since your son is involved in the stealing."

"Can you prove that?" Father's voice was firm

and ringing. Except for Mr. Karr and Paulson, the men avoided looking him in the eye. "I know there have been stories going around, but I'm talking about proof, not women's gossip. I don't go along with a lot of my son's ways—you all know that. But when you're talking about 'taking steps' against a man you better think hard over whether or not the proof is there."

"Ella Watson isn't troubled about the evidence now," Bobby Dutton laughed.

Father stared at him a moment. "I reckon not, though maybe you are."

The men remained silent. Ethridge sighed and looked around at the others. "Well, we ain't trying to be unreasonable, Martin. We could think it over a little more."

There were a few nods—I thought two or three of the riders looked relieved—and then Clayt Paulson turned on them.

"We argued this all out before," he said. "I have seen horse thieves moving through Willow Springs Canyon, and some of you saw the way a rustler named Lamar operated from there. It won't hurt to learn just what is going on at that homestead. We can hear what Mr. Tyrrell's boy and this Bill Donohue have to say for themselves."

"Ella was eloquent," Dutton joked again, and then I realized he'd been drinking. "I said, 'Ladies first,' but the other chaps overruled me.

They say she was marvelous in bed, but I can only speak of her eloquence at the end of a lariat."

"You're more of a fool than I thought," Father told him. "Were you drunk that day too? I reckon so."

"No more than usual, old boy. You should've been there. Of course that might have been embarrassing since you . . . well, you know . . . had been, what shall we say, sampling the wares?"

Most of the men hadn't expected to hear that, and they looked up in surprise. All but Paulson, who was smiling.

"I thought everyone knew that Mr. Tyrrell had visited her," he said. "Naturally he didn't pay her in mavericks like the cowboys did, but he rutted in her cabin the same as any unreliable hand."

Bobby Dutton winked broadly at my father and made an elaborate gesture of disbelief with his shoulders. "I say, that can't be true, can it, Martin? Tell us quickly that it isn't so!"

Father didn't flinch. "It's true. I would imagine some of you did the same thing."

Ethridge grunted in a strange way, for once he had talked openly of a night he'd spent with Ella. But he didn't say anything now. My father looked hard at the Thompson brothers and then at Finn Rankin—they didn't speak either. The gray morning was perfectly quiet, except for a horse snorting and saddle leather creaking when Rankin's animal moved his weight from one hind foot to the other.

"So that's how it is." Father spoke without anger. He said the words like a statement rather than a question. "I know the story Whitey Pence has told some of you, and I've already said how things were between Ella Watson and me. None of it had anything to do with this ride you men are planning to make today. I'd still advise you all to think hard before you do a thing which might get you hung yourselves."

Paulson frowned and danced the buckskin around to face Father. "Is that some kind of threat?"

"You can take it any way you want," Father told him.

"I don't take kindly to threats from a man who has been bulling over that cattle-stealing whore at Bothwell."

I'd never seen Father's face so cold, and when he answered Paulson his voice was controlled as carefully as a Colt's mainspring. "Say that again, Clayt, and I'll decide you're serious about it."

He turned his back on them without warning and disappeared inside the house. After a few moments had passed and some of the riders had begun to mutter nervously to each other, Father stepped out the door again. His six-shooter was thrust into the waistband of his trousers, the heavy cylinder dark against the whiteness of his shirt.

Paulson started to say something, but Mr. Karr cut him short. "Clayt was speaking impulsively. After all, you're not on trial here, Martin. Many of us are unhappy that this gossip about you and the Watson woman should turn out to be true. Of course the most disturbing aspect of your relationship with her is the question it raises concerning your loyalty to your friends and neighbors. But that is for the Association to deal with later. We came here to do something about the rustlers who are using Willow Springs Canyon."

"Ain't I got a right to say something first?"

I looked at the horsemen behind Karr to see who had spoken. The Senator looked around also, angry at being interrupted. "I think you better let me handle this, Pence," he said.

Moses Ethridge crossed his hands deliberately on his saddle horn. "Might as well let him have his say, Senator. I guess we wasted too damn much time now to grudge a bit more."

"Let him talk," Finn Rankin called. "It's the only thing Whitey's good at." Nobody laughed.

Now that everyone was looking at him, Whitey seemed less anxious to speak. "Well . . . I ain't worked here without seeing a few things," he began hesitantly. "Worked damn hard for what little pay I got, too. . . . Guess my boss was more interested in other things than whether his hands was well taken care of. . . ."

"Go on, Whitey," my father told Pence when he paused and licked his lips. "Everyone's listening to you now."

"Just tell them what you told me last night," Paulson called to Whitey. "You don't have anything to be afraid of."

He was afraid, though. I could tell he was worried about both Clayt Paulson, who probably had put him up to this, and my father.

"Why, I ain't a troublemaker. . . . You all know that. But I ain't one to take abuse, either. Mr. Tyrrell ought to know that. . . ."

Paulson cursed. "Tell them what you know, damn it!"

"Well, it's all true about him and Ella Watson. I swear it is. What's more, this Mr. Tyrrell ain't so high and mighty about everything as he lets on. Ask him about the sheep his older boy owns that some little Mex's been herdin' over Red Desert way. Ain't that sweet, a Tyrrell owning a bunch of stinkin' woollies!"

I could see the men's faces turn as one to Father as if he, not Whitey, had spoken. He's lost it now, I thought. Until then I'd figured he knew the others so well he might dull their determination enough that Karr and Paulson wouldn't get them to Willow Springs today—or maybe ever. Now it looked like my father was getting himself worked tighter and tighter into a corner that hadn't a way out for him, or Ira either.

"Is Whitey talking the truth about those sheep?" Moses Ethridge asked.

I expected anything but what I heard then. "No," said Father. "I reckon it's not quite the whole story. I gave Ira the money to buy sheep, so you might say I own them. I figure that's nobody else's business, though."

He said it so plain and direct that the men just stared at him. I didn't know what to think either. If what he said about the sheep was true—and I couldn't believe it was—my father was ruining himself as a Sweetwater cattleman by admitting it.

Ethridge shook his head. "I never would've thought it possible, Martin. All of us agreed to keep the sheep off the range we owned. Ain't it wrong to help your boy go against your neighbors that way?"

"I was ranching in this country before any of you men even thought of owning cattle in Wyoming," answered Father. "I helped get the Association started. I don't reckon I need to be lectured on the women I visit or the kind of stock I buy. Those sheep were grazing on the Red Desert and never hurt your cattle ranges. If you feel like I've done something wrong, you can report it to the Association and let them blacklist me. Otherwise you should keep clear of me and my affairs."

"I hate a damn sheep!" Seth Daniels shouted. "But I hate a man who owns them worse."

Father looked straight at him without moving or speaking. Suddenly I knew he had lied deliberately to shift the men's attention from Ira to himself. And I realized it might work.

"Them sheep won't hurt nobody now," someone said. "They done committed suicide one night."

"Just like old Ella done," another of the ranchers put in. "But don't it beat all, Martin—the bad luck that can plague a man! It's a real disappointment to find you was running woollies on the sly and warming the bed of a rustler-loving slut that made trouble for your best friends. Here we thought all along you was the straightest man on the river."

Bobby Dutton took a brandy bottle from the pocket of his overcoat and drank from it openly. "I do believe you're a fallen idol, Martin. What a bloody shame."

"Why don't you pass that around, Mr. Dutton?" Seth Daniels asked. "I'm cold sitting here listening to Mr. Tyrrell's troubles."

"I'm for going to Stenger's where we can all have a bracer," Finn Rankin said. "Reckon those rustlers won't mind the delay, and if they get the message and take a *paséito* out of the country it'll save us the trouble of bothering with 'em. Who knows but what Mr. Tyrrell might want to leave here too? Not that he ain't welcome to stay and let his Association blackball him. . . . Anyone else heading for Stenger's?"

Then Senator Karr began to realize what was happening. I saw him and Paulson glance pointedly at each other. Clayt backed his horse beside Bobby Dutton and said something to him, after which the Englishman put the bottle away without smiling. The Senator reined his horse around facing the men.

"I know it's cold weather to be sitting here talking," he said. "But it won't be any warmer riding out of our way to Stenger's. Obviously Martin is not going to cooperate. In fact, the Association will want to look more carefully at his relationship with Ella Watson and the stock rustlers in this valley. After what he has told us, I believe it more urgent than ever to get this business at Willow Springs settled once and for all."

He paused and pointed dramatically at the thickened, sullen sky. "I would say a hard storm is on its way. We ought to finish what we have started before the weather turns too bad."

"The Senator's right," Paulson said. "This is the best chance we will have to catch up with Donohue and any other rustlers that might be holed up together. How about it, Mr. Ethridge?"

"I don't plan to ride over here again in the middle of winter. Anyhow, we already picked up this damned Russian thief at Green Mountain. I ain't for turning back now."

"How about you?" Karr asked the Thompson brothers. "You men aren't turning back, are you?"

They both looked over once at Father. "I guess we'll ride with you," one of them told the Senator. "We lost a lot of stock this past year, what with honyockers like this Volanski butchering our steers and rustlers branding our new calves all to hell. I'm for teaching them a lesson like the one that somebody learned Ella and Averill."

"Dutton?"

"Of course I'm one of the gang." Bobby glanced at Clayt Paulson with irritation. "But I've a right to take a nip now and then if it suits me. It's bloody cold, Wallace."

"We will talk about that in a minute," Karr said. "What about you, Pence?"

"He's going with us," Paulson cut in. "Aren't you, Whitey?"

The cowboy nodded without looking at any of them, and I wondered if he was worried now about having talked so much.

Then a couple of the ranchers I didn't know very well backed out. They were from west of Beaver Rim, and one of them said they had to bunch their cattle before the storm hit. They both just started riding away from the group, passed where I waited in the saddle shed, and kept their horses going at a steady walk in the direction of the river. I'll always remember the way their faces looked passing me—white even in the cold and strained with the effort of not showing any fear, like the faces of men who had just seen somebody die. . . .

I saw the riders in front of the house watch the two men who had left until Karr said, "They might have slowed us down anyway, and besides they were not really from the valley."

Father laughed. "And besides that they couldn't stomach the kind of thing you want them to do, Wallace."

Mr. Karr ignored this, but his hand began to clench and unclench nervously against his thigh. I knew he needed Finn Rankin, Daniels, and those three other ex-cowboys now—and so far they hadn't had much to say.

"Well, Rankin," the Senator began, "I know we can count on you and your men."

"You know it, do you?" Finn smiled. "I'd say it wasn't so slick as all that."

"You and Daniels have lost stock too. I think it is very clear that all of you would benefit from our efforts to stop the losses."

"Why, that's sure true," said Rankin. "But Seth and the rest of us on Antelope Creek are planning to start a cattle company of our own. We've been workin' hard, and I figure that if we're going to stick our necks out chasin' rustlers for the Association, the Association ought to let us join and have our brand recognized. What do you think, Mr. Karr?"

I had to admire the way Rankin had worked it, but it left Ira and Volanski caught between Rankin's ambition and the demand for action being pushed ruthlessly by Karr and Clayt Paulson. Looking back on it, I think the Senator had already decided that letting Rankin's crowd into the Association was a good way to hold some control over them. Finn and his friends, on the other hand, needed bad to have their brand recognized by the Association—otherwise they couldn't ship or sell their cattle. And after all, hunting down suspected rustlers was a good way to help people forget how they got started on Antelope Creek with a running iron and a long rope.

"I believe we can admit a company like yours into the Association," Wallace Karr told Rankin. "Would any of you other gentlemen object?" When nobody spoke out Karr looked satisfied. "I think that's settled. As chairman of the Association membership committee, you have my word on it, Finn."

Apparently the Senator had lost some of his nervousness now, and he was smiling a little.

"Clayt will lead the way to Willow Springs and be in charge of taking the cabin. I will be in charge after that. Ride quietly and do whatever Clayt or I tell you is needed. Any questions?"

The men didn't move for a long moment. Then they began pulling at their hats and let the horses sidle around and toss their heads as they sensed the possibility of movement again. Paulson had started to ride off, motioning some of the men to bring Volanski along behind him, when Father called, "Clayt!"

The riders reined in abruptly, and Paulson stared around at my father, his handsome face stamped with a wild expression that I couldn't read.

"I want to talk alone with you and Wallace for a minute." Father opened the door and placed his six-shooter inside the house. "It'll be safe enough, I reckon."

Karr hesitated, then said, "All right, Martin. You men start on ahead. Clayt and I will catch up with you shortly."

I saw Paulson and the Senator rein their horses away from the main group of riders, who headed down past the house with Moses Ethridge in the lead. Father began to talk with Clayt and Mr. Karr, but his back was toward me and he spoke so low that I couldn't really hear what he was saying. I could see Karr shake his head every once in a while, though, and finally Clayt

Paulson turned impatiently to see how far the men had ridden. Soon the horsemen were out of sight.

And then it happened—so suddenly that the movements seemed unreal, as though the murky winter day was playing tricks on my eyes. I saw Father reach up and grasp the front of Wallace Karr's overcoat with both hands and start to drag him from the saddle. I think he would've done it, too, only Karr cried out so shrilly that his horse shied, jerking Father off balance. At the same time Clayt pulled his six-shooter free of its holster, kneeing the buckskin over against Father.

And I saw Paulson swing the Colt's barrel and cylinder smashing down like an ax blow on the head of my father, who had kept his hold on Karr's thick coat. Almost as part of the same motion, Clayt Paulson pointed the .44 down at the figure toppled to the ground. His horse jumped in fright, but I heard the heavy report echoing flatly from the river bluffs in the cold air.

The Senator's startled face—afraid and disbelieving—stared at me as I ran toward them from the saddle shed. And then both men spurred their horses through our yard, leaving me kneeling over the gaunt form that was my father, Martin Tyrrell—crumpled down and bleeding on the winter-hardened ground. . . .

Chapter 19

It was beginning to snow from a flint-gray sky as Cookie and I carried Father into the house. After we laid him on his bunk Cookie slashed open the pant leg above the purple-red bullet hole in his thigh, and I saw Father's eyes move jerkily under their lids. Then he was staring calmly at us as the old cook began to clean up the wound.

"You saw what happened out there, son?" Father asked me in a strangely clear voice.

"I saw Clayt Paulson fire the shot," I told him. "I was in the saddle shed all the time."

He showed no surprise at my being there. "I thought I could stop them from doing something foolish. I couldn't, though. Once they would've listened harder to me, I reckon, but not any more." His voice fell off and his mouth pulled down under his mustache, like he'd suddenly felt the pain of that bullet for the first time.

"Didn't hit the bone none," Cookie said, though I had a feeling it hadn't been the wound that caused my father to grimace that way. "Go get me boiling water and some clean cloth, Mart. You better bring a bottle of your dad's rotgut too. I'll need some if he don't."

When I'd brought everything and Cookie had finished dressing the leg we covered Father with plenty of blankets. "Gettin' hit with a .44 slug is a lot like taking a square kick from a shod horse," said Cookie. "They both knock hell out of your whole body for a spell. Best to keep warm and full of whiskey."

Father didn't say anything to that one way or the other, but he seemed impatient for the cook to finish. I was wishing he would hurry too. For now that my father looked to be better than I'd believed possible, I was beginning to realize what might happen to Ira. The thought of that wasn't very pleasant. . . .

Once Cookie had left the room, Father called me over beside his bunk. Except for the heavy mustache, his face looked drawn and somehow terribly old, as though he'd aged even more since talking to Karr's "posse."

"You know where Ira is, son?" he asked me.

"I'd guess Willow Springs," I said. "Anyway, that's where Karr and the others are headed."

He nodded like that didn't make much difference. "Mart, you stay clear of this. I'm not asking you to change your mind on what you said about me and the ranch last night. But I'm the one responsible for what's happened with Ira. I'm the one to deal with Karr and Paulson now."

I thought to tell him now was too late for him being much help. But instead I said, "I'm not a part of the TX any more than Ira is. What I said last night I meant . . . so I guess you might as well know I'm riding over to Willow Springs Canyon whether you want me to or not."

He looked straight through me. "Are you, Mart? It looks like my sons are just as bullheaded as me. One thing I want to tell you, though."

"What's that?" I asked, seeing his eyes center on me again like he wanted to hold me there by his will. And thinking back now, I know he could've held me if he'd wanted to. . . .

"Clayt Paulson's father was the best friend I had in Texas," he said then. "His mother was a Mexican woman that lived near our place in the brush country. She married a cowboy named Paulson who had ridden with me and my brothers. When your oldest uncle was murdered in cattle troubles with some people that hated us, Clayt's father helped us out just as though he was a Tyrrell himself . . . and he got shot down and killed doing it. . . ."

I watched him, feeling shut in by the log walls of the room . . . feeling angry and cheated from remembering that old Jules and Mary Lamar had been shot down too. "So you got Clayt a job with the Association and gave him the run of the TX?"

"I recommended him to the right people in Cheyenne. We needed someone like Clayt . . ."

"What would you want me to say about it?" I finally asked.

"Nothing. I wanted you to know."

That was true enough, I think—he wasn't apologizing or asking for any sort of comment from me. He just wanted to tell me how he'd tried to pay off a debt to Paulson's father. Maybe he also wanted me to know he felt some responsibility for the things Clayt had done, though I knew well enough he would still defend the Association's need for men like Clayt. What he hadn't said, though, was that Paulson had just tried to kill him and was riding with a mob to find my brother Ira. . . .

"All right, you've told me," I said, already turning away. "Maybe I can do something to help Ira or maybe I can't. I'll try, anyhow, and then I'll never come back to this damn place."

When I looked at my father again he just nodded curtly without changing expression, and I wanted to say something that would hurt him more. I wanted to make him say he'd been wrong about using Clayt Paulson to protect his range and stock, about the Ella Watson business, and most of all, wrong about trying to force Ira into thinking the same way he did about things. But I knew he wouldn't say he was wrong or probably even think it. So I left him there on the bunk, thinking I never wanted to see him or the TX again.

I went into the kitchen where Cookie was stoking up the stove. He squinted his eyes against the smoke and cursed at nothing in particular. "Hell of a thing to happen to your dad, but it's done. Murderin' bastards ain't had enough, either, so it's Ira they'll sneak on now."

"I know," I said. "They're probably well on their way to Willow Springs now."

"So?" He glanced at me and wiped his eyes on the sleeve of his flannel shirt.

It was strange how I'd become a responsible man in one short day. Cookie's question had been troubling me long before he'd asked it. But I wasn't any more certain than the "posse" about where Ira was.

I said, "When Slat rides in this evening, ask him to take the team to Rawlins tomorrow and bring Doc Parker out. He better tell the sheriff what happened, too. Not that it will do much good."

"What were you aiming to do now?"

"Find Ira," I told him.

"You'll find a power of trouble, anyhow, but I ain't the one to stop you. Looks to me like you got a lot to take care of here without proddin' around, though. It'd be different if you knew where your brother was."

In my head I kept seeing Father fall and hearing the shot echo, but it was all mixed up with the story about Clayt being his friend's son and the trouble in Texas. "Maybe I don't want any more of this place," I said. "Now is as good a time as any other to pull out."

"That's one way to play your cards, Mart," Cookie muttered. "Quit the bunch and to hell with it. Ira done it that way, so why not you too? Your dad would feel right proud, wouldn't he?"

"Look where his ranch got him," I said. "It isn't a question of quitting or not. I want to start in a country that gives a man some chance to run his cows in peace without someone always telling him what he can or can't do."

Cookie tugged at his mustache and shrugged. "Why don't you leave then? It don't make a damn to me."

"It shouldn't," I told him.

When the cook made no reply I knew it did matter and I felt ashamed of taking my anger out on him. "Thanks for helping me," I said.

"I can throw together some grub for you to take," he answered more gently. "Though I reckon you'll be too stubborn to carry it."

I went to the lean-to for a heavier coat, and when I came back into the kitchen I heard Cookie speaking to someone at the front door. It sounded like a woman's voice. In a moment I went to the big room and found a girl warming herself at the fireplace. As she turned toward me I recognized Leah Karr—I still thought of her that way—dressed in a heavy sheepskin coat and wool pants. The cold had burned her cheeks scarlet, and melted snow dampened her hair around the edges of a man's sealskin cap.

"Oh, Mart," she called. "Where's Mr. Tyrrell? We've got to keep the men from finding Ira."

"My father's hurt," I said. "Clayt Paulson shot him a little while ago in the yard."

"Shot him!" She held both hands to her cheeks and then jerked them away, as if her fingers found no warmth there. "He's hurt badly, Mart?"

"He was shot in the leg. I'm going to look for Ira now."

You had to admit Leah had grit. She didn't break down like another woman might, but her eyes flashed angrily. "I'm sorry, Mart. Perhaps my father is as much to blame for it as anyone."

"Maybe so," I said. "Didn't your husband tell you where he was going when he left to come here?"

She didn't much want to answer. "No. Did he . . . shoot your father in a fight or . . ."

"You could call it an argument over Ira, I guess. Anyway, Clayt did it when Father was looking even if he wasn't armed. That's a real change for your husband, isn't it?"

I saw I'd touched a raw place. The pain was there in her face, and I figured she'd learned a lot more about Clayt Paulson than she'd known when they married. I didn't press her, but she told me anyway.

"He's done terrible things, Mart. I can't condone them, even though he was taking orders from Cheyenne—or from my father. He feels it's

303

just a dirty job that he is suited for. He doesn't seem to think it's any worse than his helping the army hunt down renegade Apaches in New Mexico."

"I imagine so," I said. "Did Clayt tell you he shot Jules Lamar and had Meyers take the blame for it?"

Leah moved closer to the fire, shivering slightly. "Clayt didn't tell me . . . but I knew about it."

I took a chance then. "Did he tell you about shooting the Lamar girl too? She was lying in bed real early in the morning when it happened. It was a sort of accident, because he thought it was Ira there. At least I think that's what happened."

Leah was shaking her head numbly. "That's what happened, Mart. I thought he wouldn't do a thing like that. He had no reason for it except . . ."

"Except what?" I asked her.

She didn't answer. I watched the soft flakes curling down outside, and I realized I'd have to start riding before the storm worsened. "I'm going with you," Leah said then. "I've got to see your brother."

I tried to argue her out of it, but she was set on going—by herself if I wouldn't take her. "I know Clayt and my father," she said. "Sometimes I can reason with them when nobody else can. And I know Ira too."

While I went out to saddle Blacky and a fresh horse for her, Leah swallowed a little hot coffee and looked in at Father for a minute. Her face was set in hard planes when she came out to start the ride. She wanted to hear exactly how the shooting happened, and so I told her as we started away from the ranch. She listened, only nodding, and when I finished we both rode on silently. There wasn't much for us to say.

The snowflakes were thicker and falling faster now, and as the afternoon grew colder they blew across the trail in a light ground blizzard and piled up in hollows and low places. The horned larks had been gathering around the corrals when we left the ranch, and that often was the sign of a bad storm or blizzard building up. The breath of our horses was frosty, and their shoes left clean marks in the snow, which luckily wasn't icy enough to ball up yet.

I had no trouble following the hoofprints of the horses ahead of us. Though I judged Karr's men were riding hard, I figured they didn't know any more than I did about how to find Ira. Where the trail to Willow Springs Canyon forked, I saw by the tracks that the riders had bunched to talk things over, before riding on—toward the canyon. And Clayt Paulson would lead them there by the shortest way.

"I don't think Ira will be at Willow Springs," Leah said, turning her face away from the snow.

I hoped he wouldn't be there. "Why not?" I asked her.

She seemed reluctant to answer. "I saw him a few nights ago, Mart. . . . I told him what my father had threatened to do about getting rid of several men that the Association didn't like. Ira said that didn't bother him and anyway he wasn't staying at the homestead any more."

I pretended not to be surprised that she had seen my brother recently. "Do you know where Ira is?"

I could tell by her expression that she did. "He told me that he was moving to the old line camp on Beaver Rim. He's going to meet a buyer there and sell some of his horses. . . . I think Ira's leaving the Sweetwater, Mart. He's got to get away after what has happened today."

I listened to the two horses blowing in the cold air. When they shifted their weight the snow crunched lightly under their feet. The range looked gray and cruel under the blowing snow. A cow bawled eerily from a hidden draw, and the wind stung my eyes as I turned through habit to look for her.

"Did you hear me?" Leah asked. "Ira must leave the valley, and I want to go with him."

Ira leaving? It was what I'd often thought of doing too. But the controversy over him had resulted in Father getting shot. His disappearing now would seem to be an admission of guilt—an admission that he was a horse thief and had been helping the rustlers. And Leah was surely smart enough to know that Clayt Paulson wouldn't let his wife run off after my brother. Besides that, I couldn't see how Leah would have any more luck than Mary had in getting him to quit the country.

I took a deep breath of sharp air. "Where would you want him to go, Leah?"

"I'm not sure," she said. "Just away from here. You wouldn't want him to stay, would you?"

If I was honest with myself, I had to admit there wasn't much sense in him staying. Why should he wait around for someone to shoot him down from hiding or for a mob to snap his neck in the crazy sort of lynching we'd had at Bothwell a few months back? Maybe Leah had some reason for thinking he'd leave Mary and the homestead at Willow Springs, though thinking about that got my feelings all mixed up again. . . .

"We better get started for the rim," I told Leah. "I guess Ira's the one to say what he's going to do."

"But you won't try to make him change his mind, will you?"

"No, I won't. He'll have to know about Father, though."

"Of course," she said. "It wouldn't be fair not

to tell him. I don't think that should make him stay."

I started Blacky into a slow trot that got my blood moving again. Leah followed behind me, her upturned collar hiding most of her reddened face. Before long the snow stopped, and the sky to the west broke open in a ragged silverish blotch. I was following no real trail now. The land under snow swelled and tilted in strange forms that seemed unrelated to the shapes of our summer range. Wind called like an owl over the breaks near Longs Creek where antelope and cattle stood for protection. The game was warier than it would be in January or February, when the storms had a full edge and feed became short.

I remembered the meadow larks of spring and summer—and felt a longing for green and the spring work when I could ride out among the new calves. I guess it was more, too. I'd seen Jules Lamar buried on the range not far from here. I'd lost Mary to my brother and then seen her almost die in the cabin. The dissension between Father and Ira had changed our lives and almost destroyed both of them as well as their reputations. I didn't figure either one of them was completely to blame, but I still didn't believe enough in myself to make my own life much better.

Spring seemed a long time back as I strained my eyes finding the way to the line camp. The country did look different in winter . . . but I think my trouble was mostly that since last spring I was seeing darker depths and shadows in the rangeland . . . in the people I knew . . . in myself. . . .

Chapter 20

The line camp was partly hidden in a cleft weathered through the chalky limestone and brown sandstone formations tilted down on the eastern slant of Beaver Rim. Several scrub pines grew in front of the sod-roofed cabin, whose rough log walls had bleached out close to the same color as the sandy soil now covered with several inches of soft snow. A dozen head of horses were corralled in a pole pen behind the cabin. They whickered loudly when we first approached, sounding far away and unreal in the wind fluting across the rim. No smoke was visible above the stovepipe sticking from the cabin's roof, and I saw no movement yet at the doorway or window.

"I'm afraid Ira isn't here," Leah said as we stopped for a minute to give our horses a blow before riding closer. "Do you think he could have gone back to Willow Springs for some reason?"

I told her I didn't think so, but I was worried that he actually might have gone back. "He probably hasn't noticed us riding up," I said.

Our horses were nervous as we approached the camp. I still saw no sign of anyone around—inside or out. The only sound now was the wind. Then, just as I dismounted by the pines, a figure appeared in the doorway of the cabin. He was a bearded, long-haired man, wearing an old army overcoat and holding a Winchester to his shoulder. "Hold up there!" he called sharply, and then he spoke to someone else inside.

In a moment Ira appeared beside the man and motioned us to come on. I led my horse up, while Leah rode behind me. Though I didn't particularly care for the looks of things, it was a relief to know Ira hadn't gone back to the homestead.

"I didn't recognize you at first," my brother said. "Those winter clothes fooled me." He glanced over quickly at Leah and smiled, but he didn't seem surprised at all to see her there. "What brings you out this way, Mart?"

I must've looked toward the man standing behind him. "That's all right," Ira told me. "This is Bill Donohue from up on the Powder River. He plans to buy the rest of my saddle stock, and we were closing the deal."

I knew well enough who Bill Donohue was—he'd been run off one of the largest ranches on the Powder and gotten blacklisted by the Association. The story was that he'd been friendly with some of the nesters and ex-cowboys trying to get started on small ranches around Buffalo. After that Donohue did give the company which fired him something to worry about, for he knew their operation so well that he could pick up mavericks easily on a range he'd worked for ten years. And the other company hands resented his firing and would look right at him branding a slick calf without seeing a thing. Donohue had a reputation for nerve and fine good humor when drinking—and for the last two years he had been high on the Association's list of men its members wanted to get rid of.

Leah and I entered the cabin, which was dark inside and cold without any fire in the stove. As we sat down on a wooden bench along the wall Donohue began to whack up kindling for a fire. A quarter of meat wrapped in a flour sack hung against one wall, and the room smelled of saddles and riding gear piled at the foot of the double bunks. I had a feeling the two men had been about to leave the cabin when we rode up.

"You better go ahead and tell him, Mart," Leah said without looking at my brother.

"Tell me what?" Ira smiled. "Didn't you come out for the fresh air?"

"No," I said, wanting to get it over with quickly. "Father's been shot by Clayt Paulson."

Donohue stopped splitting kindling, and I saw Ira's face darken as he stared at me and then at Leah Karr.

"When did it happen, Mart?" he asked then.

As I told him of the way Father had tried to stop Clayt and the Senator, I thought I saw another shadow trouble his face. Everything had to be said, though, because I wasn't sure when I'd see Ira again if he did leave the country like Leah wanted him to. For some reason I thought he should know Father hadn't given in to any of his cattlemen friends who demanded that he help Karr's "posse."

When I'd finished, Leah said, "The whole thing has become senseless now. You can't stay around here and let that mob find you." She turned to the other man. "You're on the blacklist too. If you two are found together there's sure to be more bloodshed."

"Well, that's so, ma'am," Bill Donohue said politely, "but I'm not too sure a man's safer running than he is setting still. Especially with a snowstorm like this one building up. I'm real disturbed by that damn Paulson shooting somebody that way, but the Association isn't going to push me out until I'm ready to move."

I noticed that Leah had started biting her lower lip. "You both know it's a mob coming here. Perhaps you haven't done anything to run from, but these men won't listen to your side of the argument. When a man like Mr. Tyrrell has just been shot, why should they worry about shooting two more people?"

While the others were talking, Ira had been staring down at the patch of dirt floor under his boots. He reminded me of Father sitting in the ranch dining room after a meal or brooding over a glass of whiskey before the fireplace. I wondered if he was blaming himself some for the way things had turned out, just as Leah had felt the Senator was responsible for my father being shot by Clayt. Or maybe it was deeper, and the three of us who had grown up on the Sweetwater felt a guilty uneasiness at the way our fathers had been willing to fight and kill so they could run their cattle here. Like Father and Senator Karr, I'd usually felt they'd done the needed thing in protecting themselves from Indians, thieves, and honyockers . . . but, like Ira, I was beginning to see that we were being removed much like the Crows and the Sioux. The Finn Rankins and the Volanskis were demanding their "rights" now. Thinking awhile like that made me feel awful old—and alone. . . .

Finally Ira looked up, his face calm again, as though he'd thrashed something out for himself. "It was good of you and Mart to come here," he told Leah. "If you hadn't, we might have been caught by surprise and not had a chance of defending ourselves. I want you both to go back to the TX and take care of Mr. Tyrrell. There's nothing more you can do here now."

Leah stared at him for a moment. "Please think

about it longer," she said, turning to look at Donohue and me then. "If they've quarreled with your father that way, I'm sure they won't listen to reason as far as the two of you are concerned."

"Well now"—Donohue nodded—"you know these gents real well. You'll pardon me for asking it, but how come you to find out about them like that?"

"Mr. Karr is my father, and I'm married to Clayt Paulson."

Donohue glanced at Ira with wary, edged eyes. "It's all right," my brother told him without embarrassment. "I've known her most of my life, and she wouldn't be here unless she wanted to help us."

"That's true," Leah said. "But neither of you seems to want any help." She wasn't angry, I thought . . . just plenty worried.

I watched Ira take out his pipe and fill it carefully. "I appreciate what you've done, Leah," he said. "Bill certainly isn't obliged to stay here—I'm going to, though."

"But why?" Leah broke out bitterly. "Your staying won't help anything now."

The match Ira struck flared yellow in the cabin. I saw the snow outside still drifting down like scraps of white feather. Without any fire the room seemed to be getting colder, and I wondered if the riders with Karr and Paulson would really hunt for Ira after getting to Willow

Springs and not finding him there. Something told me they probably would if Clayt had his way. After shooting Father, he would have to make Ira appear to be a real rustler.

"I'll try to explain myself quickly, Leah," my brother was saying. "Ever since I left the TX, people have tried to say I was either stealing horses or working as some sort of spy for the cattle companies. I haven't been a thief or an informer, but that seems hard for anyone to believe. Of course I've had business dealings with homesteaders and Bill here, and I have friends who oppose the Association—though you and Mart are people on the other side of the fence that I've seen too. I consider all this to be my own affair."

Ira struck another match and tamped down the tobacco in his pipe with the matchstick. "What I want to say," he went on, "is that a man living in this country doesn't have the freedom any more to do his work and tend to his own business. I don't like what the Association has been doing, but Finn Rankin and Jack Stenger have been stirring up trouble also. Anyway, if I run away now I'll be acting like a rustler, when I am really only a horse rancher working from a homestead that seems to be in the wrong place."

"Don't you know Finn Rankin and his friends are being taken into the Association?" Leah said. "My father has been talking about doing that ever since the fall roundup. He believes those Texans are the kind of men the Association will need in getting rid of the farmers and sheepmen—and you, Ira."

"She's right about Rankin," I put in. "The Senator agreed to let his outfit join the Association while they were talking to Father at the ranch."

"And Finn agreed?" Ira asked calmly.

"Sure." I shrugged. "Why not? He and his crowd need a way to market their beef. Without an approved brand they'd go broke."

"You see? The two of you don't have anyone to help you." Leah straightened up beside me on the bench. She'd taken off the cap, and her amber hair had fallen down around her face, which was still colored from our cold ride. Whatever her marriage to Paulson was like—and she'd said enough at the ranch to give me the idea she was awfully unhappy—Leah still hadn't got over the hurt of losing Ira. You could tell that by looking at her eyes as she talked with him.

But I noticed something else too. She didn't really understand why Ira spoke of staying there instead of riding away safely with her. Which was the same as saying Leah didn't understand him at all. At least that's how it seemed to me that day in the line camp. . . .

"The last time we talked you told me you didn't intend to spend your life breaking horses at that homestead," she finally said when nothing else had changed Ira's mind. "You meant that, didn't you?"

He nodded. "I meant it. But I'm not going to run from your father and Paulson. I haven't stolen a single head of stock, and they can't force me to act like I'm guilty of rustling. You can see that, can't you, Leah?"

She looked straight at him for a moment before shaking her head fiercely. "No!" she cried out. "I can't. . . . It's foolish and useless. If you won't do anything to help yourself, I will."

I watched her stand up and put the sealskin cap back on, biting her lower lip like she was angry or trying not to cry. Then she started for the cabin door without looking at Ira again. Donohue muttered something about checking the horses and went outside also.

"Will you see that she gets back to the TX?" my brother asked me.

"I'll try to," I told him. "Maybe she had a good point about you not staying here, though."

"She had a good point, Mart. I want you to look after her until all this blows over."

"Look after her and Father both?" I asked. "After all, he told Karr's bunch he owned those sheep that Pete Rodriguez was herding for you. I guess you haven't heard about the Senator and Finn Rankin getting together to destroy the whole band and scare out the herder."

Ira didn't like what he was hearing, but it was Rodriguez he was worried about more than the sheep. "Are you sure he's all right?" he asked me when I finished the story.

"I don't think he was hurt bad," I said. "You don't have sheep any more, though."

"It looks that way. I bought them more to help Rodriguez and establish a principle than to make a profit. The Association and the ranchers in the valley have no right to keep people from grazing sheep on government land. And I didn't think Karr or anyone else would go so far as to use violence against an old Mexican."

"They did," I said, "and Father lied to his own friends to try and make them turn on him instead of you. Does that change your view of him any?"

He gave me a strange look, like I'd meant that as something more than a simple question. "I certainly didn't want him to be shot by Clayt— no matter what the circumstances were."

"Would you say that if Clayt Paulson was the one who tried to kill Mary, and Father was somehow involved in what happened to her?"

He thought hard before answering. "Yes . . . I would say the same thing. But that wouldn't mean I'd changed my mind about Father bringing most of this trouble upon himself. I still want no part of him or his ranch."

In the quiet that followed I thought it must be the cold wind blowing through the open cabin door that made me shiver, though it probably wasn't that alone. I knew I had to tell him the whole story about Father helping Clayt Paulson get hired by the Association—but Ira didn't give me a chance just then.

"Clayt was the one who shot Mary, wasn't he?" he said.

I answered almost without thinking, "That's what I've heard."

"Then I imagine that Paulson will try to get me lynched when he and Senator Karr ride up here," Ira said evenly.

"You mean he'd do that to protect himself in case you . . ."

"Not just that, Mart." Ira's voice had gone cold, and I wondered what he was thinking. Then he said, "I suppose Clayt knows I'll find out for sure someday that he shot Mary. But he's been trying all along to run everyone off that homestead of Mr. Lamar's."

"You think he wants it?" I asked.

"That's right. Not for himself, though—Karr's the one who would like to own it. He hasn't any deeded land with good water on it, and when fences go up in this country his ranch won't be worth a third as much as the TX. Unless he can get possession of a homestead with good water . . . like the one Lamar filed on at Willow Springs."

What my brother said did make sense, and I remembered my talk with Mr. Karr before the beef roundup. He'd been plenty worried about something then. Still, you had trouble seeing one of the most important men in the territory as a person who'd dirty his hands on the kind of greedy sneakiness Ira was suggesting. But I could believe the Senator might risk quite a bit to further his political career.

"That about Mr. Karr," I said. "How can you be sure it's so?"

"Add up the pieces yourself. You could ask Leah, and I imagine she would tell you the same thing I've said about Karr."

"I'll ask her," I told him, "though I'm learning the truth is sometimes pretty hard to come by. Anyhow, there's a thing you should know about before Karr's bunch get here."

"All right, I'm listening."

"Father told me . . . after he'd been shot."

"Go on, Mart."

I heard the wind come up and whine like a saw on Beaver Rim. "It's about Clayt Paulson," I said. "Father recommended him to the Association as a good man to hire for a stock detective, though I guess that isn't a very accurate name for what Clayt does. Anyhow, it seems that Clayt's father was a friend of the Tyrrells in Texas, and he helped them settle some fighting that started with a neighbor family over maverick calves. One of our uncles and Clayt's dad were killed before it was all over."

Ira's mouth went tight, like it had when we found Mary shot in the cabin at Willow Springs. "I'd heard about the trouble, but I didn't know that Paulson was related to anyone who took part in it. Did he say what Mother thought about it? I wasn't old enough to know what was going on. But I can't believe a woman with her convictions against killing would think very highly of him, when the Tyrrells were partly to blame for the bad feeling."

"No. . . . He didn't mention her one way or the other."

My brother gave a bitter, grating laugh. "I suppose he wouldn't say anything about her. But the story about Clayt's father must be true if he told you so. It sounds like the kind of thing the Tyrrells would get involved in—even the part about Father helping Clayt get a job with the Association. Maybe there was some justice in Clayt's shooting Father like he did."

"What does that mean?" I asked, not liking his last remark at all.

"It's clear if you think a little. Father got the Association to hire Clayt to protect the cattlemen's interests. Now Father finds himself outside the fence he helped to build, and Paulson has given him the same treatment the Association uses on rustlers and troublesome homesteaders. . . ."

"You forget that Father was trying to protect you today," I said angrily. "If he'd let them come after you without doing anything, Clayt wouldn't have had the chance to fire that shot."

"I didn't forget what Father did, Mart. I haven't forgotten what happened to Mary either."

"I guess not, though you'd probably say they balanced each other out."

He nodded, looking down at the pipe that had gone out in his hands. "I could say that."

"But you wouldn't?"

"No," he told me, "I wouldn't." When he looked up, though, the resentment seemed to have been smoothed from his face. "Thanks for riding over here, Mart."

"You'd thank me better by going back to the TX," I said.

But he just smiled, shaking his head. "I can't. . . . I've already told you why. If the word 'law' is going to have any meaning, it has to stand for something more than doing what will best advance your own interests or satisfy your personal hatreds. It has to stand for more than what's best for the Association or for the homesteaders. It has to mean equal justice for everyone in a country, which isn't easy to bring about. The least a person can do is stand up for himself when he hasn't broken any laws or interfered with the rights of any other man."

I said, "You're awfully serious about all this legal business, aren't you?"

"I'm very serious. Maybe someday I'll have a

chance to study law and do more than just talk about improving things. But for now I'm satisfied with letting Senator Karr show himself up for the kind of man he really is—the kind of man who talks like a Supreme Court justice but shows only contempt for legality in his actions. I'm going to let him ride up here with his mob and break the law more clearly than the worst rustler in the valley has done so far."

I didn't think he was doing the smart thing, but he'd made his decision sound final. "All right," I said. "Take care of yourself."

"You too, Mart."

So that was the way I left him, standing in the doorway of the line camp, lighting his pipe, and watching me ride off after Leah. I remember that the scrub pines by the cabin, loaded with snow, were bent like old men by the wind. Bill Donohue had saddled a couple of horses and led them outside the corral as Ira went back into the cabin. I wondered if that might be the last time I would ever see my brother alive. . . .

When I first caught up with Leah, I thought we were in for several hours of riding. I knew she would try to find her father and the men with him, but that might mean riding clear to Willow Springs or on to Stenger's—and maybe still not finding them. Even if we did find them, I didn't figure anything she said would do much to stop them. Especially when her husband had already put a bullet through one man that day.

For a little ways the snow was against our backs. But then we had to skirt a rocky gully below the line camp, and when the snowflakes hit the side of my face I felt the sharp cold for the first time since leaving the cabin. The country was taking on an unreal gray whiteness—a sort of dulling sameness—which usually meant you had to be careful about directions and the lay of the land. Heading off into the snow-swept rangeland, I had a feeling—loneliness maybe— that made me think of Mary Lamar, until not having her around was a kind of aching emptiness as sharp as the wind.

So I decided to concentrate on getting off the rim, even though there were some things I wanted to ask Leah about the Senator and the Willow Springs homestead. I didn't get a chance to ask her, though.

Before we had ridden very far a shot boomed behind us, muffled by moist air and the snow on the ground. Then I heard several more shots in succession—the slapping flat crack of rifles mixed with the softer boom of revolvers—like they'd been fired at someone's command. Then the firing became slower and more disorganized, as though the shooters weren't able to find any definite targets.

Leah jerked around, trying to see what was happening. She couldn't . . . but she guessed it.

"We're too late," she cried, her voice faint against the wind. "Oh, Mart, how could we have missed them?"

I knew it would be easy enough to miss them in the snow—especially if they had ridden along the top of Beaver Rim. It was even possible they'd been watching the cabin, while Leah and I were inside talking, and then waited for us to ride away before closing in. But I didn't tell her that. She'd already reined her horse around, putting him back on the slope we'd just ridden down. You couldn't hurry an animal uphill into the snow and wind, and Leah knew that as well as I did. In some places where the snow had drifted our horses slipped and began feeling their way over hidden rocks with their front feet before moving their hindquarters. Leah helped her sorrel by giving him plenty of rein, but you could see that all the strength had gone from her face, making the bones look frail and delicate like those of a woman who'd been sick a long time. Like Mary's face had looked the last time I saw her. . . .

The shots had stopped before we crested out a short ways from the line camp. There were men lying in the snow behind or beside several of the big rock formations in back of the cabin. You couldn't see anything moving inside the cabin itself, at least not from where we were. The thing I couldn't understand was why the firing had stopped so abruptly, and then, when Leah and I rode far enough to see directly behind the line camp, I saw the answer.

"Who is it?" Leah asked hoarsely, seeing the same thing I did.

I'd known as soon as I caught sight of the figure sitting a tall bay horse and holding the bridles of the two mounts Donohue had saddled as I left the line camp. The rider was wearing heavy winter clothing and an uncreased gray hat, worn over a scarf tied around his head to protect his ears. He was slumped a little, as though it pained him to ride completely erect, but I recognized those long legs and the way the Texas bay carried his head high on the loose reins my father held in one hand.

"Can it really be him?" whispered Leah in the silence. "He seemed too badly hurt to ride up here."

"It's him all right," I said. "He must've done it somehow." The thing I wasn't sure of was what he hoped to accomplish sitting his horse outside the cabin that way. But then I realized he'd already stopped the firing on both sides, if Ira and Bill Donohue had been shooting back at the men in the rocks.

My father had done that, apparently, by riding down to the line camp, leading the two horses he must've caught when they spooked in the first shooting. He'd taken one defeat after another since that spring of '89 started, but seeing him ride down into the gunfire must've reminded the men in the rocks of what a force he had always been in the valley. Paulson was the only one of them who could've taken a shot at him—the others would've been too startled or cowed to do anything but hold their fire and watch the tall old man walk his horse slowly down through the snow while the firing stopped.

You had to admire him for it, shot up like he was. And despite everything bad I'd heard or thought about him myself, I couldn't help being glad he was there . . . and that I had seen him sitting his horse beside the cabin where my brother and Donohue were trapped.

"You best ride out of the way, Martin," Moses Ethridge shouted down from the rock. "We ain't in the mood to talk no more."

I had looked for the Senator to challenge Father, but then it occurred to me that neither Karr nor Clayt Paulson had told the others about the shooting at our ranch. If they had, it might've stopped the whole business before the "posse" got much beyond the TX.

Father's voice was stronger than I would have expected. "Don't talk then, Mose!" he called. "You boys know you're doing the wrong thing, and talking won't make it smell any sweeter."

I heard Bobby Dutton begin to laugh drunkenly. "You do look heroic, you know,

Martin," he cried, "but what if we were to hang you too?" Someone told him to shut up, and then a little quarrel broke out among Karr's men. It finally died away, while Father sat silently and the snowflakes licked down into his face.

"You going to move out of the way?" Ethridge shouted again. "We'll give them fellows in the cabin a chance to give up, but after that we plan to take 'em the hard way."

"It'll save the trouble of a trip to court *either* way!" someone in the rocks called. "They can have all the say they want once we get some rope around their necks. . . ."

"Ride on while you got the chance," hollered Seth Daniels. "You wouldn't give a damn what happened here if it wasn't your boy mixed up in it."

There was some more arguing among the men, and Leah whispered, "I better try to find Father up there. Maybe I can make him listen to me."

"Just a minute," I told her. "I'm not even sure he's still with them."

Before she had a chance to say anything else my father began to play his hand. And I won't ever be able to forget what he did in those next few minutes on Beaver Rim. Maybe it was what his whole life had been building up for—I don't know. More likely, the moment just came and he was ready for it, the same way he'd been ready for all the troubles of his times. All of them except my mother dying and Ira leaving the TX. . . .

As Leah and I watched, Father turned his horse around and paused, his stern face tilted up momentarily toward the rocks. "I'm taking these two men into Lander myself," he called. "If you've got any evidence against them you can take it there and try to convict them. But if you're thinking of taking shots at them when they come from this cabin you're going to have to kill me pretty well too."

There was silence . . . followed by shouts and curses from Karr's men, but nobody fired a shot. If there had been some gunfire then, I don't think my father would've had a chance. But there wasn't . . . and he'd already started riding, his back to the rocks, and led the horses around to the door of the line camp. I saw him draw the Winchester from his saddle scabbard and hold it across the pommel of his saddle—though it wasn't pointed at the cabin. When he spoke to the two men inside his voice didn't carry up to where Leah and I were.

Then the quiet became complete. There was no movement in the cabin. The horses in the pole corral had calmed down and stood with their rumps to the storm. The men with Karr were just watching my father, until gray sky and snow seemed to blanket everything and kill all sound. I had the feeling you get after watching snowflakes too long as they fall toward you when you have to ride into a storm—heavy-eyed and a little sleepy, yet still knowing how dangerous it is to feel that way.

I'd gone two days and a night without any real sleep, and waiting those few moments to see what Ira and Bill Donohue would do, I had difficulty keeping my eyes focused. The cabin began fading farther and farther back into the snow—then suddenly jumped closer with my father huge and swollen out of proportion, before my vision quit playing tricks. Ira arguing with Father, the nester Volanski butchering that beef in his shed, Clayt Paulson and Father riding together along Cottonwood Creek, that ugly turkey buzzard hunting for something dead while circling above Split Rock, Old Man Lamar's gray eyes turning hard as he spoke about Paulson staying off his land, and then Mary holding tight to me under the willows where we swam in the Sweetwater—they all were alive and haunting in my head like pieces of dreams. Until finally there was only Mary whispering something, her mouth by my ear, but no matter how hard I tried I couldn't make out what she was telling me. . . .

Leah brought me back, saying, "They're coming out, Mart!"

I shook my head to clear it, seeing then the two figures in the doorway . . . watching them move out deliberately to the horses. They weren't in view of the cattlemen yet, but already Father had sidled his bay right up behind their mounts. Ira and the other man swung up into their saddles, looking small now against the snow.

A shout went up from the men with Mr. Karr when the three riders appeared in full view just beyond the cabin. I could hear threats from the rocks, and I waited for the first shot, feeling almost like I was one of the three horsemen riding at a slow walk away from the line camp. And then they were a quarter of the way across the open ground that ended in a protecting ledge and some more scrubby pines. "Maybe they can make it," Leah cried softly, and as she said it I heard a voice shouting down—almost a scream that could only belong to Mr. Karr. "Stop them, you men! Can't you see they're getting away?"

"Why don't you take a shot at 'em, Senator?"

Moses Ethridge swore and yelled at somebody to bring up their horses from the other side of the rim, but I didn't hear anyone answer him. Another voice shouted, "Looks like he's really going to take them to Lander. You can't shoot him for that, Senator!"

"I'm in charge here," answered Karr, "and I want them stopped. Where's Clayt?"

I heard a man call for Paulson, but as far as I could tell there was no reply. That bothered me for some reason, though I knew the confusion among the cattlemen was helping Father, who now was two thirds of the way across the exposed whiteness.

Watching the three clumped-together figures put their horses up a little incline that marked the last few minutes they would ride in sight of Karr's "posse," I felt like something bad was sure to happen. My throat was dry and aching from the cold, yet I began to feel sweat on my skin under the heavy clothes. I remember saying over and over to myself, "Nothing's going to happen. . . ."

When the shot came I flinched hard, but still I saw a tiny spume of snow kicked up just to one side of my father's horse. The report echoed dully across the cleft in the rim. Jerking my head around, I saw the bit of smoke above where the rifle had been fired. I turned back, expecting other shots to follow at once, but instead a new argument broke out among Karr's men.

For what seemed like an awfully long time I watched the three riders make their way slowly toward the rock and trees that would give them protection. And at last, without another shot being fired, they disappeared behind the ledge.

For a few moments I was afraid to try to speak. My heart was hammering, and I realized the muscles in my back were tensed up as though I'd been expecting a bullet myself. While I sat there trying to tell what the cattlemen in the rocks were arguing about Leah grew restless.

"I'm going up there, Mart," she said.

"All right," I told her. "If you can get Mr. Karr and Clayt to act sensibly, there may not be any more trouble. I better ride along with Father and Ira."

She nodded, still looking worried, and heeled her horse up toward the rock formations. I waited until I heard her call out to Karr, and then I started Blacky around the line camp. I hadn't got much past it when a six-shooter fired, sounding a little faint from down the rim, and right along with the soft echo came a second report. That was followed immediately by a final shot—making only three in all—sharp with a heavy flat ring to it. Even at a distance I recognized that last sound, for I'd heard the same report more times than I could count and fired rifles of that bore myself—a .38-55 like Ira's single-shot Ballard and my father's Winchester. Then it was quiet except for the little squeaks Blacky's hoofs made in the snow and the noise of his blowing. . . .

One question kept running through my head, and that was whether Clayt was with Mr. Karr in the rocks on the rim. I looked around as the Senator, Leah, Moses Ethridge, Rankin, and the others came riding down toward me.

And Clayt Paulson wasn't with them.

Chapter 21

We found Paulson's body sprawled in the snow, his buffalo overcoat making him look like a dark hide thrown down carelessly against the whiteness. His horse stood at the edge of the clearing with the bridle reins dragging. The tracks made by the buckskin as he bolted off were already filling in with fresh snow. Something dark glistened in Clayt's outstretched, ungloved right hand, and when we dismounted beside him I saw it was the .44 Colt he'd always took so much pride in.

Finn Rankin was the one who rolled the stock detective over and opened the overcoat so we all saw where the bullet—fired by my father or Ira—had passed through the pocket of Clayt Paulson's wool shirt at about heart level. When Rankin had taken the six-shooter from Clayt's hand, he rubbed the wet blue barrel thoughtfully against his mackinaw for a moment before clicking the cylinder around.

"Paulson shot twice at somethin' himself," Finn said then, as if it wasn't of much interest. "Ain't like him to miss, though a .44 don't hold up too well against a rifle at any distance."

The men grouped around. Gloves were taken off and cigarettes rolled with cold fingers. Some of the riders squatted down on their heels as was their custom when thinking something over. Behind them, tired horses breathed noisily and clinked their bits occasionally when shaking their heads. But where we gathered around Clayt Paulson the air was quiet and heavy, so that a man's voice sounded unnaturally loud. . . .

"Our rustlers have left a clear enough trail," said Mr. Karr, who still was sitting his horse. "If one of you will go back with my daughter and poor Clayt's body, the rest of us should have no difficulty finding the men we want."

A few of the cattlemen stirred and looked back at where the honyocker Volanski was shivering numbly on the horse my brother had been accused of stealing and selling without a bill of sale. I saw Leah move around him to get near the Senator. She seemed very cold and tired from the last few hours in the wet snow, and when she spoke she had trouble controlling her voice.

"You can't mean that, Father," she said. "What did you expect would happen when you started shooting at Ira and the man with him in the cabin?"

Karr frowned deeply. "I know you are upset, Leah, but this isn't a matter for emotions any more. We are after justice here now. Clayt's murderers will have a chance to give their side of the argument . . . I promise you that."

"Justice?" Leah glanced around at the men. "How can you say the word with a straight face after the things that have gone on the last few months? Was the hanging of that woman at Bothwell a part of your justice? Or killing those sheep the Mexican was herding for Ira? I think you should use another word for what you're after."

The Senator made a stiff gesture toward the body in the snow, as if he was ending a speech. "Do you think I have liked all of this any more than you or these cattlemen have? But someone has to take the responsibility for stopping unprincipled thieves like those who have killed your husband."

Leah faltered, her eyes turning uncertainly to me, so that Karr thought he'd gained an advantage over her. "This thing isn't your concern, Leah," he said more softly. "It isn't a woman's business. I think we could prevail upon Mart to take you back to the TX while we see this thing through."

Finn and the others were still non-committal, but I'd had all I could take. "Listen to me," I told Mr. Karr, my voice coming out stronger than I'd expected. "This has gone far enough. All of you decided a long time ago that Ira was guilty. The only way he's helped Donohue or any rustlers is by not reporting their whereabouts to the Association. That makes him guilty as hell, don't it?"

"I think you've said enough," the Senator told

me sharply. "Naturally you want to defend your own brother, but it appears clear to me that he and Donohue have just finished killing a man."

"I didn't notice you being worried about Ira getting killed in the cabin a while ago," I said.

Karr turned to Moses Ethridge and Bobby Dutton for support. "That was not the same thing at all. Clayt was a lawman doing his job to protect our stock, and your brother and William Donohue were known troublemakers. We had no choice but to take action against them. We did not know your father would choose to obstruct our efforts and help bring about Clayt's death. God knows we tried hard enough to reason with him back at the TX."

"Well said," Bobby Dutton spoke up, "well said, Senator. I for one am pledged to justice for our friend Paulson. Let's hang the whole lot who were in that cabin, as well as this Volanski fellow, and be done with it."

I didn't wait to hear what Ethridge might say. "Why don't you tell your friends about the way Clayt shot Mary Lamar?" I asked Karr. "And about what happened this morning at the ranch when you and Clayt stayed back to talk with Father alone?"

The Senator was so astonished that he couldn't answer at first. Then I saw him straighten in his saddle and his face become even more determined as he realized I'd actually seen the way Father was shot, not just him and Clayt riding off afterward. It looked to me like he'd already decided he could smooth everything over without much trouble. After all, I was pretty much of a kid, while he was a lawyer and politician known all over the territory. And what bothered me even more was knowing he really might be able to convince the cattlemen that Clayt hadn't tried to kill Mary and my father.

Moses Ethridge glanced at me before turning back to Karr. "The boy here says you've got something to tell us. Let's hear it, Senator."

"Are you taking orders from me or a Tyrrell boy?" Karr asked coldly.

"Neither just now."

"I see that," snapped Karr. "I have nothing to tell you, and I suspect the boy has nothing worth while to say, either."

"You're wrong as hell," I told him. "This morning when you and Paulson stayed behind to talk with my father I saw everything that happened from the saddle shed. There was an argument and Clayt pulled a six-shooter and fired. Father was unarmed, so Paulson wasn't taking much of a risk."

The men muttered to one another in surprise. It was pretty plain that they didn't like not hearing about this before. "Is that what happened, Senator?" Ethridge asked.

Karr didn't answer, and I could tell the men

had expected him to deny what I'd said. Even Bobby Dutton kept quiet this time—though it could've been that the brandy was working out of him by now. Most of the cattlemen stood around stiffly, their eyes red from the wind as they stared at the Senator.

Moses Ethridge blew his nose slowly and then asked, "Clayt the one shot that Lamar girl, Senator?"

Karr was gazing off toward Beaver Rim as though he might find something more to his liking there. "Apparently," he murmured, shrugging.

"You told him to?"

The Senator turned back and pulled himself erect in his saddle. "I am not on trial here, men. I did not shoot the half-breed girl."

"Was it Paulson took a shot at Mr. Tyrrell this morning?" asked Finn Rankin.

This time Karr himself faltered, breathing heavily . . . before nodding. "Tyrrell tried to pull me from my horse, but Clayt protected me. That was all."

"No, not quite all," said Leah. "A year or so ago my husband became involved in some bad debts in Cheyenne, and Father settled them for him. After that, Clayt would do anything my father asked him to do. So old Mr. Lamar was shot down and made to look like a rustler. And then his daughter was shot when she was mistaken for Ira Tyrrell, who was helping her hold a homestead with good water that Father wanted. This morning it was Martin Tyrrell who would've died if Clayt's horse hadn't been frightened."

"That's enough, Leah!" Karr shouted. "You're tired and hysterical. These men sympathize with what you have been through, but these wild accusations aren't helping anything. I'm guilty of nothing except doing my duty to protect the horses, cattle, and land of honest men from unscrupulous outlaws."

"Ira isn't an outlaw," I told him, "and Mr. Lamar never branded any more mavericks than the Two-Bar-K or the other outfits did."

"I think my opinion on that is worth more than yours," the Senator said.

"Why didn't you or Clayt tell us what he done to Mr. Tyrrell?" asked Moses Ethridge.

"I didn't think it wise to bring up the subject just when we were closing in on the rustlers. Perhaps I was wrong not to have mentioned it."

"You damn sure was wrong!" said Rankin. "I suppose that was why you was dead set against letting Mr. Tyrrell take those fellows into Lander for a trial. Clayt's itchy trigger finger would've come in for some discussion there, I reckon."

"Now look here, Finn," Karr began. "Someone had to make the decisions. It was not an easy job for me either."

"The hell you say, Senator," Rankin told him. "We all would've been in bad trouble if Martin Tyrrell had got killed by a posse we was part of."

"That's so," agreed one of the Thompson brothers sullenly. "I never would've rode up here if I'd knowed Paulson shot Mr. Tyrrell that way. Would you, Mose?"

Ethridge frowned and shook his head. "Ain't likely I would've. Paulson must've had a lot of poison in him to do a thing like that. Maybe him shooting that 'breed girl was an accident, but why would somebody want him to bushwhack old Lamar, anyways?"

"I'll tell you, Mr. Ethridge," Leah said clearly. "So my father could take credit for getting rid of the homesteaders and other people who opposed him on the Sweetwater—the so-called rustlers, who might or might not be dishonest. Of course he also wanted to gain some good water at Willow Springs before he sold the Two-Bar-K. But if you knew my father like I've finally come to know him, you would see how badly he wants to make a reputation for himself. Next winter he'll be helping the homesteaders if they have the most votes. Is it the governorship or a place in the United States Senate you want for yourself when Wyoming becomes a state, Father?"

So there it is, I thought, remembering my talk with Mr. Karr at his ranch before the fall roundup. He'd hinted at his ambitions then, and now Leah had thrown them into his face before the whole valley. I thought he'd be angry or try to deny the accusations she'd made, but I was wrong. I guess he did have a sort of twisted pride that kept him from stepping back now that the cattlemen were balking at his orders and Leah was questioning his very character as a man.

And watching Mr. Karr as things started to go against him, I knew he would never admit to anyone that he'd destroyed several lives along with his own integrity. Instead he gestured at the men with one arm held as stiff and threatening as a sword. "I have given years of my life to this territory and the Stock Association," he said. "Martin Tyrrell belonged to it reluctantly, but I helped give the Association power in the territorial government."

The Senator paused dramatically and seemed to be daring anyone to contradict him. He had reined his horse right up beside Paulson's body in the clearing, and as he began to speak again little skiffs of snow were being blown down like white birds from the branches of the pine trees behind him. "Where would you be without the Association to protect what you own? Where would you be without detectives like Clayt Paulson to put some fear into stock thieves? I can tell you. You would already be broken men without a damn cow or acre of land in Wyoming. . . . So the thanks I get is having you all turn against me when I try to drive the rustlers from your very doorsteps. Turn against me, by God, when I want to find the murderers of this man who helped all of you hold onto this valley. If I have done anything wrong, then you stand just as guilty. Isn't that so?"

No one answered, which seemed to encourage him. "Leah is right that I plan to be an important man in this state!" Karr shouted. "Why shouldn't I? I have taken the responsibility for accomplishing things that none of you had guts enough to do. Is this the thanks I get?"

"Now wait a bit, Senator," Moses Ethridge tried to put in.

"I'm not finished! You men will hear me out whether you like it or not. You have a choice to make here and now. Either you follow me and bring back Clayt's murderers or you lose the protection of the Association."

Mr. Karr's lips were clipping out the words under his military mustache. I had the feeling he'd handled men this same way as an officer during the war, only these men weren't in uniform and more than twenty years had passed since the fighting. Still, you had to say he had a desperate persuasiveness about him. I guess you had to admire that even if you hated him. The men stirred a little—they were worried all right.

"Well?" he demanded. "Which will it be? I can tell you that if you desert me now I will never use my influence to help a single man of you. And I assure you I will have influence."

When Karr said that I took a deep breath and stepped up by his horse. "He won't have any more influence than any of the rest of us," I said. "My father was the first man to ranch along the river, and he helped most of you get started. As for Ira, he never stole a thing from any of you."

The Senator jerked his horse around in front of me. He was really angry now—you could tell from the way his voice went high-pitched and wild. "I won't hear any more lies from a Tyrrell!" he cried, and in the next moment I felt his riding quirt come stinging down across my shoulder. Leah screamed, and I jerked back from him, pulling the old six-shooter from the pocket of my mackinaw. The hammer clicked loud in the cold. The Senator saw the barrel level up straight at his chest, and his hand holding the quirt for another blow came down slowly.

"You'll hear me," I said. "You'll listen until I finish, Mr. Karr. This dead man here was the son of my father's best friend in Texas. That's right. . . . I didn't know the whole story until Father told me this morning, but I imagine there are still folks in the brush country who can tell you why the Tyrrells were in debt to Clayt's dad."

I saw the expressions on those faces in front of me shift a little in surprise at what I was saying. Karr was caught off guard too. "So you can figure my father doesn't feel very good about what has happened," I said. "And for all any of us know he may have been the one who had to kill Clayt. I heard the shots, and it was Clayt who fired first. If my father did have to shoot him, you can figure he thought plenty hard before he pulled the trigger."

The cattlemen looked silently at me and then shifted their eyes over to Karr. Finn Rankin took a final drag at his cigarette and flipped the brown butt thoughtfully into the snow. No one spoke.

"Another thing you ought to think about," I went on, "is that Ira and Bill Donohue are being taken to Lander. If any of you have charges against either man you can make them there, like my father said. And if you've got something to say about Clayt Paulson getting killed, you better ride into Lander and say it."

I took a step back and lowered the six-shooter away from Karr before letting the hammer down. "I guess I'm finished now," I said. "But I'll have some cards to play if you try to stop my father from taking Ira and Donohue to Lander."

The men continued to stare at the Senator. "Hell," Rankin finally said, "it'd be too late to catch up with them now anyways."

I looked at Moses Ethridge, who pulled out his red handkerchief and wiped his nose hard. "Court in Lander wouldn't convict any of 'em. Can't say Paulson was a great friend of mine neither. Anyhow, it's too damn cold up here." He straightened suddenly and stalked off for his horse. Then others started to move away from Paulson's body.

Karr looked as if he didn't believe what he was seeing. He began shouting something about Volanski. Ethridge grunted and dug into his pocket for his knife. He didn't look at the Senator as he cut the rope from Volanski's hands and told him to get the hell out of the Sweetwater country.

One of the Thompson brothers brought Paulson's buckskin over and tied the detective's body across the saddle. "You and Mrs. Paulson better ride on back with us," he told Karr. "It'll be close to dark before we get much past Stenger's. Might be more snow, too . . . you can't tell on a damn day like this."

The Senator just sat there grim-faced on his horse, while the men mounted up and started riding back for the line camp, where the trail led off the rim. The wind had died down, and you could hear cold saddle leather loosening as the horses moved slowly across the clearing. Then Leah started her horse after the others.

"Are you coming with us, Mart?" she called back to me.

"I reckon not," I told her. "I'll cut straight across for the TX."

"All right," she said.

So I sat there watching Mr. Karr stare at the

long spot Clayt's body had melted in the snow. He licked his chapped lips, looking like a tired old man who'd been out in the cold too long and suddenly wanted a warm place to lie down. I couldn't feel sorry for him, though. Then Karr looked up at me, his eyes not angry or hateful— just empty and unbelieving, a broken man's eyes—and spurred jerkily at his horse until the animal moved away. I watched the strung-out riders walk tired horses into the scrubby trees at the edge of the clearing. And then in the gray afternoon and silence it seemed like they hadn't ever been there at all. . . .

Chapter 22

A week later Cookie and I went to Lander to attend the coroner's inquest into Clayt Paulson's death. During the first part of the hearing neither Wallace Karr nor the Association lawyers tried to discredit Father's testimony that he had shot the detective in self-defense up on Beaver Rim. I don't think any of the cattlemen with Karr—or the Senator himself—wanted to admit publicly that they'd been "out to get" at least three men that day. And the Senator described only half of what had actually happened, so that even now you'll find a few people who will tell you Wallace Karr drove the rustlers from the Sweetwater without firing a shot.

When Ira was called on to testify, though, it was a different story. I thought he'd have something to say about Paulson and the way Karr's bunch had attacked him and Bill Donohue at the line camp. And I was right.

My brother started off by telling about what had happened at the cabin and how Father had ridden in to stop the shooting and get him and Donohue away. He said Clayt Paulson must have been working down toward the line camp from the north and not known the three of them were riding out. Clayt had been very surprised to see them, he thought, and was still mounted on the buckskin with his rifle in a saddle scabbard. A moment later he had turned his horse to face the three men and drawn his six-shooter, firing first at Martin Tyrrell, who carried his Winchester across the front of his saddle and might have seemed at the moment to be the most dangerous man. It was long range for a .44 Colt, and Paulson's first shot had missed. My brother said he had pulled his Ballard from its scabbard then. But as he was trying to take aim his horse had sidled around, which was about the moment Paulson had fired a second shot . . . at him this time and, Ira thought, not missing by far. That was when my father had shot Clayt Paulson in the chest with his .38-55 Winchester, the bullet striking, as the coroner had already testified, very near the Association detective's heart. The frightened buckskin had bolted away from the falling man. . . .

"That was the way Paulson died," Ira told the coroner's jury, "but I would hope what happened on Beaver Rim will serve to keep the same thing from occurring again."

I won't forget the look of the cattlemen and their lawyers in the polished hearing room as my brother spoke that way to them—men who had never thought of themselves as being wrong in any of their actions on the Sweetwater or in the Association's Cheyenne offices. They sat there—in their shining shoes, fine suits with only the top coat buttons fastened, white boiled shirts, and cravats tied in the latest fashion—and stared at Ira like ranchers who had just noticed some new kind of locoweed growing in their best pasture. But the Lander men that made up the jury were listening with plenty of interest.

"Senator Karr was leading a mob that might easily have murdered three men," Ira went on, "and the Association as well as Clayt Paulson stood behind him. If he feels no guilt himself, he should be even more guilty in the eyes of others. And if the Association can say it feels blameless in the killing and ruining of honest men as well as stock thieves, it should be tolerated even less than the Clayt Paulsons and the organized rustlers operating from places like the Hole-in-the-Wall. In my own mind, though, the question isn't which of us here are to blame for the trouble on the Sweetwater. . . . Rather it is whether we have the integrity and self-respect to see that the trouble ended when Paulson died up there in the snow."

My brother sat down then, among objections from the Cheyenne lawyers, and he wasn't asked for any more testimony. Several of the men in that hearing room weren't very pleased, and the Senator's face was set so hard with anger and strain that a person might guess he'd been frostbitten. My father's expression didn't change a bit, and he sat perfectly straight in the varnished wooden chair like it was a slick-fork saddle. But the thing I noticed most was that he still looked as proud and unashamed as he had before Ira testified.

The coroner's jury ruled the shooting was self-defense, and there was no trial. And even more damning to Wallace Karr, no one filed charges of any sort against Donohue or my brother. . . .

When he first came back to the ranch after the inquest, Father never talked with me about Paulson, the Senator, or Ira. But he stopped the heavy drinking that had gone on ever since my brother left the TX. He was more like his old self now, though Doc Parker told me his health had been broken by the gunshot wound and that long ride he'd made through the snowstorm while taking Ira and Bill Donohue from the line camp into Lander. I could see for myself that physically he was becoming weaker rather than stronger. I knew he hated weakness, especially in himself. And yet he seemed untroubled for long periods which were occasionally broken by black spells, when he kept to himself as though some grim fight was going on inside him.

I understood something about black spells myself, for Cookie had told me of a talk he'd had with Ira outside the hearing room in Lander. My brother had told him he was planning to take a job in the office of a Lander attorney and rent a place for Mary in town. After Cookie left me, probably knowing I'd take it hard, I felt as I had one April when I swam in the Sweetwater during runoff and the current caught me. I'd been pulled under and thrown downstream so swiftly the breath went out of me in one choking, cold slap of murky river water. Once I saw a team of horses swept down that same way, the buckboard twisting over and dragging them off their feet, but I'd been lucky and gotten thrown near enough the bank to catch a willow stab. Now, though, I felt numb and helpless against something I didn't know how to fight. When I heard nothing from Mary in the days that followed I tried to put her and Ira out of my mind—and didn't succeed very well.

A few weeks after he'd returned from Lander

my father took me to the ranch office and started telling me things he thought I should know about the TX. It was after midnight when he finished and sat back in his chair with his bad leg stretched out before him on a stool. He gave me a cigar and lit one for himself.

"I reckon you could run the place all right, Mart," he said almost gently. "Better than I did, maybe."

I watched his face, thinking I'd see some bitterness there, but I didn't.

"Cookie tells me your brother is planning to make a career of the law," he went on carefully. "He'll never want any part of this ranch, and I was wrong wanting to change him. Your mother always said I had a failing that way. Once it's gotten half grown you can't change a cow, or a man either. Or a country. . . ."

He eased his leg to a more comfortable angle and absently flipped ash from his cigar into the brass spittoon. "I've done a few things I'm not very proud of, Mart, but I've been paid back for them one way or another. Like with Ira and Clayt . . . Ella Watson . . . and your mother."

"What about her?" I asked him.

His eyes, mottled gray like pale turquoise, were seeing something else when he looked at me. "Your mother? She was a fine woman with good breeding and strong feelings about right and wrong. When your uncle was murdered she tried to stop me from paying back blood in more blood. It was the only thing she asked that I wouldn't have given to her, and the killings that happened afterwards while she was in a family way made her a person I didn't know at all. I was young enough to be falsely proud, and I didn't try to see her side of it. I went off with a trail herd to start the ranch here, leaving her expecting you and wondering if I would come back. You were born all right, but she died. . . . Sometimes I've tried to blame you for something I felt guilty about. . . ."

He let the cigar die out without relighting it. "When Clayt shot at Ira up on the rim that afternoon I knew someone had to kill him. Your brother had reason enough, but I couldn't let him settle a thing I'd started myself seventeen years ago in Texas and made worse here on the Sweetwater. Your mother was right, Mart, and I've no one but myself to blame for any of what's happened. . . . I reckon all this makes a sorry story—just as sorry as what Wallace Karr did trying to make Ira out to be a rustler."

"Maybe so," I said.

He nodded, frowning deeply for a moment with his eyes squinted up as though he was facing north again on some hot, dusty cattle trail. "I made a ranch here without anybody's help, but I ruined my own life doing it. The country here and in Texas was all open for the taking once the

Indians were gone. I took my share of the range and tried to make of it what I thought I wanted. But I reckon the country made something different of me too, and so I'm paying now for the sorry way I left your mother that last time in Texas . . . the thing I did by getting the Association to hire Clayt Paulson . . . the headstrong way I've treated Ira and you. . . ."

Then he said, "You could sell this place and get a fresh start somewhere else. I wouldn't blame you for doing it."

I thought of all the trouble I'd seen at the home ranch, on our range along the river, in Willow Springs Canyon, up on Beaver Rim. None of it made a pretty story, any more than our country or way of life was pretty. Or what Father had just told me about himself and my mother. . . . But a man had to start in somewhere and try to make things better than before, didn't he? I wasn't sure.

"Anyhow, Mart," I heard Father say, "I'm not asking you to keep the TX. I reckon you'll know the right thing to do when the time comes. I was lucky to have you and Ira both for sons, though I've been too damn proud and selfish to say it before. Someday you can tell Ira I said that . . . if you think he'd be interested in hearing it."

That night must've been the first and last time he admitted the mistakes he had made and what they'd cost him. And I knew it hadn't been easy for him to tell me he'd been wrong. We both sat there for a long time, and then I recall very clearly that he reached toward me with one of his calloused, rope-hardened hands. . . . And I shook hands with him before leaving the office. . . .

After that his grimness and dark moods were gone—or else he hid them from me—and whenever the weather was good he walked confidently around the headquarters and corrals, using the crutch he'd got in Rawlins when his leg began troubling him. In the evenings he would often call Cookie to the front room, and I'd hear them talking about the old days in Texas and trail drives they'd made or heard about. One morning in January when Father didn't come to breakfast Cookie and I found him in his room, where he'd gotten himself dressed for the day's work before he died in the same uncomplaining, abrupt way he had lived. . . .

Cookie and I did the needed things together. My father looked larger than life, resting on his bunk with black boots touching the footboard. We stood there without talking—I don't know whether it was for minutes or much longer.

"I'll nail a box together for your dad," Cookie said at last. "It won't be much, but he never cared where he unrolled his soogans anyways."

"All right," I told him, and in the early afternoon, when I'd helped the cook as much as I could, I saddled Blacky and rode up toward

Beaver Rim until my head cleared and my body got tired out.

So it was finished, I thought later while coming down off the rim. Or was Father's dying the beginning of a different way of life rather than the ending to an old way? Maybe both, I figured, though I wanted time to mull it over more carefully.

The afternoon had cleared off blue and cold, with a false warm brightness from a low winter sky already dropping toward the South Pass end of the Wind River Mountains. That was one direction I could ride if I wanted to leave the Sweetwater country and the TX a long ways behind me. On beyond South Pass was the Union Pacific Railroad and trains going east or west. Or I could ride instead along the mountains toward Jackson's Hole . . . or turn up north for the Owl Creek Mountains—through a desolate sweep of badlands fit only for outlaws and locoed wolfers—on a trail that would take me into Montana or Canada. Anyway, it would be easy enough to leave the TX the same way Ira had. . . .

Blacky began walking faster as soon as we sighted the river—pale and lonely-looking with its slaty skim of old ice. Somehow I felt I might meet Pete Rodriguez with his wagon and sheep moving along the far bank, but I knew inside me that was only a sign of how tired I was. Rodriguez would probably never get any sheep of his own. Even then, he wouldn't dare show up in the Sweetwater Valley with them.

As it turned out, I was right. I never saw the little Mexican again, and the next time I passed by Stenger's, Jenny had left too. I was glad of that, in a way, because I wouldn't have wanted her to lose the life from her warm brown body—the way Ella Watson had when they pushed her swinging off to die against a lariat noose. It might have happened to Jenny, along with Jack Stenger, because there was plenty of bad feelings around from the time of those hangings at Bothwell until several years after the Association hired Texas gunmen and invaded Johnson County to drive "rustlers" from the Powder River. That was in '92, and I was too busy with my own work to stick my nose into it one way or the other.

Of course a lot of people will still claim the Association was right and that Clayt, like Tom Horn, was a great man of the kind we needed in those days when Wyoming was a territory of grass, open range, and large ranches sprawled over the best grazing land in unowned claims as big as whole counties. I guess you'll always find men who think they can solve all their problems by just joining an Association and hiring a Clayt Paulson. . . .

Not long after Paulson was killed the Association began trying to make him sound like a heroic lawman who'd been murdered by stock thieves and outlaws. But Leah Karr wrote a letter, published in newspapers across the territory, in which she called him a hired killer and told the true story of his death. She went down to Denver after that, and I think she was always happier there than in Wyoming.

Once I stopped to see Leah, after she'd married a well-known Colorado politician, and she was just as beautiful as ever. When she first came to Denver, Leah told me, she'd hoped Ira would write to her or make a visit there. But he hadn't, and she said her marriage gave her everything she'd ever wanted. I think that was almost true.

The Senator ran for the United States Congress in the first election after Wyoming became a state in 1890. He wasn't elected, even though he'd sold the Two-Bar-K by then and started up his law office in Rawlins. I think too many people recalled him being with Clayt Paulson when my father was shot at the TX . . . and what Leah had said about him that afternoon when Clayt was killed on Beaver Rim. I always remember Wallace Karr as he looked when Finn Rankin and the Association ranchers refused to hunt down Ira, Bill Donohue, and my father. I suppose it was the first time his word hadn't been taken as law. At any rate he left Wyoming after the election, and no one complained when he pulled up stakes. Maybe the new state had started to outgrow Senator Karr and his kind. At least that's what I'd like to believe. . . .

But that afternoon in January after Father died, I wasn't thinking much of Clayt or the Karrs. I kept hearing my father and Ira—their quarrels, my talks with Father at the ranch and with Ira by his corral at Willow Springs after he'd started living on Lamar's homestead. As Blacky jog-trotted through crisp snow lumpy with sage, I thought over the things they had believed and stood up for. Though he'd talked of my selling the TX, Father would want me to take hold with the ranch and run it the same way he had—like his own father and brothers had done with land in Texas—holding and building it with sweat, a Winchester, and blood if necessary. And probably bloodshed had been necessary in his time.

I knew it wouldn't have seemed necessary to Ira, though. He'd warned my father that the Association was aggravating the tension between homesteaders and established cattlemen, and he had thought we were trying to graze more land than anyone had a right to hold. So Father had died in part from their quarrel. . . . And what was I going to do with the ranch that had come between them?

When Blacky reached the flats of wild-hay meadow where the river straightened, I saw our cattle scattered out to feed. The wind had swept snow from patches of the dry grass, and the reddish Shorthorns were in good condition. It would be a different story in February and early March. But maybe, like Ira and I had planned, a man could work up more hay land and irrigate from Longs Creek and the Sweetwater: By putting up hay for emergencies, cutting the number of head on the TX, and breeding for better quality cattle, I might not need as much land as Father had tried to control. Already there was talk of barbed-wire fencing in our country, and it had been used for years all the way up from Texas to the Laramie Plains. I didn't like it, but I could see where it would put a stop to some of the quarreling over grazing land and mavericks.

I rode through the cattle slowly. Gray clouds behind me were coloring up with orange and streaks of purple. I heard a bull bellowing in the white willows ahead and the bawls of cows sounding close and then echoing far away. In the morning I could catch fresh horses and pack some supplies. I could just start riding away, and there would be time later to think about selling the TX.

Then I was on high ground where I could see the ranch buildings and pole corrals. I stopped Blacky and sat there, thinking about the work it had taken to haul logs and put a headquarters and bunkhouse where there had been only sage and a lonesome wind. I thought of my father standing bareheaded on the porch of our ranch, while the men from the valley who had been his friends accused him of being disloyal to the Association. Remembering that and the way he'd faced Karr's "posse" again in the snow on the rim, I felt the last of the resentment I'd built up against him go dead inside me. He was no longer—as he'd once been—my ideal of everything a man should be. But on that one day in November when his whole world began pulling him down like quicksand in a river crossing, I'd finally seen the same kind of will and strength that had gone into a brief generation of trail drivers, outlaws, lawmen, and pioneer ranchers.

Maybe being strong enough to build and hold a ranch in Wyoming wasn't enough in 1889 to bring him much honor, but I knew that right or wrong he'd been more of a man in some ways than I or the small ranchers like Finn Rankin could ever be. And that I had to accept him, just like he was, as my father. . . .

I kept sitting there on Blacky while I watched the night move down the bluff above the river and thought of Ira and Father facing each other in the spring-warm, dusty corral those ten months past. They were so different in what they believed that sometimes I'd had trouble seeing how they both belonged to the same family. Maybe it was time more than anything else that had separated them, though, for in standing on their own feet, in spite of everything, they were both Tyrrells. . . . And suddenly I thought, *So am I.*

I drew cold air into my lungs and all at once felt very clearheaded. I wasn't my father and I wasn't Ira. I was Mart Tyrrell, and I owned a ranch in Wyoming Territory. That was all, but that might be enough. The next few years would tell the rest of the story, I guessed. And after a while I started Blacky down the trail leading to the TX headquarters.

A kerosene lamp lighted up the windows in the bunkhouse as I heeled Blacky into a lope. The winter rangeland disappeared beneath the old gelding's hoofs, and the ranch buildings loomed up in the night, as solid and familiar as Father's shape at the head of our table each evening at mealtime. . . .

When I had unsaddled and fed Blacky, I found Cookie waiting for me at the corral gate. "While you was gone I took care of most everything left to do," he said as his twisted fingers whittled on a plug of tobacco.

I told him I'd been riding up toward Beaver Rim to think things out.

He grunted and spit his old tobacco into the dead snow. "Yeh? Don't surprise me none," he said curtly. "You stayin' or sellin' out?"

"I'm staying, Cookie," I told him.

He nodded, but then I saw him look closely at me. "Runnin' things the same way your dad did?"

"No. . . . My way."

"Figured as much. Shows I was wrong about you."

"How's that?" I asked.

"Meaning you got more sense than I figured, that's all. I thought you might try to wear your dad's boots, and they damn sure wouldn't fit you or nobody else around here. What's more, I'm glad of that, which don't mean I didn't admire Mr. Tyrrell."

"I admired him too," I said.

The little cook stared at me intently again. "I believe you did at that," he muttered then. "Come on and eat the cold grub I saved for you. Shame to waste it on the damn magpies."

I'd come home to the Tyrrell ranch—to the land that belonged to my father, to my brother Ira, and to me. . . .

There isn't much more to tell about that year which started in the spring of '89. We buried Father on the sandstone bluff across the river from the house. I was riding every day that winter—too bone-tired each night to do more than fall quickly asleep in Father's bed or a bunk at one of the line camps. During the days, though, I had plenty of time to wonder how Mary Lamar was doing and whether she might someday appear at the ranch in a buggy driven by my brother.

But Ira didn't come back to Wyoming until a few years later, when he'd finished law school in the East. He set up practice over in the Lander Valley and lived in a place out of town where he could keep a couple of good mares and train their colts when he had the time. From what I heard, though, he didn't have much time to himself once he'd handled a few cases. People found out Ira wouldn't take a client he didn't believe in, and once he did take on a case, he had the kind of mind and convictions to make a jury see the rights a man should have and be allowed to hold to. Mostly he took cases involving honest homesteaders, small ranchers, and sheepmen that a few of the bigger cattlemen were still trying to run off the range, or Indians that some white man had tried to swindle. I guess some of them couldn't pay very much or very promptly, but I figured Ira was living the way he thought was right for him—without cheating or stepping on the toes of anybody else. That was just his nature. And I'd found out a lot about how I wanted to live from him and my father both. . . .

In the weeks right after Father died the weather wasn't too bad, but I still recall that first winter as the hardest time I ever had on the TX. I had a lot to learn about running a ranch and not much time to learn it. Green-up came, though, like it always does, and one morning when I went out to saddle Blacky I heard the meadow larks sing full and clear from off toward the river.

As I stood listening by the corral I saw a rider coming up on the wagon trail. I waited, conscious of each breath I took of the light Wyoming air. I didn't move until I was sure my guess was right and Mary Lamar held up one hand in a wave. Then I walked toward her through the spring-damp sage and young buffalo grass.

"It's good to see you," she said from her horse.

I thought she looked much the same as she had the spring before. Those hollow, wasting shadows the lung sickness had made around her eyes and cheekbones when I last talked with her at the Reservation were almost gone. Her hair was again tied in thick shining braids, and below the collar of the velvety purple blouse her throat was shaded a smooth light tan. Maybe she was a little thinner and still worn out some from getting over the bullet wound and fighting with consumption. Maybe she was a little older and more of a woman than I'd remembered.

"How are you, Mary?" I said. "I've been thinking a lot about you."

"I'm almost well. . . . My mother's brother rode out beyond the rim with me, and all the rest of the way I smelled the Sweetwater in the wind."

"I thought you might've moved into Lander," I said.

She smiled in a way I couldn't understand at first. "No . . . I don't ever want to leave here now, Martin. That's what I came out to tell you. But I didn't know whether you would want to see me."

"You didn't need to worry," I told her. "I've been hoping to see you. . . ." I wanted to say it a lot plainer than that, but I made myself go slow this time. "Have you seen Ira lately?"

She wouldn't look at me then. "Your brother left to begin law school in the East. He promised he would send you a letter once he gets settled. He said he would be very busy for a while."

I heard the meadow larks flute again. "When did he say that?" I asked her.

"He came to see me after the trouble with Mr. Karr and Clayt Paulson was finished, and I told him . . . not to stay in Lander because of me. I told him I didn't need him now because you . . ."

Her face looked thoughtful and shy for a moment, and I knew she was still a part of the Sweetwater country that wouldn't be much different to me no matter how the times changed or who ran stock along the river. I kept remembering the way she had walked up the path to Lamar's cabin carrying water from the spring, her moccasins light and sure on the ground like she belonged there without needing to build a fence to prove it.

Then I heard her say, "I'm here, Martin. Isn't that enough to speak for me?"

"Yes," I said, holding her waist and pulling her down from the saddle. "I reckon it's enough for me."

It was the first time I'd seen her cry, and I held her there, her tears wet on my face, listening to the meadow larks and the Sweetwater crowding its banks with runoff from the blue mountains . . . and seeing the fresh green of new grass beginning to color our rangeland again.

And it was enough.

Center Point Large Print
600 Brooks Road / PO Box 1
Thorndike ME 04986-0001 USA

(207) 568-3717

US & Canada:
1 800 929-9108
www.centerpointlargeprint.com